Lynn,
Thanks for your
support

Charles

BE SAFE

BE SAFE

CHARLES GIRSKY

I would like to acknowledge my wife, Lois, for always being there, and Debbie and Kelly, members of my writing group.

PUBLISHED BY IVY HOUSE PUBLISHING GROUP
5122 Bur Oak Circle, Raleigh, North Carolina 27612
United States of America
919-782-0281

ISBN 1-57197-301-X
Library of Congress Control Number: 2001 132669

Printed in the United States of America

The speedometer was nearing eighty-five as she hit the send button on the mobile phone that came with the rental car at LAX. "Pick up the phone! Pick it up!" she yelled into the receiver.

Finally a mechanical voice said, "You have reached Ajax Imports. Our office hours are from 8 A.M. to 5 P.M., Monday through Friday. Please leave a message and your call will be returned when we re-open. If this call is of an urgent matter, press the star key and number three key. Your message will be forwarded as soon as it has been completed."

"You rotten pieces of shit! You told me someone would be there twenty-four hours a day." Tears came to her eyes as she took a deep breath and continued, "I'm in Los Angeles. I'm headed north on the 405 Freeway in a rented Lincoln from Avis. I am positive that they're somewhere behind me, I just don't know how far. I'm headed to the apartment in Woodland Hills and will try and make contact from there. Listen carefully. It's not the Cubans. It's someone with connections into some of the highest offices of the government. The guy in charge is an ex-general named . . ."

Throwing the phone down she shrieked, "Get the fuck out of my lane." She hit the high beams and drove around the car in front of her. She grabbed the phone again. "I'm approaching Wilshire Boulevard and you've got to get me some help. These guys are going to rip off millions, shit, I hit the . . ." She grabbed the wheel with both hands as the car spiraled and hit the divider for a second time. The car was now on its side and she kept trying to right it by turning the steering wheel in the opposite direction. Her leg felt like it was on fire and her only thought was verbalized, "I'm going to die."

Chapter 1

I had just heard for what seemed like the tenth time on the twenty-four hour news station that the Clippers had blown an eight-point lead with just a minute and a half to go and lost in overtime to the Lakers. It was 1:15 A.M. and I was returning home to Thousand Oaks after a business dinner in San Clemente. Jerry Morgan and his wife Susan had brought a female friend with them to the dinner. They thought I would like her. More and more people were trying to fix me up lately. I guess they thought twelve months was long enough for me to sit home and feel sorry for myself.

My wife, Marcia, passed away last February. She fought a brief battle with cancer that seemed to spread faster than a rash picked up in the steaming jungles of Southeast Asia.

Tonight's winner of the "who gets to date Aaron Carlyle sweepstakes" was Karen Williams. I estimated that she was about five or six inches shorter than my six-foot-two-inch frame. Her body was hidden behind a business suit that made her look both professional and desirable at the same time. She owned her own investment firm and I had the impression that she did very well. Jerry and Susan made sure I heard that more than once. What I was being told was she was not in need of a man with money, but was looking for someone who enjoyed the same things that she did. I'm sure in the future I will learn what they are. Jerry and Susan were hoping that I was that someone.

I had driven past the exit to LAX and past the car dealerships with the balloon arc bobbing in the breeze. Even at this time of night the colors caught my eye. Glancing at the rearview mirror, I caught the headlights of what looked like a police car speeding up behind me.

"Just what I need!" I said, attempting to slow the car without having the brake lights go on. The car behind me hit its high beams twice and then pulled out of the left lane and moved into lane three. As it came alongside me, I noticed it was a late-model Lincoln driven by a woman somewhere between thirty and forty. She was going at least eighty-five miles an hour.

The woman was gripping the wheel with one hand while talking into a mobile phone. As her car passed me, she pulled the wheel back to the left to reenter the fast lane. At that point, I touched my brakes, slowing down to what seemed like a crawl. I never looked at my speedometer because my eyes were now riveted on the Lincoln that had moved just ahead of me.

We were just passing the Wilshire ramp when she must have caught something out of the corner of her eye. Her head turned right and the car moved ever so slightly to the left, hitting the dividing wall with a glancing blow. There was a shower of sparks as she started to correct and then in what looked like an over-correction, the car again hit the wall and flipped over on its side. It was like watching a slow motion film. The car went sliding up the 405 Freeway at what looked like the same speed as when it passed me. It flipped again and started spinning like a top. When it hit the wall for the third time, it came to a stop. It was amazing that she didn't hit another car, or maybe not so amazing since at that time of the morning there weren't very many cars on the freeway. Cars started to pull over to the side to see if they could help, or maybe just to look, I don't know.

I pulled over and dialed 911 on my mobile phone. I explained to the operator where I was and what had happened. She asked for my name and the type of car I was driving. When she asked if anyone was hurt, I realized the woman had not climbed out of the car and that among the six or eight bystanders, no one had gone to her aid. They were all standing there gawking. I jumped out of my car and ran to where her car had come to a stop. The driver's side was on top and when I opened the door and looked in, I saw that the woman was alive, but bleeding. I freed her from the seat belt and started to pull her out. She reached over for her purse and struggled against the air bag as I lifted her free of the car. I laid her down on the pavement and used my jacket to cushion her head.

She looked up at me and said, "Thank you. Are you a brave man?"

I heard the words, but somehow converted them to 'you are a brave man.' No one had said that to me since Vietnam.

"Thank you," I replied. "Please lay still. Help will be here soon."

She looked at me for a second and then said, "What is your name?"

"Aaron." I answered. She showed a lot of guts asking questions. Marcia always did that from the first day I met her in Vietnam.

"Aaron," she replied as her voice seemed to get weaker, "Please watch my belongings until I get out of this mess."

I tried to smile as I said, "Don't worry, I am also honest." I turned to the people standing behind me. "Are any of you a doctor?" No one answered as I heard the sound of police sirens coming up behind us. One of the people in the crowd yelled, "The car is on fire."

I looked up as flames started to appear as if by magic.

A policewoman came running up, knelt down beside me and shouted, "We have to pull her back!"

I lifted the woman and started to carry her at almost the same time the car blew. The rush of hot air pushed the three of us at least fifteen to twenty feet. The policewoman looked like she was running into the bushes and I felt myself being pushed further back along the pavement with the woman in my arms. I ended up on the grass with the woman lying on top.

As another policeman ran to help us, I heard the woman saying, "Don't forget."

Three police cars pulled up right ahead of a fire engine and an ambulance. The firemen had the burning car under control in what seemed like a matter of seconds. One of the medics that arrived in the ambulance was saying, "Be careful. She may have a concussion and she definitely has at least a broken leg."

One of the firemen said to me, "You look like you might need a ride to the hospital."

As far as I could tell, nothing hurt and no bones were broken. I told him, "If I feel bad in the morning, I'll go see my own physician."

One of the police officers handed me my jacket. It looked like it had been run over by all the cars on the freeway. I put it on to see if it was ripped when I remembered the injured woman's purse that she had given me for safekeeping. As I picked it up, a little notebook fell out. I walked over to the ambulance that had the woman in it. The officer in charge stopped me to ask me some questions about what had gone on.

"Is your name Aaron Carlyle?"

I nodded yes.

"I have you as the one who notified 911 about the accident."

The policewoman who was first to arrive came over and was taking notes. She had light brown hair, green eyes and no ring on her finger. The dirt from being thrown into the bushes only helped to accentuate her shape. I felt myself staring and turned to the sergeant as the ambulance started to pull away. Even though all of this was going on, I stood there wondering if she was married.

"The woman asked me to hold on to this purse and I really don't want to keep it for too long. I don't have the slightest idea if I'll ever see her again and really don't know what to do with it." I was standing in front of the officer in charge, but talking to the lady cop.

He looked over at the policewoman and said, "I am opening the purse for identification purposes and want a witness just in case there's something valuable inside."

He sounded like a pompous ass showing off for the good-looking lady cop.

Upon opening the bag, the first thing we all saw was a stack of hundred dollar bills that looked like they would choke the proverbial horse. The wrapper on the outside said $50,000 and we all stared at the number as the officer kept turning the money over and over. He looked inside the bag again and pulled out another stack that was identical to the first. There were five stacks for a total of $250,000. "Holy mother of God," he said to no one in particular. He looked up and yelled out to one of the other cops, "Bring me an evidence bag." He put the money in the bag and had the woman officer with a nametag "Novak" sign the closed bag beside his name. They did not ask me to sign the wrapper on the bag.

"What about me? I feel a little obligated. She gave me the bag to hold."

"Don't worry, everything will go into a larger bag that you will be asked to sign."

He was talking to me like I was a two-year-old. I could feel the hairs on my neck start to stand up straight.

"How about not sealing the bag until we look inside the purse and maybe seal the whole thing?"

The sergeant looked at me with open disgust, but he reopened the bag and found nothing else exciting or out of the ordinary. He read the license and wrote down the address and phone number. Aloud he said, "Well Carol Sellars, you'll certainly have a lot of explaining to do in the morning."

"Is there anything else? You have my name and address and I'd like to go home. If Ms. Sellars asks, you can pass it on." As I walked to my car, I remembered the notebook in the pocket of my jacket. I turned back towards the sergeant and Officer Novak.

They didn't see me coming and I heard him say, "A quarter of a million dollars! You and I could have had a ball with just one of those packets."

I decided to call the hospital in the morning and return it myself rather than face the two of them. Since I had parked behind the accident, they had to stop traffic to let me through and I noticed the policewoman sitting in one of the vans that I had thought pulled over to help. She was a good-looking cop, maybe almost as pretty as Karen, the woman I had met earlier. She was on a mobile phone and I found myself hoping she was talking to a boyfriend and really couldn't stand the sergeant. The thoughts going through my mind about the lady cop told me Karen Williams was probably going to get a call sooner than later. As I went down the Mulholland Grade, I started thinking about the accident and I almost missed the exit from the 405 to the 101 going north. For some unknown reason, I couldn't stop thinking about the lady cop. Her hair picked up the light of the moon as she moved and her shape probably irritated the hell out of her partners' wives. I wondered if she was married and didn't wear a ring or had a boyfriend. All of a sudden, I felt guilty. First, I felt guilty earlier tonight with Karen and now with Officer Novak. I hadn't thought of another woman since last year and now there were two of them I was fantasizing about. I was going to have to do something about this.

Chapter 2

I had gotten in the habit of having a scotch and water before turning in, but tonight I didn't need it. A year was a long time and maybe Susan and Jerry were right. Maybe it was time to get on with my life. I had given up setting the alarm clock when Marcia died. There seemed to be a little clock inside of me that woke me every three to four hours. At first, when I started waking up, I looked at the other side of the bed thinking that Marcia had gone to the bathroom. After a while, I just lay there and stared at empty space beside me.

Thirty minutes had passed when I finally came out of my reverie. I shook my head and looked at the television. One of those infomercials was advertising a 900 number and a bevy of good-looking women that promised great phone sex. Just as I hit the off button, I was positive one of the women was the lady cop. I didn't bother to turn it back on. I was doing a great job of fantasizing.

When I opened my eyes, I couldn't believe it was 6:30 A.M. I dragged myself into a shower and after what seemed like forever, I finally got the temperature right. For over ten minutes I let the cascading water run over my body. Walking back into the bedroom, I clicked on the television and half-listened to the news as I dressed for the meeting that I had scheduled with Scott and Tom. Our armed response security firm had clients all over Southern California. We had to decide what we could reasonably tell our stockholders in our upcoming annual report. Three years ago, we had taken the company public, which allowed all of us to bank some money and provided Marcia and I some five-star vacations. Marcia's aunt had an expression that popped into my head: "Man plans and God laughs." I was thinking about her aunt when the television caught my eye. They had a story about the accident. I was referred to as a heroic bystander. They didn't use my name or Officer Novak's, but they gave her credit, which was fine by me. The story ended on a sad note: The woman, whose name they didn't use, died after an emergency operation for internal injuries. The camera shifted to the weather girl who promised another glorious day in the Southland.

I turned off the television and walked into the kitchen. I noticed the red light blinking on my answering machine. I picked it up wondering how I missed it last night. It turned out that the call was only forty-five minutes old. The police had called and asked me to call back as soon as possible. It had something to do with last night's accident. I wrote down the number and called from my car phone on the way to the office. When I told the policeman who I was, he connected me with a Sergeant Dan something. His last name was muffled by what sounded like a donut trying to be eaten. Sergeant Dan asked if I could stop down and identify my signature on the property bag before it was opened. The accident report told of a large sum of money and police procedure stated whoever signed the bag should be there at the opening. This sounded a little strange, but my social calendar being what it was made the decision easy.

I asked, "Will the two officers be there?"

He replied, "At least one of them will. They both went off duty around 7 A.M. Would 4:30 P.M. or 5 P.M. be convenient?" He gave me the address on Wilshire Boulevard and continued, "Thank you, Mr. . . . Carlyle," and hung up before I could say another word. I found myself hoping the right officer would be there.

When I arrived at the office, I found Scott pacing the hall and Tom in the conference room with the Wall Street Journal spread all over the table. Their compassion and strength over the past year was a real test of friendship. Our sales had slipped a little, probably due to my mind being elsewhere, and with our sales had gone some of our profits. The stock price of the company had risen from the initial price of $19.00 to a little over $30.00, but had fallen over the last quarter to somewhere between $25.00 and $27.50.

Three years ago when we went public, we were each allowed to sell fifty thousand shares of our own stock. After brokerage fees and taxes, we each had about six to seven hundred thousand dollars.

Tom believed our upcoming annual report had to show confidence in the future and wanted us to not only have a report from the president explaining the last year, but a report with pictures of Scott and himself extolling the future. They both wanted to include pictures of the newest Sony camera and maybe the front and rear doors of four or five of our larger or more well known clients. Our lawyers told us to be cautious with our forecasts and projections and today's meeting was to decide how best to proceed. If we did some smart things, this might be the year we would be able to sell a couple of hundred thousand shares of stock.

Scott started by asking for a detailed report on how last night's meeting went. I had the distinct feeling that he knew about Karen being there.

I talked about the meeting and casually mentioned that I thought I might ask Karen out on a social basis. The smug expressions on their faces told me I was probably right. When I told them about the accident, they both thought I was out of my mind to stop on a freeway and get involved. The meeting went well and in fact, the entire day went well. There was a report of a break-in at one of the electronic companies we serviced and it was decided that aside from the patrol cars that toured the industrial park, we would try and talk the customer into some motion detector cameras. We had found in the past, once one company in an industrial park did something, the others seemed to follow. It's always nice to have pictures in case it's an inside driven theft.

The office seemed more upbeat than it had over the past year. Maybe it was the first time I paid any real attention to it. Last night's dinner and then the woman dying in the accident had certainly started me thinking about more than losing Marcia.

Chapter 3

I left the office in Newberry Park around 3:10 P.M. for the trip to Westwood. Traffic was light, aside from the normal congestion up the grade on the 405 Freeway. I approached the Wilshire exit at 3:50 P.M. The stock market report was on and the Dow was up thirteen. The NASDAQ was four and a half higher. As I was exiting the freeway, I noticed a beige Ford in front of me getting off at the same time. I thought it was odd since that car had been leapfrogging me since at least Woodland Hills when I first noticed it. I pulled into the visitor's parking lot and saw the Ford at a meter about half a block away.

As I entered the building, I started laughing at myself. One visit to a police station and I started acting like Dick Tracy's sidekick. I normally can't tell one car from another, and if this one didn't have one of those note holders stuck to the front window, I wouldn't have noticed it at all. I thought they were illegal when attached to the front window. When I was in Vietnam, I was assigned to the Military Police during the last six months of my tour. One of my functions was to check the security at the buildings we had people in. In Nam, we not only checked the buildings, but cars, trucks or anything a bomb could be stashed in. We questioned everything. It was a tough habit to break.

I told the officer at the front desk I was looking for Sergeant Dan something and he knew exactly where to direct me.

"It's on the second floor, third door on the right." He handed me a visitor's badge and pointed at the stairs. He picked up the phone and I heard him say, "That fellow you were asking about is on his way up." The lovely Officer Novak greeted me at the top of the stairs.

She smiled and asked, "Do you remember me?"

In civilian clothes, she was a knockout. She wore a light blue silk blouse and a pair of dark blue slacks. She wore an open, bulky, button-down sweater over her clothes. If she was trying to hide her shape, she was doing a terrible job. She wore very little makeup, which highlighted just how pretty she was. All in all, she was a welcome sight.

"I certainly do. I heard on the radio the woman died."

"Yes, she did. When we transported her, I didn't think she was that bad off. You can never tell."

She escorted me to a conference room and introduced me to Sergeant Dan Rossner, a six-foot guy with a hard body who rose and shook my hand.

"Hi. I want to thank you for coming down." As he pumped my hand, I noticed three other men in the room. His grip felt like a vise and I promised myself I would start working out and lifting weights the first chance I had. Not that I was in bad shape, but maybe running three to four miles, four times a week was just not getting it done. On the conference table they had the sealed bag with my signature on it. Seeing the bag made me ask if she had any family, and instead of an answer, one of the other three men in the room asked, "Can you tell us your version of what happened?" He was the tallest and I didn't like the way he jumped into the conversation.

"As opposed to whose?"

He just stared at me, so I continued.

"Did Carol Sellars have any family?"

This time the smallest of the three men asked, "How come you know her name?"

A second look at him made me think of a Sumo wrestler. He wasn't squat, he wasn't bald, but he had a thick neck, and the muscles across his chest and his body movement suggested he wasn't someone you poked fun at in a bar.

"Who are these three people?" I asked of Sergeant Rossner.

He looked over at Officer Novak and said, "Sally, maybe you could get us a soft drink or something."

She nodded. "We have Coke, Diet Coke and Sprite. They only cost fifty cents. If you're out of change, I can get you some black coffee. It's not the best in the world, but it generally gets your heart pumping in the morning."

I replied, "It's not morning."

She answered just as quickly, "That's when the coffee was made."

I smiled. She had a quick sense of humor.

The sergeant said, "My treat."

Something was really starting to bother me. The third man was just sitting there with a shit-eating grin on his face absorbing what was going on almost like he was laughing at what was transpiring. It was then that I realized the other policeman wasn't there. Maybe these three guys were investigating him.

"Where's the other officer that was at the accident?" I looked at their eyes as they digested the question. Sally looked around the room at the sergeant and then at the ceiling.

To me, it looked like she sighed in relief when the sergeant said, "Get us three Cokes and three Diet Cokes. One of the guys will help you carry them." She shook her head and walked out the door without saying a word. The tall internal affairs guy walked out of the room behind her leaving me with the Sergeant, the Sumo wrestler and the one I decided was in charge. I looked at the men still in the room. "Do you want to start over again?" I asked.

The little one said, "That's a good idea. Would you like to tell us what happened last night as you remember it?"

I looked at him and said, "That's not what I had in mind. Did she have a family? Where is the other cop? Since you already have my version of what happened, I would like some simple answers. While you're at it, you could start by telling me who the fuck you are and what the hell is going on."

There were a few seconds of silence. I was trying to decide what to do next, as I'm sure they were. The door opened and Officer Sally entered. She was followed by a man that looked how a typical cop should. He had gray hair, stood about six-foot-one, and was more than a little overweight. The top two buttons of his shirt were open and a tie hung loosely around his neck. The sergeant and Sally stood and retreated to the back wall.

"My name is Captain Beckman." He reached out to shake my hand. His grip was firm and dry, and he looked directly into my eyes as he spoke. "I wanted to thank you for coming down. I understand you did a heroic thing last night. It was a shame she died. We're still trying to find out if she had any family. The address on her license was incorrect." I looked at him and wondered if the room was bugged. He came in just as things looked like they were getting ugly and defused a tense situation. I glanced around the room. Nothing jumped out at me, but I knew a bug could be almost anywhere. The man that left with Novak walked in with an armful of soft drinks.

The captain turned and said, "I'll take a Diet Coke. I'm watching my calories. When my wife was alive, she was always telling me that a calorie here and a calorie there would some day add up to a whole bunch of saved calories that I could turn in for a piece of apple pie and ice cream for dessert." His eyes lost focus for a moment and I could sense loneliness. It looked like he almost finished the can in one swallow when he turned and said, "Mr. Carlyle, have you met these other gentlemen yet?"

I then thought again about the room being wired and said, "No, not yet."

He turned to the three of them and said, "Do you people get business cards working for the federal government? Why don't you either give him a card or your name and organization and let's get on with the meeting." The silence in the room could be cut with a knife, and if looks could kill, the captain was dead. No one moved. I sat there stunned. I felt a constriction in my chest that could only be relieved by taking a deep breath, and I was afraid to take that breath. Finally, the middleman that looked like he was in charge smiled and held out his hand.

"Mr. Carlyle, let me introduce myself and my fellow government workers. My name is Paul Roland. The gentleman on my right is Ken Carlett and the fellow holding the sodas is Terry Flores. We work," he continued, "in a small obscure division of the Treasury Department. Our function in life is to chase down large sums of money that seem to appear out of nowhere. One of our people on duty last night read the accident report about the money that was found. We were told you were the only person that approached the car and spoke to the woman. Our first thought was that you knew her."

"Why didn't you tell me who you were when I walked in?" I questioned.

"What you did was very heroic, very stupid, or you knew the woman. We wanted to find out which was the right answer." He looked at the other two men and said, "Terry, introduce yourself and ask Mr. Carlyle your questions."

He handed me a business card that said only "AJAX IMPORTS" on the first line and "TERRY FLORES" on the bottom.

I smiled; this division of the federal government was so obscure that they didn't even give out their name.

Terry had put down his soda and had taken a notebook out of his jacket pocket. He asked, "What were you doing on the freeway that late at night?"

I told him about Jerry and Susan, leaving out the part about Karen Williams. As I told the story, I kept glancing at Captain Beckman. I kept wondering if he had started dating. I had a feeling he had and I felt more uncomfortable about having to be fixed up. I looked more than once at Sally Novak and I was sure I didn't want her to know people were trying to pair me up. I felt a little foolish. I didn't even know if she was married, dating or what. I reached into my pocket, took out my wallet and retrieved the receipt from last night's dinner.

"Okay, Terry, we had dinner at the Surf's Up restaurant in Solana Bay. It looks like they took my American Express card at 21:13, which I think is about 9:15 P.M."

"Did the woman say anything unusual?" he asked.

"Yes she did. She asked, 'Are you a brave man?' when I pulled her out of her car."

At that point, Agent Carlett chimed in with, "What was your answer?"

"I thought she mixed up the words and meant 'You are a brave man,' so I just said thank you. She then said, 'Aaron, could you please watch over my belongings until we see each other later?'"

"How did she know your name?" Paul asked.

"Oh I forgot. She asked my name right before she asked me to watch her stuff."

"What else have you forgotten to tell us?" asked Terry.

There was something about the way he asked the question that made me not want to answer it. I asked instead, "There was another officer at the scene of the accident last night. Where is he?" I turned to officer Novak and asked. "What is your partner's name?" Every eye turned to the back wall.

Sally pushed herself away from the wall and said, "Sergeant Garret isn't my partner."

"He's in court today," Dan Rossner said. "Why are you asking?"

This was the first comment he had made since the meeting started and it seemed a little too fast, like he was covering up something.

"He made a comment to Sally about how they could have a ball with that much money. I thought you might be investigating him."

"He thought you might say something," replied Rossner. "Are you filing a complaint?"

This statement bothered me more than the first one and I didn't know why. Something was wrong. I wasn't asking the right questions.

"Did she have any family?" I asked.

Paul Rowland, whom I assumed was in charge, answered, "We don't know. The credit card she used to rent the car at LAX was reported stolen three weeks ago. We don't have the slightest idea who she really is, where she came from, where she was going or what she was going to do with the money when she got there. We were hoping you had some of the answers."

I shrugged my shoulders. "I'm sorry, but I can't help you." They were lying. If they were telling me the truth, the credit card would have been refused.

Terry looked at the receipt again, copied down something from it and asked the names of the people I had dinner with. I omitted Karen's name and again felt awkward.

As everyone started to leave I asked, "Is the money real?" They jumped liked I hit them with a cattle prod.

"Why would you ask that?" Roland asked.

"I don't know," I answered. "That much cash seems odd. They looked like brand new bills."

"We checked," he said. "They're real."

"When did you check? I thought this was the first time you opened the bag." Not a muscle moved on anyone's face except for Sally's. She blinked.

"I guess it doesn't matter," I said. "If it's not claimed within how long, sixty days, ninety days, it reverts back to me. Since everyone here has now heard this treasury agent, who works for Ajax Imports, say it's real, there shouldn't be any question as to who it goes to, that is unless you locate her family."

"You rotten piece of shit!" screamed Agent Carlett. "We knew you had some kind of angle."

Roland held up his hand stopping Carlett in mid-sentence. "That brings up an interesting question, Mr. Carlyle. What did you do in Vietnam that got you discharged in Cambodia? Did it have anything to do with drugs of any kind?"

"Fuck you," I answered with a smile on my face. I turned to Sally and apologized for my bad language. I turned back to the three of them and said, "You guys should broaden your horizons. Drugs weren't the only thing for sale over there."

I looked at Captain Beckman and said, "It's been a pleasure. If you have some time I would love to buy you a beer. Otherwise, I'm out of here. You know where to reach me." I walked to the door and hesitated for just a second. I wanted to see if they were going to stop me. I turned the handle of the door and exited like I didn't have a worry in the world. I didn't, but everything about the whole meeting bothered me. I stopped in the men's room to catch my breath and use the facilities. As I left, I ran right into Sally Novak.

"You didn't ask me if I wanted a beer."

I smiled at her and said, "How about dinner?"

"As long as it starts with a drink, the answer is yes."

We left the building and I suggested Matteo's. It was the only restaurant I could think of in that part of the city. It was a place where I used to take customers. The food was great. It also held a lot of personal memories about Marcia. I hoped I was up to them.

Chapter 4

As we reached the street I asked, "Can I offer you a ride?"

"I was hoping you would ask. I was dropped off by a neighbor earlier this afternoon."

I held the door open for her. She stopped before entering and said, "Hi, my name is Sally. I know yours is Aaron." She held out her hand and I reached for it and clasped it in both my hands.

"Hi Sally," I replied. I hoped my face didn't show my reaction to our simple touch. All of a sudden, my mouth had gone dry. I felt like a teenager out on his first date with the prom queen. Her hand was soft and dry. I smelled a flowery sort of perfume or hand cream. I couldn't seem to get my thoughts together. I guess I held her hand too long, because she smiled and withdrew her hand, and it felt like she had to yank it from my grip. I stammered an apology and went to the driver's side of the car. My keys were slow in coming out of my pocket and Sally leaned across the seat to open the door. She was still leaning in my direction as I entered and I couldn't take my eyes off of her breasts that strained against the blouse she was wearing.

She pulled back as I started the car and I told her, "You'll have to excuse some of the things I either say or do tonight. I haven't been out on a date for a long time."

She laughed and said, "Don't worry about that. Before the night is over, I may say or do something I might regret in the morning."

I smiled. I wondered if the double meaning was on purpose.

Matteo's is only about ten minutes from where we started and we made some small talk about the weather, the Dodgers and how clean they kept police headquarters. They have valet parking at Matteo's and one of the valets opened her door as I got out on the street side. As I started around the car, I noticed the beige Ford again. There must have been a dozen or so cars behind me because I hadn't noticed it before this. I tried to get a look at the driver, but the back window was filthy, as was the license plate, although I was able to get the four numbers after the first one. It should be enough for one of my people to find out whom it belonged to.

Sally asked, “Is something wrong?”

“Just someone getting a little too close.” We entered and it was like I had stepped back in time. Nothing had changed. The picture of Frank Sinatra, the chairman of the board, still hung in its place of honor. There was a story going around some years back that when Frank Sinatra’s mother was missing in a plane crash, Matty was with him in a small plane looking for the downed aircraft. Los Angeles has a way of telling stories, either fiction or fact, that grow in the telling. I nodded at the mâitre d’ and asked for a table for two. I told him I didn’t have reservations and would wait at the bar.

“There is no need to wait, Mr. Carlyle. I can seat you immediately.”

I was surprised that he remembered my name. It had been at least a year and a half since I had eaten there. We were shown to a table toward the front of the restaurant, which was another surprise. These tables were usually reserved for show people. Sally looked impressed. I just assumed business wasn’t so good. The waiter took our drink order, a beer for Sally and a Merlot for me.

The mâitre d’ delivered the drinks and as he put them down he said, “Mr. Carlyle, I am sorry for my lack of manners, but I feel I must tell you how sorry we all were when we heard your wife passed on. She was a charming lady that we all liked and will miss.”

I thanked him for his condolences. He lifted a glass of wine he had brought with him and said something in Italian that both Sally and I took as a toast. We lifted our glasses and drank.

He then said, “Finish your drinks and I will return with our specials for tonight.”

I looked at Sally and asked, “Are you hungry?”

“Starved,” she replied.

“I’ll tell you what,” I said to the waiter. “Why don’t you just surprise us?”

He smiled as he walked away. “You will not be disappointed.”

Somewhere in the middle of dinner, a party of six was seated next to us. I recognized Don Rickles, but the names of the others escaped me.

Sally looked at them, leaned across the table and said, “There’s Sonny and Cher.” We both looked at the table next to us just as Sonny turned and looked our way.

He smiled and said, "Good evening." I knew by the look on Sally's face that I had chosen the right restaurant. We talked about a million things, but not once about the accident. I handed the waiter my credit card without looking at the bill and he promptly handed it back.

"Please inspect the charges," he asked.

I looked at the bill and across the front of it was written, "Welcome back, we missed you." I felt my face flush because I had not expected this. I reached into my pocket and took out two twenties; there was no sense stiffing the waiter. We walked out of the front door just as Harry Belafonte stepped out of a chauffeured limo with a beautiful girl on his arm. Sally squeezed my arm and said, "Look, there's Shari Belafonte. I wonder who she's with." My car pulled up and two valets held the doors for us.

"Where to?" I asked.

"I live in the valley. It's two blocks off of Topanga Canyon Road. Is it out of your way?"

"I go right past there on my way home. I can always slow down and let you jump as we get close," I joked. We got on the freeway at the same exit that the accident had occurred the night before. It didn't seem like it had been less than twenty-four hours since we had met.

"Are you married?" I blurted out. Smooth, I thought to myself.

"Not anymore. He was killed in the line of duty about eight months ago."

"Was he a Los Angeles cop?"

She hesitated a second and answered very softly, "No, he worked for the federal government." We rode in silence for what seemed like about five or ten minutes.

"Are you a policewoman?"

She hesitated a little longer. "I am, but not for the L.A.P.D."

"Do you work for Ajax Imports like those three men back in the office?"

She thought for a second. "Yes, but I am not like them. We work for the same department, but I hope to God I never become like them."

"What the hell is going on?" I blurted out.

"I can't tell you that," she replied.

"Is that why you went out with me, just to get information?"

She didn't look at me as she answered. "Do you have any?"

I felt the blood rush to my face as I answered much too loudly. "Any what?"

"Any information about the accident."

"I don't even know what we are talking about. I stopped to help at the scene of an accident and all of a sudden I find myself knee deep in a pile of shit so high I can't even figure out where it came from."

"I was there," she replied. "What I can tell you is that the lady was involved with something illegal. What it was, I don't even know. I was on the freeway trying to catch her when the accident occurred. We were told she blinked her lights right before she passed you and crashed. I was given instructions to find out if she was meeting you."

"You could have checked me out and found out anything you wanted to know. Why the charade?"

"This is my exit. Do you want to come in for a cup of coffee so we can finish talking?"

For the first time tonight, I didn't know what to say. I hadn't been alone with a woman for dinner in over a year, and now she invites me in for coffee.

"Sure, why not. I haven't been sleeping too well anyway." Hopefully, I sounded blasé enough that she wouldn't notice my discomfort.

Chapter 5

She lived in a detached house six or seven blocks away from Chatsworth State Park. She got out before I was able to open her side door and proceeded up three steps to her front door. She opened the door with a key from her purse.

I jokingly said, "You should have an alarm system. I could get one for you wholesale."

The inside was clean and neat, almost antiseptic. The first thing she did was to walk over to a picture on the bookshelf and put it face down.

"It's a picture of my husband. You are the first man I have invited in since he died and I feel a little uncomfortable with his picture standing there." She removed her coat and I noticed a revolver attached to the back of her belt. She took out some coffee from the refrigerator, poured some into a coffeepot and asked me to have a seat. She said she would be right back. I sat there taking in the furniture or lack thereof. There was a sofa about eight feet long, a recliner, a television, a tape deck, a bookshelf loaded with a few books and a coffee table. The room had more than a sterile look to it. It felt strange.

Sally returned at the same time the coffee was ready. She came back wearing a cotton bathrobe, like the kind Jane Wyatt wore on *Father Knows Best.*

"I just had to get out of what I was wearing." She poured some coffee and asked me, "How do you like it?"

I wasn't sure if she was asking about the bathrobe or the coffee. I decided to answer the safer way, "Black."

She walked over to the table between the couch and the television set and put down the two cups of coffee. I sat on one end of the sofa and she sat on the other.

"This is very tough for me," she began. "About thirteen months ago, we started hearing stories about the Cuban government or some part of their government that was going to attempt to create a major crisis for the United States. The rumor was unsubstantiated, but came from a source that had given us good information in the past. Before we could even find out how it was supposed to happen, the source we had been using for years disappeared. All efforts to find him failed.

"My husband was given the job of trying to reconstruct what the source had found and finding out what was supposed to happen. This was the first time we were going to be apart for any length of time. Rumors about Cuba are always followed up. My husband had some contacts in the Cuban community down in Florida, so he started to ask some questions. Stephen, my husband, was required to file reports every forty-eight hours. His first reports were about a group inside the Cuban government. There were no names, nor mention of how they were going to somehow raise hundreds of millions of dollars inside of the United States." She hesitated, "After six reports, my husband was found dead. There was a car accident on the Long Island Expressway right before the entrance to the Queens Midtown Tunnel. A few months later, a second agent was assigned—you met her briefly last night. All of a sudden, we stopped getting reports from her. We didn't know what happened to her until her credit card was activated at the Avis counter at LAX. We were minutes behind her when she had the accident. You know the rest, except that the police sergeant from last night has now disappeared. He never went home and his car is missing."

"This is quite a story. It sounds like a Tom Clancy novel."

"I wish it were. My husband would still be alive. We still don't have the slightest idea of what is happening. Obviously, the money was to be used for something, we just don't know what. The only thing we can think of is that it was a payoff to someone."

"How come you decided to tell me?" I asked.

"I believe you just happened upon the scene and everything you told us is the truth." She hesitated and looked at the bookcase with the turned over picture. "There are some things I would like to ask you."

"What do you want to know?" I asked.

She stood and walked over to the tape player. She inserted a tape, hit the play button and turned to face me.

"Do you miss your wife?"

In the year since Marcia died, no one had ever asked me that question.

Chapter 6

I looked at the clock on the shelf. It was 9:30 P.M. It was the same time last year that I received the phone call from the hospital about Marcia.

"Mr. Carlyle, please hurry back!"

"Is something wrong?" I asked the voice on the phone. I had only left there thirty minutes ago.

"Please hurry." I realized that she didn't answer my question.

I was on my way in less than three minutes. I used my car phone to call Scott, my Vice President of Sales. He, along with Tom, my Vice-President of Finance, were the brothers I never had.

Scott's oldest daughter, Caroline, answered the phone. "Dad!" she yelled, "Uncle Aaron's on the phone."

"Is Marcia okay?" he asked anxiously.

"I don't think so. She didn't even open her eyes when I was there earlier. They just called and asked me to return."

"Constance, get dressed!" he yelled to his wife. "We'll be there in twenty minutes."

"Call Tom and for God's sake, drive carefully."

I pulled into the parking lot and found a space almost at the front door. I was out of the car sprinting when the front door opened outward and Marcia's doctor stopped me.

"Aaron, we've done all we can. I've administered some painkillers, but she's been calling for you. She's been very brave."

I ran up the three flights of stairs rather than wait for the elevator that always seemed to take forever. One of the nurses sitting at the front desk was crying and the other one couldn't look me in the eye. I went straight into her room. There was a third nurse holding her hand. She got up and left as I entered.

I sat on the side of the bed. "Marcia," I whispered. Nothing happened. "Marcia," I said again. Her eyelids fluttered, but she couldn't open them.

"Aaron," she whispered back. "Aaron?"

"I'm here, I'm here." I said rubbing her hand.

"Don't forget to water my plants."

"I will, but just until you get home."

"Aaron, you've always been an optimist, starting from when we first met in Nam."

"Haven't I always been right?" I whispered back.

A little smile seemed to appear on her lips.

"That's why I love you." She was quiet for a few seconds and then took what looked like a deep breath and sighed.

Almost simultaneously, one of the machines started ringing and the doctor and two nurses came running in. I stepped back as the doctor listened with his stethoscope and a nurse felt for a pulse. I looked away. There was a spider climbing the wall heading towards the ceiling. I wondered if it was a sign of some kind. The walls were an apple green that matched the vertical blinds in a blandness that only happened in hospitals. My feet felt like they were rooted to the floor. I was afraid to make a sound. After a long minute or two, they both stopped and looked at me.

The nurse whose name escaped me said, "I'm so sorry."

Sam Gordon, our doctor and friend, had tears in his eyes. "Some day, we'll figure out how to fight this." He squeezed my hand as they both exited the room.

I was left standing there. Marcia was gone and I was alone. What should I do now? I asked myself. I looked at the bed. She looked so small and fragile. For the past year, we both knew the outcome. I lived in a state of denial. I was sure she would somehow pull through. I sat on the bed and held her hand. I felt tears running down my face. From somewhere behind me, I heard a movement and turned to see both Tom and Scott standing there.

"She's gone," I muttered. "I don't know what to do."

"Don't worry," Tom said. "We're here for you."

I didn't want to leave, but I could feel Marcia was no longer there. In the hall, I found Mary, Tom's wife, and Constance, Scott's wife, sitting on a bench crying. Like their husbands were my best friends, they were Marcia's. They rose in unison and came over to me. The three of us stood with our arms around each other and cried like babies.

Chapter 7

Sally interrupted my reverie. "I asked if you missed your wife."

I nodded. "She was the most breathtaking woman I think I had ever seen, but she was more than that. She became my friend, my love and my reason for being. I find myself thinking less about her every day and sometimes it bothers me. My friends tell me that I have to get on with my life. I don't know if I'm ready."

She stared into the empty coffee cup.

I asked, "How are you doing?"

"About the same. The days aren't bad, but the nights are terrible. I lie in bed wanting to hold on to someone or something. I want to be a woman again, but I'm afraid."

"Afraid of what?" I whispered.

"I don't know, maybe of getting hurt. Maybe of getting involved."

"I'm not a good one to give advice. I've been mourning for a year, but I know at some point you have to move on. I know I do. I guess it's just knowing when." I stared at the shelf and the down-turned picture. Without speaking, Sally rose and picked up the empty cups. Slowly, her feet took her to the stove where she stood staring at the coffeepot. It looked like she was trying to digest what I had said. She walked to the counter, picked up the container of coffee, put it into the refrigerator and placed the cups into the sink.

She walked back into the living room, still without talking. She picked out another tape and put it into the machine. The music immediately filled the room. I recognized "Madam Butterfly" sung by Maria Callas. Sally turned off the light and walked in my direction, still without saying a word. The lights from the street highlighted her frame and she seemed to float across the room. Her hand was held out in front of her as the music filled the room. She still hadn't said a word, and I wasn't sure what was expected. She started walking towards the bedroom putting pressure on my hand to follow. As we entered the bedroom, she turned, put both of her hands around my face and kissed me lightly on the lips. I reached for her as her hands dropped to her waist. She untied the belt around her robe, and I held my breath as the robe fell to the floor. The music continued first with Carmen and then with melodies that sounded familiar. I took off my tie and started to undress as Sally uttered her first words in what seemed like forever.

"Let me," she whispered.

My mouth was like cotton, my ears were filled with some of the most sensuous sounds I could ever remember hearing and my mind was petrified that I wouldn't remember what to do. It had been over a year since I had had sex with anyone and the experience was unsettling. My hands were all thumbs as I looked for the snaps on her bra. Afterward, I thought the people that believed Ravel's "Bolero" was sexy should listen to Maria Callas. She was intoxicating. I felt guilty, I felt exhilarated and I felt like a new person. I left Sally's around 12:30 A.M. We hadn't slept, we made love or had sex—I wasn't sure which. We talked about Marcia, we talked about her husband and we talked about our lives, as they were today and what we thought they would or could have been. We never said we loved each other. In some way, it was like two trains passing in the night, both stopping at the same station at the same time for water. When I left, I started to say that I would call, but she put her fingers on my lips and said, "No promises."

It was a thoroughly strange and enjoyable night, one I was sure I would remember forever. As I started my car, I noticed another car starting just up the block as its headlights went on. I wondered if he was going home or to work.

Chapter 8

There weren't many cars on the freeway heading out of the valley this late at night, but the traffic building up on the way into Los Angeles looked enormous. I had only gone three exits before I realized I was being followed. I had slowed down as I reached for a bottle of water, which was on the seat next to me, and I noticed a car about two to three hundred yards behind me slow down.

I exited at the Calabasas off-ramp and pulled into a Chevron station. The car behind me exited the freeway. When the driver saw where I was headed, he proceeded past the gas station into an industrial park. It was the same car that I thought was following me earlier in the day. I decided that I had had enough of this shit. I used my car phone to call the office. We had over twenty cars with two men in them patrolling the area. My security company was different than many of the others in Los Angeles. We took pains with the people we hired because we were an armed response company. The phone was answered on the first ring and I recognized the voice of the duty officer.

"Carol, this is Aaron. I need some help. I've been followed since early this afternoon and I need some of the men to help put a stop to it."

"Where are you, Boss?"

"I'm at the Chevron station on the north side of the freeway at the Calabasas exit. The car just pulled into the industrial park by the Griffin building."

"Hold on," she said as the phone went silent. Her voice came back. "The cars are rolling. I'm patching you through to them. We have two cars less than thirty seconds away with four more less than a minute behind them. Do you want the sheriff's department notified?"

"Hold off on that until we get this guy and I can figure out what this joker wants. Here comes the first unit."

"Be careful, Boss. Scott will skin me alive if something happens to you."

The first unit pulled up with the second right behind them. A third car pulled up and Tuloc jumped out of the driver's side. He was joined by one of the biggest black guys I ever saw. I was starting to get a rush. I hadn't been out with the men in over two years. Two more cars blocked the street. No one was getting out of the industrial park unless they could fly.

"What do you want us to do, Mr. Carlyle?" asked Tuloc.

Even though I'd been to more than thirty family functions over the years, Tuloc has never called me anything but Mr. Carlyle in public. In private, I was Uncle Aaron. Min, one of my closest friends, was his uncle and would never sit still for a breach of etiquette. I explained about the beige Ford. I told the men I wasn't even sure how many people were in the car. There were eleven buildings in the industrial park along with the local courthouse. My company had contracts to service five of the eleven. By this time, six more cars had joined the group. Tuloc's partner motioned to six or eight of the men and they started to follow him. He turned to Tuloc and said, "Tuloc, you take some of the men and go down the right side. I'll take the left." He pointed at some of the other men and told them to block the street after four of the cars started in. The men driving the four cars were told to drive ahead of the group and block two driveways on each side. I promised myself to find out his name as soon as this was over. He had great leadership qualities that I was sure we could put to good use.

I yelled at the men, "Be careful." I felt foolish because these were trained private investigators. The four cars drove into the industrial park with the men following on foot. They hadn't gotten fifty yards down the street when I heard the sirens. I don't know how, but I knew they were headed toward us. I knew Carol didn't call them and I wondered how they found out. This was really starting to piss me off.

My men's cars blocked the first black and white car that arrived. It was a highway patrol van driven by an officer who was obviously flustered. He hadn't expected to see men in uniform and he started yelling, "What's going on here? Who's in charge? Someone better start talking." He stopped, looked around and walked over to me. I was the only one not wearing a uniform.

"Are you going to answer me?"

"I'm in charge. My name is Aaron Carlyle. I am the president of Be Safe Security and we cover six of the buildings inside of the park. We think we have someone trapped inside and we were just going in to find him. We certainly could use your help."

He turned around. By this time, another fifteen or twenty officers had come running up. Their cars were backed up to the freeway. He was looking for someone and found him at the back of the ever-growing crowd of men.

"Captain, you better get up here. I think we've got ourselves a situation."

The captain walked up to where the group was standing. He stood about six feet tall, had graying hair and his nose looked a little crooked. He surveyed the area, shook his head, looked at the officer and then at me. He smiled and said, "Hello Aaron."

"Hi, Barry."

"Long time no see," he countered.

"I've been out of circulation."

"I'm glad to see you back at work. We were getting worried about you."

Captain Barry Sands was only a sergeant five years ago when he answered a silent alarm call on one of the buildings that we were protecting. I happened to be out checking on the men and arrived about the same time he did. I was standing beside my car as he and his partner opened the door to check out the building. As the door opened, three men wearing masks and carrying shotguns ran out. The last of the three men turned and aimed the gun at the two officers. I must have started moving when I saw the door open because I reached the man aiming at the police just as he pulled the trigger. The sound was deafening, but I hit him just hard enough so that he missed both of the men as they were regaining their balance. Barry got off two quick shots, hitting the man I had hit as he again raised the gun. The other two men with masks had turned and both fired in our general direction. Barry coolly got off three more rounds and both men fell.

It turned out that I was hit in the soft part of my ass by a ricochet. I was lucky; the other officer had taken a hit in his chest. He was rushed to the Westlake Hospital emergency room where he died two days later, leaving a wife and two little boys. I had Carol, his wife, put on my payroll the day before he died, which gave her benefits far beyond those covered by the police. Barry's bullets had killed one of the crooks and to this day he never forgave himself for not killing the other two. That night had started his promotions and a friendship with me, built on mutual respect.

"Who are you looking for?" he asked.

I motioned him away from the men and told him the story starting with last night.

"That figures. We received a call from an Agent Roland at Treasury telling us one of their men was being hassled by some home boys."

"I wonder why the hell they're following me."

"We got him, Mr. Carlyle!"

Barry and I turned as Tuloc and his partner were dragging a man dressed in jeans and a tee shirt towards us.

"What happened to his face?"

"He had a gun," Tuloc answered. "Michael took it away from him."

I walked over to the man and pushed him against the side of one of the cars. "Why the hell are you following me?" I shouted.

Barry hesitated a few seconds to see if he was going to answer and when it was obvious he wasn't going to say anything, he stepped in between me and the man my men had captured.

"Don't hit him, let me do my job. We'll see if we can get anything from him and I'll call you later."

Barry took him by the arm and asked, "Do you have some sort of identification?"

The man shook his head. "I left it in my office."

Barry turned and asked Tuloc to turn him over to one of the police and they would take over from here.

"That's some combination you have there. You better tell your men to start moving their cars. I'll give it the old college try and get back to you as soon as I have some news."

We shook hands and started to leave.

"Say hello to Carol for me," Barry said.

I smiled and said I would. He had been dating Carol for over two years. It was supposed to be a secret and maybe it was. His wife had left him for a dentist three years ago. The cars started pulling away as the men went back to their patrol routes. They only had another couple of hours before the shift would be over.

I yelled over to Tuloc, "Tell Michael I'd like to see him this afternoon."

Tuloc waved an acknowledgement as his car started down the freeway entrance. I called Carol and told her I was headed home and would be in the office around 9:30 A.M.

"Scott called. He said to give him a call when you get a chance."

"Sure. By the way, Barry said to say hello. He led the charge from the regulars." There was no answer and I realized she was afraid to say anything incriminating on an open line.

"Is he still overweight?" she asked.

I hesitated a second and said, "I thought he looked pretty good. Life must be treating him well."

I felt her smiling as I heard her say, "Base out."

I arrived at the office at 9 A.M. I gave Emily, Scott's secretary, my cleaning and asked her to have the cleaners pick them up. My secretary had left about four months ago and I never got around to replacing her. For the second time in two days, I found Scott and Tom waiting for me in the conference room. As I walked in, Scott jumped to his feet and yelled, "Are you freaking crazy?"

Tom chimed in, "You must have lost all your marbles."

"Slow down and let me explain what happened after I left here yesterday." The story took almost forty-five minutes. Neither of them asked a question nor spoke until I finished. I had left out the going to bed part of the story, but Scott, true to his nature, asked, "How was she?"

After a few seconds Tom said, "We can turn this into a big plus."

I looked at him questioningly.

"We let the word out that Aaron saw something that wasn't right and pulled out all the stops. The customers will love it."

Scott continued, "Maybe we can get it into the papers."

"That's not a bad idea," I said, "but make sure, if it gets in the newspapers, that it includes a picture of Tuloc and his partner, Michael something."

"You must mean Michael Harran. He's been with us about four months. He put in his twenty with the San Jose regulars and decided he had enough. If we ever open up in that area, he's a good candidate to head it up."

I told them I had asked him to stop by this afternoon since he did a great job this morning and I wanted to thank him personally.

"He's about five weeks short of his six-month review and raise. If you want, I'll join you and give it to him today."

I looked at Scott and said, "That's a great idea." What Scott had really meant was that is his job, not mine.

Tom had been doodling on his yellow pad and as he looked up he asked me, "What do you think is going on?"

I shook my head. "I really don't know. It obviously has something to do with the money and Sally said the Cubans were involved, but for the life of me I can't figure it out."

"Do you believe what she told you?" asked Scott.

Both Tom and I looked at him. All three of us remembered the other time we had dealt with the government. It was not something you put a lot of trust into.

Chapter 9

Scott's secretary knocked on the open door. We all turned in her direction.

"They ran a trace on the plates of that Ford that you had a problem with this morning."

"What did they find?" Scott asked.

"It's registered to a company called Entertainment, Inc. and it's located in Burbank. A further check found that Entertainment, Inc. is owned by That's Entertainment, housed in Westwood. The only problem we now have is the address for That's Entertainment is the Federal Building on Wilshire."

Tom thanked her for the information and asked her to close the door on her way out. As the door closed, Tom looked at us and asked, "What have we gotten ourselves into this time?"

"I guess they were telling me the truth," I answered.

"Or a part of it," Scott chimed in.

"I'll have to check with Barry and see what he found out," I answered.

"Maybe we should have Carol find out for us," Tom said absentmindedly.

I looked at my two friends and said, "That's one hell of a secret I'm keeping." I stood and told my friends I would call Barry and get back to them with any information. As I reached the door, I stopped short and asked them if they knew a florist that delivered, which brought forth another round of laughter. I shook my head and headed to my office. It was the first time that I could remember laughing that much. The phone was ringing as I entered and I pushed the hands free button.

"Hi Boss. How about taking me off of the speaker?"

I recognized Carol's voice, but before I could acknowledge her, she continued, "You know I was worried stiff this morning when you called. I don't know what I would have done if something happened to you."

I looked at the phone in my hand. Something was wrong and I didn't have a clue what it was.

"Why don't I meet you and put your fears to rest," I whispered.

"I was hoping you would say that. Can we meet at the motel your overweight friend owns?"

She was talking about Barry's condo. Something was wrong. I threw out a question. "How much time do you have before the kids get home?" I was trying to find out when we should meet.

"About an hour and a half," she countered.

"Sorry, but I have something to do at the office. How about tonight?"

"Do you understand everything that I said?" she asked in a voice that was an octave higher.

"I understand. You know this relationship had to end eventually. If you have a problem and want to quit, I'll understand."

"I need the job. There won't be any trouble," she slammed down the phone.

I looked at my watch as I hung up the phone. Scott walked in and told me Michael Harran was outside. I asked him to close the door a second. Putting my finger to my lips, I motioned him into a seat and took out a pad.

"Do we have any equipment that can detect illegal listening devices in the office?" I wrote the question in big block letters. His eyes had a look of alarm.

"You said you needed a florist," he said as he nodded.

"I want to send roses to the woman I had dinner with last night, unless you think it's old fashioned."

"Just give me the address and the spelling of her last name and I'll have Emily get them delivered today."

Those were the words he said, but his eyes were moving all over the room. I repeated the spelling of Sally's last name twice as I handed him the tape from my voice activated recording machine.

"Now that the important stuff is taken care of, let's call in Michael."

"Here is his review form. I'll be back in about fifteen minutes," Scott murmured as he put the tape in his pocket.

In an office about three miles away, the three government agents and Sally were listening to the tapes of conversations being held at Be Safe. "I knew he was a sleaze ball," Agent Carlett said to no one in particular. "He gives Sally some cock and bull story about not being with anyone for over a year and he's banging some secretary at the office."

"Sally, I wish you hadn't hit the off button when you put on the music." This time, it was Agent in Charge Paul Roland that spoke. "Are you sure he didn't say anything that we could use?"

"I told you that I don't believe he's involved," Sally answered a little more quickly than she had wanted. She knew they couldn't hear what went on, but the whole conversation made her uncomfortable.

"Maybe he turned off the listening machine when Sally left the room," Carlett said.

"I wouldn't put it past him," Agent Flores joined the conversation.

Roland turned to Sally and said, "Well, he's sending you flowers. There are two possibilities—one is he's setting you up and the other is he knows nothing. Let's find out which possibility it is and if it turns out that he knows nothing, we'll get rid of him. If he's involved, let's find out what the fuck is going down. Get the rest of his office wired, all the phones and all the rooms. If we don't get anything in seven days, we'll try something else. Sally, you go home and wait on Romeo. You two get ready for twenty-four hour surveillance."

"How about some help?"

"Roger's got a busted nose, but I'll try and get two or three more people."

Sally opened the door and turned back into the room. "I still think this is a dead end."

Roland shrugged his shoulders and said, "Maybe, but it's the only lead we've got."

After Sally left, Carlett said, "I don't trust that bitch. I think she turned off the mike."

Flores said, "You're just pissed that he scored after you've been trying for six months."

"Stop it," said Roland. "Today's problem is what happened to the missing cop, Garret, and I'm not so sure he did."

"I think he met with Carlyle afterwards. We were lucky. Sally was so close; it stopped whatever they had planned, and for the record, I think he did."

"Tell me again why you think he's involved?" Roland asked Carlett.

"Something happened in Nam that got covered over that he was a part of. Almost every time that happened, some sort of drug operation was being covered up."

"That's another thing we have to find out about. I'm having a problem getting the records opened."

As I walked out of the conference room, Emily waved at me to stop at her desk. She was on the phone taking down Sally's address and as she put down the receiver, she asked if there was anything special I wanted written on the card. I felt my ears warm and said, "No, just 'Thanks for joining me for dinner.'"

As I started to walk away she said, "The cleaners found this in your pocket." She handed me a little notebook. I stared at it for a second before I remembered where it came from. The book had fallen out of the purse I was holding for the woman in the accident. I opened the book and looked inside at a series of numbers and letters that made absolutely no sense. I stuck it in my pocket and drove over to Barry's condo twice, doubling back to make sure I wasn't being followed. My paranoia was starting to bother me. Since I was about thirty minutes early, I parked two blocks away from Barry's condo and I opened the little book. I again realized the entries were written in some type of code. There were four rows. The first row had a six-digit number that was obviously a date. The second row was groups of four or five letters that meant nothing to me. The third row was three digit numbers and the fourth row was again a date. Each page had six entries and there were four pages with writing on them. I decided to show the book to Tom to see what he could make of it before I returned it to the police. I walked over to Barry's place and knocked on the door. He greeted me with a smile, but I could tell something was wrong. I followed him into the kitchen.

He motioned towards the refrigerator and said, "Help yourself to a beer."

I opened the door and took out a Coors Light.

Barry started in right away. "What the hell did you get yourself involved in? I spoke to Captain Beckman and off the record he tells me these are bad people. That's why I had Carol call you. They have some kind of clout that goes as high or higher than anyone Beckman knows. His Sergeant Garret has disappeared and when they went to his place to find him, they found it in shambles. They have initiated an all-city search, which will be expanded tomorrow when they can call in the FBI. To make things even worse, about a half hour ago I received a phone call, again off the record. They found the body of Sally Novak. She was beaten and then shot."

I had been listening to Barry and trying to digest what he had been saying, but I wasn't prepared for that. I sat up and said, "That's impossible. I was with her last night. I had just come from her house when I noticed the car following me."

"It's no mistake. I've had it verified."

"Do they know who did it?" I laid my beer on the table with a shaking hand. I felt like I was going to be sick.

"No, but they have a tape recording. It seems the house was wired. They have the whole thing on tape, but from what I've heard, it had to do with the evidence bag from the scene of the accident."

I sat there, my mind going in a hundred different directions. "The money, it must be the money."

Barry looked at me for a few seconds and then said, "I guess so. We have people getting murdered for a whole lot less."

We sat there in silence.

Barry asked, "How are you handling this?"

I stared at him. It was just like Barry. No bullshit, no pussyfooting around. He just asked the question.

"I don't know. She was the first woman I've been with in over a year." I shook my head; there was nothing to say. I got up from the couch, shook Barry's hand and headed towards the door.

"Be careful. We really don't know what the killers were after and we don't know what is on the tape. They could decide to ask you some questions if they haven't found what they were looking for."

Chapter 10

I left and headed back to my office. My mind was going around in circles. My first impulse was to call someone, but I couldn't figure out who that someone was. I started to talk to myself, trying to figure out what was going on.

I certainly didn't trust the people Sally had worked for. I wasn't even sure I trusted the L.A.P.D. I looked up suddenly and stared out the rearview mirror. I just realized I hadn't been paying attention to what I was doing. Two quick right turns showed me that I wasn't being followed. I decided to get something to eat before going back to the office. I hit my phone and called out "Office."

The phone was answered on the second ring. "Be Safe Security, how may I direct your call?"

"Hi, this is Aaron. Can I speak to Tom, please?"

There was a brief hesitation.

"Sorry, Aaron. Tom is busy right now."

"Okay, how about Scott?"

"Sorry, but Scott is also busy."

"Put me through to Emily, Scott's secretary."

Without even taking a breath, she replied, "Emily is busy. I think you should call back later or come on in."

I shook my head, bewildered. "Is there anyone besides yourself that's not on the phone?"

"Nope. I was told to tell you that anyone you asked for is busy on the phone."

"I'm glad to see we're busy," I said sarcastically. "If anyone asks, tell them I'll be in around 3:30 P.M."

"Sorry, Boss, they want to see you before then."

"Who wants to see me before then?"

"Scott and Tom."

"Are either one of them off the phone yet?"

"They will be by the time you get here."

"In that case, I'll be there in about fifteen minutes."

"I'll see that they get your message."

The connection was broken, leaving me staring out the front window wondering what the hell was going on.

Ten minutes later as I approached the office, my car phone rang. I touched the receive button and said, "This is Aaron."

Scott's voice came out of the speaker, "How far are you from the office?"

"Less than five minutes. What's going on?"

"Meet Tom and me over at Roxie's. We're pulling into the parking lot now."

Roxie's was the local twenty-four-hour deli. It was frequented by many of our people. The food was good; they served humongous portions and didn't charge an arm and a leg. I pulled into the parking lot just as Scott and Tom were walking in the front door. They stopped, waved and waited for me to park my car. Through the window I noticed Tuloc sitting at a table by the front door. Michael Harran was at a table by the kitchen and there were at least three more of our men sitting at other tables inside the dining area. We were shown a table in the middle of the room and it was then that I realized our men were at every table surrounding us.

"Is something going on?" I asked, motioning to the men seated at the tables.

Scott said to Tom, "Why don't you bring him up to date."

Tom acknowledged with a nod of his head. "We found some very sophisticated listening devices around the office. There were two different kinds. There was one in each of our offices and one attached to your private phone line."

Scott then continued, "We left them in place so whoever is bugging us won't know we found them. These are not run of the mill ears. They are voice-activated and they have a range of about three and a half miles. We don't know when they were installed, but we both think it has something to do with the accident you were involved in two nights ago."

I looked at my two closest friends and brought them up to date with what I had found out from Barry.

There was a waiter standing about ten to fifteen feet away. Tom motioned him over and ordered a cup of coffee and danish.

Scott said, "I'll have the same. What about you, Aaron?"

I was sitting there thinking about what was going on when Scott repeated the question.

"Aaron, do you want something to eat?"

“Just coffee,” I said to the waiter.

When he was out of hearing range, Tom said, “I think that it gets worse. The accident happened two nights ago. It wasn’t until last night that whoever is behind this knew they had a problem of some kind. That means the bugs had to be installed sometime early today. I don’t believe they could have gotten a court order that quickly and I don’t know how they got them installed with all of our people walking around.”

The waiter arrived with their order and while he was there, we didn’t say a word.

“It has to be someone from the cleaning service,” I said as soon as the waiter was out of hearing range. “I will contact Min and have him run a check on all of his people”

“I haven’t seen or spoken to him in over three months. How is he doing?” asked Tom.

“How is he doing? He’s the same old Min. It’s been nine years since we met him and he doesn’t look a day older. He’s still as active as ever. He calls every other week or so to find out how everything is going. I think he misses Marcia, but is afraid to show how much.”

My mind wandered back to the first day we met Min.

Chapter 11

Havoc was the order of the day. Six months prior, I was on patrol when Charlie opened up on us. The lieutenant was downed along with half the platoon. Luckily, I was up in front and the initial firing took place behind me. My college education went for naught. Instead of ducking behind the trees and waiting for the shooting to stop, I yelled for the four men up front to follow me back to the fighting. With all of our hollering and shooting, the enemy took off running. They put me in for a medal and gave me a battlefield commission to second lieutenant. For five and a half months I was assigned to the security section of the Military Police. The duty was great and then the shit hit the fan. It became obvious to anyone with half a brain that we were pulling out. Headquarters people were boarding planes as quickly as we could land them.

I was put in charge of loading or destroying everything of any value inside our consulate. Over the last three days, helicopters were landing on the roof, twenty-four hours a day. We could hear Charlie coming in from the south of the city. Some die-hard regular soldiers were trying to pick off their leaders and stop the inevitable from happening. The helicopters kept landing, but not as frequently as earlier in the week. They were taking out the last of our nationals and some South Vietnamese big shots.

In reality, everyone who was important left two days before. The people that were still there were the good guys. They were the ones that had put their lives on the line and hadn't skimmed a whole bunch of money off of the top. During the last year, the politicians living in and around Saigon had established a new meaning to the words "Fat Cats." There was no doubt in my mind that there were many Americans lining their pockets with the waste that was being perpetrated on the people back home. There were drugs that disappeared from the docks before they could be distributed to the hospitals that ended up on the black market at astronomical prices. Food, guns, trucks and tanks were missing after coming off the boat.

I had just put a match to the last of the classified papers as a helicopter got ready to take off. It carried the final "civilians," as we laughingly called the local CIA agents. The warrant officer flying the copter yelled, "There's only two more on the way. Make sure you're on the next one."

That left three Marines, about thirty Vietnamese people and myself on the roof. Down in the courtyard, there were nine more Marines and a shit pot full of South Vietnamese. With each helicopter capable of carrying twenty-five people, a bunch were not getting out. Some of the people were starting to get the same feeling. Shots broke out in the courtyard as people started to break in the gates.

One of the Marines looked up and yelled, "What should we do?"

I looked around. I was the ranking officer in the compound. I turned to the other Marines and said, "Follow me! We've got to get out of here." When I reached the bottom, I yelled for the other Marines to follow me. "Take as much canned goods and ammunition as you can carry." Earlier, I had noticed there was a back door along the wall leading to the jungle. At one point, we had picked up two of the South Vietnamese troops and as we went through the back door, I motioned for one of them to hang some grenades from the handle. If someone else was coming through this door, I wanted to know it. It was only two or three blocks to the jungle and surprisingly, there wasn't a soul in the streets. We no sooner reached the safety of the trees than we heard a loud cheer. We all turned and stood there as the flag of the United States went down and the flag of the people that had won was raised.

I felt anger, rage and shame all at the same time. One thing was for sure, there were no more helicopters coming back to get us. We were left behind to fend for ourselves. I wondered if the government would consider us M.I.A. or deserters. At this point, I didn't really care.

One of the Marines was looking at a map. "I think we should head towards the water," he said.

I looked over his shoulder at the map. Vietnam is shaped like an elongated S. It's the size of Italy or maybe New Mexico. China lies to the north, Laos and Cambodia to the west and the South China Sea to the east and south.

I looked at the two Vietnamese men. "My name is Lieutenant Aaron Carlyle. It looks like I'm in charge of this group. I have no objection to you two joining us, but if you do, remember, I'm in charge."

In all the time I had been in Nam, I never was able to look at any of the Vietnamese and tell what they were thinking. This time was no exception, except one of them smiled. All of a sudden, I wasn't even sure they spoke English. I pointed to the one who smiled and said deliberately.

"Do . . . you . . . understand . . . me?"

"Yes . . . I . . . do," he replied as slowly as I had asked the question.

He started to laugh. It was infectious. "You speak English," I said between the first sobs of laughter I remembered in over a week.

He held out his hand. "My name is Min." He pointed to the other Vietnamese man. "His name is Giac. His English is not so good as mine. We are prepared to follow your orders and help you get out of Vietnam with one condition."

"Which is?"

"When we are beyond the reach of the men from the north, you will help us get to the United States."

I turned and looked at the other Marines. We could certainly use their help, but I didn't know how to answer their request. Two of the men stepped forward.

Lieutenant, my name is Scott and this ugly guy on my left is Tom. We've been together for about eight months and gotten to know each other pretty good. I have some suggestions." He stopped and waited on my reply.

"Go ahead," I said. "I'm willing to take all the advice and help I can get."

"The first thing you need to do is take off your bars, just in case. Secondly, say yes to the two Vietnamese. They know the territory. I'm sure the government will let them come with us."

Two explosions interrupted him. We all turned and looked back at the Consulate as the cheering turned to screams.

"Thirdly, let's get the hell out of here. That was the back door," Scott yelled.

Min stepped forward and held out his hand. "Lieutenant, do we have a deal?"

Chapter 12

Scott began to rise. "Let's get back to work. We have an annual report to work on and some customers to visit explaining what happened last night. I also have some ideas on how we might be able to trace the listening devices."

Before Tom and I could get off our chairs, a commotion started about twenty feet away. A well-built balding man had entered the restaurant and moved to take a seat somewhere in the vicinity of where we were sitting. Tuloc asked the man to please sit at one of the other tables with the explanation that he was expecting some friends. The man kept walking until he reached the table right next to the one we were sitting at, pulled out a chair, turned to Tuloc and said, "Tough shit, Chink, first come first served."

Tuloc replied with a smile on his face, "I very sorry, but I not understand the words that you say."

I smiled. Tuloc was an English major at UCLA and his answer in Pidgin English had the start of a very funny conversation.

Tom said, "Let the boys handle it," as we headed towards the exit.

Tuloc bowed to the balding man and said, "So sorry for confusion, you have table, but when you order food I think you find shit not tough."

Tuloc turned and started walking towards the three of us. The balding man rose to his feet as if he was going to follow Tuloc when Michael Harran placed a hand on his shoulder and said, "I wouldn't. Why don't you just order something to eat and think of this as a learning experience?"

Scott walked to my car and said, "I'll ride back with you. Tom has to make a stop first."

As I turned out of the parking lot, Scott started talking. "Tom and I are concerned."

I held up my hand and nodded towards the phone booth outside of the restaurant. The balding man that Tuloc had the run-in with was on the phone speaking animatedly to someone.

"Interesting," I said. "You were saying?"

"We're not so much worried about whoever is after the money. We figure that they'll disappear sooner or later, but we're not sure how this lady cop's death is going to affect you internally. It's been a little over a year since Marcia died and this was the first woman you've been with."

I was reminded of something Marcia had once said about a sentence that was a question and a statement. I thought back and it came to me, "Is that an interabang?"

Scott smiled. "I remember the day we were going to run that ad. Better safe than sorry. Really, how is it going?"

I thought about his question for a second and then I answered, "The truth is, I feel terrible. I'm sorry she's dead, but for some reason I feel just as bad about the woman in the accident. The sex was good, but it was just that—sex. I tried to feel something when I left Barry's, but I just couldn't. I tried to psychoanalyze myself and kept coming up with absolutely nothing. Maybe it was because there is something in the back of my head that says all she wanted was information, or maybe all I am is a piece of shit."

By this time, I had arrived at our company's parking lot.

Scott leaned over, put his hand on my shoulder and said, "Just remember, pal, Tom and I are here if you need us."

As we got out of the car, Tom came walking over. He glanced at Scott who nodded his head up and down and said, "Let's get some work done."

I looked at my two friends and felt tears welling up in my eyes. "You chicken-hearted bastards. You made Scott do all the dirty work." I put my arms around both of them and we all started laughing.

As we entered the building, I mentioned I would call Min on my cell phone and get back to them when and if he had any answers. I passed Carol at the front desk and winked at her.

She smiled and said, "I have a call for you."

"Anyone I know?"

"I don't know. She says her name is Karen Williams."

"Take her number and tell her I'll call her back in less than five minutes."

I took the number from Carol and walked back out to the parking lot. I didn't want anyone listening in on this call. I had omitted her name from the report I gave the police and didn't want to get her involved. She answered on the first ring.

"Karen here."

"Karen, this is Aaron Carlyle returning your call."

"That was quick. For a second, I thought you were going to duck my call."

"Why would I do that?"

"I don't know, but I received a phone call from Jerry and he told me some police had called and asked about Monday night's dinner. It wasn't until after they had hung up that he realized they never asked about me."

"On the way home, I witnessed an accident that got very involved because I pulled the woman from her car. They asked me what I was doing there at 1 A.M. and I told them I'd been out to dinner with Jerry and his wife and didn't add your name. I decided there was no reason to get you involved."

"That was very nice of you. Now I wonder if you can do me another favor."

She made the question sound like I had done her a favor by not including her and there was no way I could turn down whatever she was going to ask me. I waited for her to continue.

"This Friday, actually tomorrow, I have to be in Santa Barbara to visit a client. My appointment is at 11 A.M. and will probably run until 3:30 P.M. or 4 P.M. I'm driving up in the morning, but I don't feel like driving all the way home that night. I expect to be passing the Thousand Oaks/Westlake area between 5:30 P.M. and 6 P.M. and wondered if you could suggest a nice hotel in that area."

"There's a Hyatt at the Westlake exit. I'll have my secretary make reservations for you and I'll make sure she guarantees late arrival in case your business appointment runs late."

"Thanks. What's your secretary's name? I'll have to send her a thank you note."

"Actually, she's not my secretary. I haven't gotten a replacement yet. Her name is Emily, but I'll tell you what. I'll make the reservations and instead of a note, how about having dinner with me?"

"You don't have to do that," she replied.

"I know I don't have to, but I would like to. You better say yes or you'll find yourself without a room. Dress is casual and I'll pick you up at 7:15 P.M."

"That sounds great as long as I'm not putting you out."

I told her again it was no problem and hung up the phone. I went back inside the building and before I had taken ten steps, Carol waved at me.

"Call Barry. He said it was urgent."

I turned back towards the parking lot and said to no one in particular, "I should put a phone booth out here." I dialed Barry's private line. He answered on the first ring.

"Sands."

"Barry, it's Aaron. What's up?

"What's up? I wish the fuck we knew. Your friend Agent Roland and his crew of merry men, have all just turned up dead."

"What do you mean dead?"

"D.E.A.D. Dead. I received a call fifteen minutes ago from the L.A.P.D. They called me because of my involvement last night. It looks like a professional job. The story they are telling is that it was related to an investigation they were working on, some sort of Cuban attempt to screw with the United States. They also found their missing guy. He's not dead, but close. From what they've been able to get from him, there was something in the woman's purse and that's what everyone is after."

"The notebook," I said aloud.

"What did you say?" asked Barry.

"Nothing, I was just thinking aloud."

Barry continued, "It is probably hitting the television news as we speak. By tomorrow, it will be a major story in every major newspaper in the world. They are counting six dead and one almost."

"Where are they getting six?"

"The three guys you met, your woman friend, her husband and the lady in the accident."

"So the story she told me about her husband was true."

"At least that part of it. Listen, if I hear anything else, I'll give you a call. Look out for yourself. We don't know if it's over."

"Thanks for the call. I'll keep in touch."

I started back inside when I remembered I had to speak to Min. I made a U-turn and walked back out onto the parking lot. On the second ring, the phone was answered with a terse request.

"Who is calling and who do you wish to speak to?"

"This is Aaron Carlyle and I wish to speak to Min."

"One second please."

It seemed less than that when Min picked up the receiver.

"Aaron, it is a pleasure to hear from you. I was just getting ready for my daily massage. Why don't you come over? I will tell her she has another customer tonight."

I pictured Min getting a massage from one of the absolutely gorgeous woman that seemed to always be around him.

"It sounds tempting, but this is business. When will you be finished? We have to talk."

Without a second's hesitation, he replied, "I will be finished as you walk in the door. I will have some food prepared and we will eat as we talk."

"You've got a deal. I'll see you in about forty-five minutes."

I didn't bother going back into the office. A phone call to Emily would let everyone know where I was and where I could be reached.

Emily seemed out of breath when she picked up my call.

"This is Emily," she whispered.

"Is everything all right?" I queried.

"Everything's fine. I was at the other end of the office. What can I do for you?"

"I just remembered I promised someone that I would make reservations for them at the Hyatt for tomorrow night."

"No problem. What's their name? I'll make it."

All of a sudden I felt self-conscious. "On second thought, I can do it. Just give me the number and I'll call it in."

"Boss, don't be an ass. Suppose I just make it under the name of Karen Williams and whoever shows up can use it."

"How did you know it was for Karen?" I stuttered.

"Give me a little credit for knowing what goes on around here," she laughed. "I'll use your credit card number to guarantee late arrival. Anything else you need?"

"No, I don't think so. If Tom or Scott asks, I'm off to see the cleaning service."

"Boss, what about dinner?"

"Who said I was taking her to dinner?" I asked defensively. After a slight hesitation, I continued, "How does the club sound?"

She didn't answer right away. "Not bad, but how about Boccacio's?"

I took a deep breath, thought about it for a couple of seconds and said, "A little too fancy. I told her to dress casual."

"The club it is. We'll hold Boccacio's in reserve for a later date."

I started laughing. "Thanks Auntie Em. I'll see you tomorrow."

The trip to Min's was uneventful. There was no earth-shattering news. The Dow was up thirty-five and the NASDAQ was up eleven. I promised myself to find out how we were doing.

Chapter 13

One of the things about visiting Min was that very little ever changed. There were always four cars parked at the corners with two men in each car. The cars weren't new, they weren't conspicuous, and they were just there.

In all the years that we had been friends, I never asked and Min never volunteered the answer to my unasked question. Why did he need this type of protection? I parked my car at the curb at the exact same time that a young Vietnamese boy walked down the three steps from Min's front door.

He bowed his head and said, "Mr. Carlyle, I would be most honored if you would allow me to park your car. Uncle Min has asked that you go straight in. He is expecting you."

"Thank you." I handed him my keys as I turned and walked up the stairs. The door opened as I reached the top step. A very beautiful young woman with long jet-black hair stood with a tray holding three drinks.

"The glass on the left contains oolong iced tea, the one in the center, Evian water, and the glass on the right is a gin and tonic."

"Thank you, Soo Kim. My throat is parched. I will take the iced tea." I could see that she was pleased I remembered her name. She was Min's granddaughter.

"Please follow me." She led me to the living room where a picture of Min's parents hung over a table, which had two hot plates with six covered dishes of food.

"Please make yourself comfortable. My grandfather will join you shortly." She no sooner finished the sentence than Min came walking into the room.

"Aaron my friend, it is very good to see you. Have you thought about the massage we spoke about?"

"I thought about it, but I decided I would rather join you for dinner. Maybe next time."

"As you wish. I have found that as I get older I need one every two or three days. If you visited more often, I am sure we would find the time."

I smiled. "I was here three weeks ago. If I came more often, I would probably become a nuisance."

He smiled back, "My people have a saying, to visit with one's friends is never a bother."

I laughed out loud. "I think you make up half the sayings your people have, but thank you for the kind thought."

Min pushed a button on the side of his desk and Soo Kim came back into the room. This time, she carried a tray with hot towels. She put the tray on the table in the middle of the room, picked up a pair of tongs and handed us both a towel. Silently, she picked up the tray and held it for me to put the used towel back on the tray.

She then turned to Min and did the same thing except as she took his towel she said, "I will leave you gentlemen alone, but grandfather please do not overeat. Mr. Carlyle, I am putting you in charge of watching him."

Min scowled at her, but she just stuck out her tongue and left the room.

As the door closed, my friend started to smile.

"Children nowadays have no respect for their elders. My people have a saying . . ."

I held up my hand. "Min, my people have a saying. The apple doesn't fall far from the tree. Your granddaughter is very much like you, except she is beautiful."

He nodded. "You are right, she is beautiful. Now let us eat."

We both filled our plates with shrimp, rice, lamb and fish dishes. Eating at Min's was always an Epicurean delight. Over the years, Marcia and I had done this many times. During those times, I learned that business was never discussed until dessert was served. Min surprised me.

"I have heard you have some personal problems," Min began in a discreet tone. "I hope your visit to me means that in some small way I can be of assistance."

I started with the crash and told him everything up to my meeting with Scott and Tom. I told him the story about the Cubans that Sally had told me, but left out the part about the bugs and the notebook. He listened without saying a word.

When I was finished, he looked at me like Sydney Toller, the original Charlie Chan, used to look at suspects and said, "You have left something out. The government or the police could handle what you told me. There must be more to the story."

I rose and said, "There is no more. I don't understand what is happening." I walked over to the doors that opened to the backyard. "It is very nice outside. Would you mind if I walked through your garden?"

Min stood. His face had grown darker. He understood that I wanted to finish the story outside, but was offended when I was afraid to speak inside the house. As we walked out the back door into the garden, I noticed someone already entering the room and taking away the dirty dishes.

When we were a safe distance from the house, I turned to Min. "You're right. There is another part of the story. Sometime between Tuesday night and Wednesday morning someone put listening devices into our office. We found four of them after Barry alerted me to the possible problem. Our first thought was that it had to be one of our people, but after we went through all the people and the times that they worked, we decided that it had to be one of yours."

"It is impossible. These people are trusted employees of mine."

"Inside your house, people move about as if they were listening in on conversations. Isn't it possible one of them has sold out to the Cubans?"

Min digested what I said before he replied. "I understand what you are thinking, but for the Cubans to get to one of my people in such a short time I find outrageous." His teeth were clenched together. There was a twitch on his forehead. I had never seen Min this upset before.

"I thought of that, which is why I wanted to finish the conversation outside. I have never asked why you need the guards outside your door. I have never asked where you got the money to open gas stations or for that matter the cleaning service. You and I have been friends for eight years and friends trust each other. We always have and I see nothing that could change that. My only thought was that you have made an enemy that has infiltrated your business. That same enemy, in a strange quirk of fate, has now become my enemy and as such this situation was very easily accomplished."

Min stood absolutely still. It seemed to me that he didn't even blink. After what seemed like minutes, but was probably only seconds, Min nodded. "You are of course correct. We are friends. In the eight years that we have known each other you have never pried into my affairs and in fact we have become very much like family. We have together shared good times and together we have mourned the bad times. It is only fitting that I tell you of my background before we met and how I have managed to achieve the lifestyle in which I live. Let me refresh our memories of a time gone past."

He sat on one of the lawn chairs and motioned for me to do the same.

Chapter 14

He began, "We shook hands, you and, I agreeing to work together to escape from the soldiers from the north.

"It did not seem important that I tell you when we first met what my rank or status was. Getting out of Saigon was the most important thing at that time. It was promised by your government, which is now mine as well, that I would be taken care of along with General Giac in the event that South Vietnam was to fall to the enemy. I was a two-star general. I was in charge of the area to the north of Saigon. I reported to General Giac who was my commander in charge of both the territories to the north as well as the south of that once lovely city. We had been given instructions to report to the U.S. Consulate for evacuation, but upon arrival, we found that we were being treated as common soldiers and not allowed access to the grounds. Luckily for us, I had been a college professor prior to the conflict and knew enough powerful people so some of our families were able to get out on earlier aircrafts. Our rank enabled us to make sure that they left with enough money and jewels so that wherever they landed, there would be enough to get started. Giac and myself had some debts of honor that had to be taken care of before we left, which was the reason we were not on the earlier aircrafts. Our leaving with you was a sign from Buddha that what we had done was correct.

"Our deal with your government was a little different than yours. Aside from allowing us to keep the money, and their honoring of your promise to help us get to the United States, they had to help us locate our families and have them transported to where they delivered us. To avoid people asking too many questions about how so many Vietnamese ended up in the same place, they requested and we agreed that the Giac and Min families be located in different parts of our new country. As you know, Giac moved to Colorado where his family is thriving."

I listened, fascinated, as we stood and walked through the exotic flowers and colorful rose bushes.

"You remember two years ago that my friend died and I became what you Americans call the Godfather for both families' business interests. Our combined family worth is now in excess of fifty million American dollars. The money has been earned honestly with hard work and careful investments. One of our investments was in a security firm whose stock went up over thirty-three percent, and while it is down a little right now, we expect big things in the future. As to the reason for guards, we found that when Giac and I repaid our debts of honor, some people were overlooked. We had decided to let those people go on with their lives. They were forced to stay in that country and that was punishment enough. We were not sure that they all think as we do. Over the years, we have been attempting to find out if these people are still alive and if they are, if they are willing to forget the past. We have not yet found out about all of them."

Min stopped and took a drink of iced tea from the glass he had been carrying since dinner.

"What are you going to do if you find some that will not forgive or forget?"

He looked at me for a second and then shrugged his shoulders. "It has to end." He paused. "Somehow."

Min's granddaughter came outside and said, "Grandfather, it is starting to get a little chilly. Do you need a jacket?"

"Thank you for asking, but we will only be out here another few minutes." She bowed and returned to the house.

It was time to reflect. I thought about what I had learned about my friend and he was thinking of what I had said.

"We must look elsewhere. It cannot be a Cuban." Min spoke with a vicious tone that I had never heard him use before. "If you had said that there were Vietnamese involved, I might be tempted to have my closest relatives take another look, but it would be beyond any stretch of the imagination to think that any of my people would be involved with Cubans."

"I can only repeat what I've been told. Out of friendship, could you please have your nephews take a look at the people that were in our building? We now know how to locate the listening devices and will be able to handle that part of our problem, but until we find out who installed them, I think we are both at some sort of risk."

He thought for a second and then nodded. “It will take a day or two to check out everyone, but I will get back to you.” He stood and we both walked back into the house.

“Aaron, tell me, have you met any nice women yet?”

I smiled, “In fact I have. I am meeting her for dinner tomorrow night.”

He smiled knowingly. “I know of a very good restaurant when you think the time is right.”

“When the time is right, you will be one of the first people I call.” We shook hands.

“Be careful, my friend.” He whispered the advice.

“You too,” I answered in kind.

My car was parked at the curb with the motor running as I came out of Min’s home.

One of the guards said, “We had the car washed and filled with gas while you were inside. Uncle Min has just purchased a new gas station and asked us to make sure that the service was as he expected it to be.”

I turned back towards the house. Min’s granddaughter stood on the steps.

“Soo Kim, tell your grandfather that I said thank you.”

She waved and entered the building. As I started the drive home, I thought to myself, a washed car filled with gas always seems to run better.

Chapter 15

The ride back was uneventful. There were no accidents, no cars following me, no ghosts from days past. It had seemed that wherever I went this past year there was always something to remind me of Marcia. Tonight felt different. Nothing seemed familiar; there weren't any memories, good or bad. It was odd. I pulled up in front of my house and got out of the car to pick up the newspaper from the driveway. As I straightened up, I noticed a man standing on the corner about one hundred yards away. He wasn't looking in my direction. In fact, I didn't even know why he caught my eye. We stared at each other as if we were each looking for something. He started walking away down the hill on which I lived. I had seen hundreds of people do this all the time. My house was located on top of a hill along with six others. People were always walking up and down getting their exercise. I stared at his back as he disappeared from view. There was something familiar about him, but I just couldn't put my finger on it. I shrugged my shoulders and drove the car into the garage. My phone was ringing as I entered the house.

"Hello?" I said into the receiver.

"Aaron, where have you been?" yelled Tom.

"I was visiting with Min. I left word with Emily."

"Emily's been in an accident. According to the police, someone ran her off the road."

"Was she hurt?"

"She's listed as critical, but when I spoke to the doctor he said they expected her to recover."

"Did they get the person who was driving the other car?"

"That's what makes this so strange. An eyewitness told the police that the other car stopped, a man got out and took her pocketbook. The police are listing it as a robbery."

"Robbery? Who the hell crashes into someone just to rob them?"

"That's what I thought. I've ordered round the clock guards until Emily is strong enough to tell us what happened."

"Do you think this has something to do with my problems?"

"I don't think so, but that's why I put the guards at the hospital. Just for the record, they're our problems."

"How is her family handling it?" I asked, not acknowledging his comment.

"Her son is at the hospital and her daughter is driving up from Carlsbad. I'm sure they'll be all right. While I have you on the phone, what did Min have to say?"

"He doesn't believe it was his people. Maybe if we were involved with Vietnamese, but definitely not Cubans. I asked him to take another look and he agreed. I was thinking about the listening devices and I think we should take them out. Let's tell whoever they belong to that we're as smart as they are if not smarter."

"You're probably right. I'll get in touch with Scott and have them deactivated first thing in the morning. I'll talk to you tomorrow. Get a good night's sleep."

I hung up the phone and hit the on button for the television. The story about the deaths of the federal agents was just starting. It ran as I had heard it from Barry, except that the government spokesman was attributing it to a drug bust gone badly. As I listened, the story seemed to make sense. The Attorney General was promising to quickly apprehend the people involved and a reward was offered for information leading to the arrest and conviction. Sally's death wasn't mentioned and I assumed they were keeping that part of the story quiet.

The rest of the news was what I had heard on the radio in the car. The Lakers won, the Clippers lost and the stock market was up twenty-seven and a half points. I made a mental note to check on the price of Be Safe stock in the morning. Every time I listened to the radio this week the stock market was up. I wasn't planning on selling any in the near future, but a rising stock price benefited the rest of the employees. I remembered when we went public. Marcia was concerned that we wouldn't get a good symbol. BESF was the symbol the broker that took us public submitted to the SEC for Be Safe. The only thing that could have made it better would have been five letters, BESAF, but this wasn't half-bad.

I crawled into bed, used the clicker to turn off the television and just as my eyes began to close, I started to think about something that had happened. Whatever it was eluded me. I tried to remember if it had to do with something Barry said, the death of the treasury agents, Sally, Min or maybe the guy I saw outside. After a couple of minutes, I gave up and fell asleep. I tossed and turned most of the night. Exhausted, I finally dragged myself out of bed before the sun rose. I hit the clicker as I walked inside to shower and the first thing I heard was that it was going to be a great Friday in the Southland. This has had to be one of the quickest weeks I could remember. Showering, I tried to recall the thought that escaped me last night. My mind kept jumping ahead to tonight's dinner with Karen, which reminded me about Emily. I picked up the phone and called the regional medical center. The operator thought it was a little early, but put me through to the nurse's station. The only information the nurse would disclose was that the patient was in serious but stable condition, and doing as well as could be expected. I asked the operator, "Are any of the family around?" After a few seconds Emily's daughter picked up the phone.

"Hi, this is Aaron Carlyle. How's your mom?"

"Mr. Carlyle, thank you for calling. She's awake and starting to recognize us. It looks like she'll be fine. The doctor told us he is going to upgrade her condition to serious, which sounds a lot better than critical."

"Sounds great, but I don't want to keep you. When you get a chance, tell her I called and said she could have the day off, but I expect her back at work on Monday."

"Mr. Carlyle, I don't know if she'll be able to be back by Monday."

"I'm only kidding. Just tell her not to worry and I'll stop by to say hello when she can have visitors."

"Thank you for calling. I'll give her your message."

Her voice had a concerned edge to it. I guess I shouldn't have kidded around.

Chapter 16

The gloom at the office was so thick you could cut it with a knife. There was a big fish bowl with money in it and a card to be signed. I dropped in a twenty and signed the card. Scott came walking down the hall.

"They found the car that ran her off the road. It was reported stolen yesterday in Encino."

"I guess it would be too much to think someone saw the person that stole it."

"The police are checking, but you're probably right."

Tom walked up and said, "The men that stood vigil at the hospital last night are refusing to sign time cards."

"Why?"

"Some of the men said they weren't busy anyway, but the story I am getting is that if word ever got out that they took money for watching over Emily, they'd have to get new families. She seems to be very well liked by the men."

"I thought of something last night. Step into the conference room a second and let me tell you my idea."

Scott and Tom preceded me into the conference room. I looked around and mouthed the word, "Bugs?"

Tom spoke up, "I had them all removed last night. I personally went through the place this morning to see if they were back and they're not."

Scott asked, "What did you want to talk about?"

"How about sending Emily to some training sessions and making her your assistant H.R. director?"

"Why should I lose a great secretary?" Scott almost shouted.

"Probably because you do a great job training them," replied Tom.

"Okay it's settled," I said. "The only thing left to decide is who tells her and how much more she gets paid."

"If it's okay with you guys, I'll tell her. She was my secretary," Tom said with a faked surrender in his voice. "By the way, while you're out shopping for a new girl Friday, see if you can find me one." I felt a momentary twinge in my stomach. It was another break from the past year's period of mourning.

"Tom, do me a favor," said Scott. "I'm going to visit three companies in Calabasas where Aaron had that run-in the other night. Ask personnel to have at least five or six secretaries here by 2 P.M."

"Will five or six be enough?"

"I only need one or two, but after I pick, I want Aaron to have a choice."

"I hate interviewing secretaries. You know that."

"Indeed I do, but I wasn't the one who thought it would be a good idea to give up Emily. It shouldn't take more than four or five hours. See you soon. I don't want to be late for my appointment."

With that, Scott headed for the door whistling "Tonight, Tonight" from *West Side Story.*

Tom smiled and I turned around and faced him. "Everyone is a comedian. Is there anyone that works for the company that doesn't know I'm going out for dinner tonight?"

With a sarcastic grin, Tom answered, "I don't think word has gotten to the day shift. They don't come on until 10 A.M. Don't worry, I'll take care of getting someone to keep track of things so you won't miss your appointment."

"Thanks. Now let's see if we can get back to business," I said, grinning. The day went by fast. Scott came back late in the afternoon with several signed contracts for the installation of video surveillance equipment from two of our customers and another contract for drive-by and armed response from a third. I looked at demographics and competition up in the Bay Area since that was where the next location was planned, while Tom went down to the hospital to visit Emily.

At 4:30 P.M., I left. I had already decided to stop at the hospital before I picked up Karen. The Regional Medical Center was only six miles from my office, but thanks to the traffic, it took almost thirty minutes to get there. By the time I arrived, visiting hours were over and I had to use my identification to get upstairs. I walked to where Tuloc was sitting and asked how everything was going.

"It's been very quiet," he replied. "I saw Mr. Greenberg leave about fifteen minutes ago and when I looked in, Emily was asleep."

"I'll take a quick look. Maybe she was just dozing." I stepped quietly into the room and looked at Emily. She seemed to be sleeping and I didn't want to disturb her, so I started to leave.

"Hi, Boss." I heard what seemed like a whisper. I turned back.

"Hi, Em." I replied. "How are you feeling?"

"What can I say? It only hurts when I laugh." She forced a smile. "Tom just left, I think. I don't have my watch. He told me what you guys decided to do with my future. I have to tell you I love it."

"I'm glad. I think you'll do a great job. I spoke to your daughter earlier. I hope she knows I was kidding about the day off."

"It's okay, I don't think she was operating on all cylinders when you called. I explained it, my husband explained it and after Tom got finished, I think she understands. I would ask you to sit down and visit a spell, but if I remember correctly, you have an appointment."

I looked at my watch. It was already quarter to six. "You're right, but I have plenty of time."

"Boss, you're full of baloney. Get out of here before I call for my bodyguard and have you escorted to your car." She started laughing and winced, "That hurts."

"I'm out of here. Now you can stop laughing and get some rest." I leaned over and gave her a kiss on the cheek. "I'll check in on you tomorrow."

"Give me all the details of how your date went."

"It's not really a date, just a sort of business . . ."

"Yeah I know," she interrupted. "Go on, get out of here."

I waved and left the room, pausing to check in with Tuloc. "Have you seen anything out of the ordinary?"

"No. What are you looking for?"

"I'm not quite sure. Maybe a man about six-foot-one with a slight build and, I don't know, something else, I just don't know what."

"I'll keep my eyes open and when Michael gets here to relieve me, I'll tell him to keep awake."

"Thanks, it's probably nothing, but something's been bothering me and I can't put my finger on it."

I waved good-bye as I headed down the hall. Looking at my watch, I realized I would have to hurry if I was going to shower, shave and pick Karen up on time.

"Bring me up to date on what you have found out so far about the Be Safe people." The voice on the phone was used to giving orders.

Ex-Los Angeles police detective Phillip Corwin, who was the owner and sole employee of Corwin and Associates detective agency, took a deep breath before he answered. "The company is run by three guys. Aaron Carlyle is president, the vice president of sales is Scott Miller and the vice president of finance is Tom Greenberg. They've been in business about seven years and if you can believe their annual report, they seem to be doing pretty well. Carlyle lost his wife about a year ago and is still doing the single scene, although we haven't identified any singles yet. The other two are married with kids. This guy Aaron stopped to help a lady involved in a car accident the other night and wound up involved in some kind of drug operation. Everyone we have talked to seems to like him and he has a lot of friends inside of the police community. All three of them have money in the bank, not a lot, but enough to live comfortably. We've only been checking since Wednesday. If you can give me some idea what you are looking for, maybe we can dig deeper."

"No, what you have given me is fine. Per our agreement, you will destroy any and all records of this investigation. It is about 6:30 P.M. now. In forty-five minutes you will receive an envelope with the one hundred thousand dollars in small bills that I agreed to pay your company, minus the ten thousand I sent you up front."

The instructions were given like an order, which bothered Corwin. He wasn't used to taking orders over the phone from someone he had never met. He knew he was getting upset and thought to himself, *For one hundred thousand dollars I can learn*. He replied, "You know, I feel bad. It seems like very little information for so much money."

"The information that you have given me confirms what I had heard from other sources. Believe me, it is well worth the money. Don't forget to destroy any records you have before the money is delivered."

The message was again delivered in precise, clipped words. He could learn very quickly to not like this guy.

Before he could say anything else, the phone went dead. He said aloud, "This was the easiest money I ever made and I never even got to meet the client."

The client, as he was referred to, faced the four men in the van that were listening to his end of the conversation. "Be at that idiot's place in forty-five minutes. After he has convinced you that he destroyed all the papers, make sure he never talks to anyone again."

"What about Aaron Carlyle, sir?" asked the tallest of the four men. Sweat was starting to appear on his balding head.

The leader sat there thinking for a few seconds. They were parked about a half block from Carlyle's house.

"I've owed that son of a bitch something for a long time. I just don't think this is the time to get even. He's not going anywhere. The notebook looks like it was burned in the fire when the car turned over. Our first move in the stock market went off like a charm. If anyone had the notebook or knew where it was, we would have picked up some other movement in the stock besides our people. We pushed all the buttons to create stress. We bugged his place of business, crashed into the secretary, took care of those morons from the government that were investigating the accident and still the book never turned up. I'm going to take one more look at this guy tonight and in six months when we're finished, I'll come back and settle up."

Chapter 17

"The telephone number of the Hyatt in Westlake," was my response to the nasal question, "What city please?"

"They have an 800 number. Please hold on."

"Hold it," I shouted into the phone. "I can't use the 800 number."

"800-228-3360," replied the automated voice.

"Shit," I murmured as I hit the disconnect button.

I looked at my watch and decided I could still make it on time as long as traffic remained light. Ten minutes later, I pulled into my driveway. After showering, shaving and getting dressed in record time, I headed out the door. At the last second, I picked up the little notebook that I kept from the accident. As I backed out of the garage, I noticed the man I had seen the day before. We stared at each other as I drove by.

"He doesn't look familiar. I wonder why he bothers me," I said aloud. I stopped the car halfway down the hill, took a little camera out of the glove compartment, and turned the car around. He was nowhere to be seen.

"Where the hell did he go?"

There was a van parked about a hundred yards away. I drove past it and wrote down the license number. I'd find out on Monday if the van belonged to someone in the neighborhood.

I arrived at the front door of the Hyatt at 7:10 P.M., a full five minutes early. I got out of the car and threw the keys to one of the two young kids in valet uniforms standing in front.

"I'll only be here five or ten minutes. I have to pick someone up. Don't let the car get too far away."

"Don't let it get away at all," came a voice from behind one of the columns.

I turned as Karen came into view. I had forgotten or maybe hadn't realized how pretty she was. She was wearing dark brown slacks and a white silk shirt with a multicolored silk scarf around her neck that highlighted her green eyes.

"Am I late?" I stammered.

"Absolutely not. I think it's terrible to keep someone waiting, so I came down a little early."

I walked over to her side of the car to open the door before I realized the valet had the keys. I turned to the one with the keys and said, "Throw." The kid with the keys stood there mesmerized. It was as if he had never seen a beautiful woman before.

"Hello, how about the keys?"

The boy looked around and realized I was talking to him.

"Let me get the door for you, Ma'am." He came running, staring at Karen, and ran right into me.

"Sorry, sir," the boy said without taking his eyes off of Karen. My handing him a dollar bill didn't even get his attention.

"Thanks for your help."

He finally turned towards me and nodded his appreciation.

As I started to pull away, Karen said, "That was nice of you. This must be his first day on the job."

I laughed, "I'll bet. How is your room?"

"It's very nice and thank you for the flowers."

"Flowers?"

This time Karen laughed, "I guess I should be thanking your secretary. Did she forget to tell you?"

"She was in an accident last night right after she made the reservations."

"I'm sorry to hear that. How is she doing?"

"I guess it was touch and go for a short while, but I saw her this afternoon and she wants a blow-by-blow description of everything that goes on tonight. I suppose it means she's doing better."

Karen smiled and said, "I'll just have to watch myself. I didn't know I was going to dinner with someone that might kiss and tell."

I felt myself starting to blush, and Karen, noticing my discomfort, said, "I'm only kidding."

I looked at her straight-faced and asked, "Does that mean I can kiss and tell?" We both started laughing as I pulled the car into the long driveway at the country club.

I thought to myself, *this dating could become fun.* The club didn't have valet parking, but I found a spot to park without a problem. We entered a marble-tiled foyer and heard the piano playing a Scott Joplin tune.

"Name please," the woman from behind a four-foot podium asked.

"Aaron Carlyle."

"Here you are," she said as she circled my name on the list in front of her. "We have a table by the window reserved for you. Please follow me."

Karen followed the woman to the table with me right behind her. I couldn't help but notice both men and women trying to get a better look at Karen without being obvious. I held the chair for Karen as the waiter rushed over and asked if we would like a drink before dinner.

We both ordered a glass of Merlot.

"Perhaps you would like a bottle? We have a fine wine list."

"Why don't you select a good one for us? We trust your judgment."

"Of course, sir. You will not be sorry."

As the waiter walked away, I asked her, "How did your day go?"

"Not bad," she replied.

When I didn't respond, she continued. "You know I invest money for clients based on their short and long term financial goals. When they engage my services, there is no charge. I collect a fee on all transactions, plus a one percent surcharge on all profits. Today I signed up a new client and before the market closed, there was a paper profit of over ten thousand dollars."

"He must be one happy fellow. Do you do this well for all your clients?"

"Yes I do, and he is a she. The majority of my clients or about sixty percent of them are women. Their husbands have either died or divorced them. They need help planning for their future. My clients have been averaging over a thirty percent increase per year over the last five years. That's enough about my work. Tell me the story about this accident you witnessed."

"It's really bizarre. I was doing about seventy-five." I held up my hand and the waiter was back with the wine. He poured a little in a glass for me to taste and stepped back awaiting my answer.

"This is very good. I'm glad I let you decide."

"I'll let you savor the wine before I return with our specials."

"Please continue with the story," replied Karen as he left.

"Where was I, oh yes, I was doing seventy-five miles an hour when a car came speeding up behind me like a bat out of hell. There was a woman behind the wheel. Her car hit the divider wall, turned over and slid on its roof for about two hundred yards. I stopped, called the police and eventually pulled the woman out of the car before it exploded."

"How awful. Is she all right?"

"Her name was Carol Sellars and she died at the hospital from internal injuries. When I pulled her out, she asked me to watch over her purse, which I turned over to the police. It contained two hundred and fifty thousand dollars in cash. It also had a notebook that I inadvertently kept. I should have turned it over to the police, but I forgot about it."

"That's fascinating, but you haven't said why you left my name off of the report you gave to the police."

"It was a man thing. I was more than a little self-conscious of it looking like I was being fixed up with a date."

Karen thought that over for a couple of seconds and then said, "I don't think it's a man thing. I told Jerry I hated someone fixing me up—even if it wasn't a date, it gave the impression of almost being one. That's really the reason I called you. I wanted to prove at least to myself that I didn't need people to find me someone to go out with."

Before I could answer, the waiter was back. He went through the specials, but my mind was elsewhere.

"I'm ready," said Karen as she looked at me.

I blinked. I hadn't been listening. My mind started racing to catch up. I was thinking about how hard it must have been for Karen to be so honest.

As the waiter left after taking our order, I continued my train of thought out loud.

"It took a lot of guts to make that phone call and even more to tell me why. It probably would have taken me at least another three or four days to get up the courage."

Karen smiled. It was something she did very nicely.

"Finish the story. What was in the notebook?"

I took the book from my pocket. "I don't know. It's in some kind of code. Here, take a look."

I handed it across the table to Karen and continued, "I think six people may have been killed because of this book and I can't for the life of me figure out why."

Karen's eyes widened. "Killed?"

"When I was at police headquarters, I met a policewoman who told me a story about Cubans trying to destroy the U.S. economy, but with only two hundred and fifty thousand dollars, I am leaning towards the FBI story of a drug bust gone bad."

Karen reacted to the words, "met a policewoman." Then her eyes focused on the first page of the book. "This isn't in code. It's a list of stocks with their prices."

"What? What do you mean a list of stocks?"

"Here, take a look."

I moved to the chair right next to her. "WWSI stands for World Wide Service, Inc. Their stock on Tuesday was about two dollars and fifty cents. Today it closed over nine dollars. The next one, SCOA stands for Specialty Corporation of America. The book says five dollars and twenty-five cents, but it has next Monday's date on it. I don't know what the stock price is today, but it must be close. I recognize some of the symbols, not all of them, but they are stocks."

I sat there dumbfounded. "I don't know how I missed them."

"Don't feel bad. None of these stocks are on anyone's must-have lists. They are part of the thousands of over the counter stocks that sometimes are only there to set a valuation on a company for inheritance purposes."

Karen continued, "If I had purchased two hundred and fifty thousand dollars worth of WWSI on Monday or Tuesday, it would have been worth over nine hundred thousand this afternoon."

The one-sided conversation stopped while the waiter brought us our salads.

After he left, Karen continued, "This book looks like it's giving instructions to buy and sell stocks on certain dates. Using the first results that I know, this, if followed, and assuming it continues to be accurate, could be worth ten to twenty million dollars."

Karen started to eat her salad and I picked up the conversation.

"If there were ten or twenty people doing the same thing in different parts of the country, the total could come to maybe a half a billion dollars."

"Where did your friendly lady cop say this was coming from?"

"She said it was started by Cuba to destroy the American economy."

"I doubt five hundred million or even a billion would put a crimp in America, but it would certainly make someone very rich." Karen stopped for a second to make sure that she had my attention. "Have you thought of investing on Monday morning when the market opens?"

I put down my fork. "No, I hadn't. Until you looked at the book, I didn't even know what all the letters and numbers meant." We both continued to eat our salads in silence.

"Is it an easy thing to buy one hundred thousand shares of a two fifty stock?"

"It's not easy, but it's not that hard either. All the exchanges have rules. If the amount of shares traded on any given day goes much above the average, the stock comes up on a list. At the same time, if the amount of trades causes the stock to go up over a certain amount, the stock gets highlighted. People that own the company or more than a certain percentage of the company stock are restricted from trading unless they file 13D-1 forms. Saying all that, there are a lot of people out there that will try and bend the rules. We are talking about significant sums of money."

"That's some business you're in. How do you manage to keep your sanity?"

She shrugged her shoulders.

"How did you get into financial planning?" I continued.

"After I graduated from the University of Arizona, Paine Webber recruited me to work in their investment banking division. After three years, I took a leave of absence to go back to school to get my Master's in Business. I was lucky. I applied to Stanford and was accepted."

"It's not usually luck. Brains have an awful lot to do with it."

Karen again dazzled me with her smile. "I think . . ." She stopped as the waiter returned with the main courses. The waiter put Karen's down first.

Karen said, "That looks wonderful."

"I'm sure you will find it to your liking."

I watched the waiter's reaction. Karen had a great way with people. I could understand why she was successful.

"You think what?" I asked as the waiter left.

"I think my father would have liked you. When I was at Stanford, I met Terry, my ex-husband. I brought him home to meet Dad and all he talked about was how pretty I was and what a great shape I had. He never once spoke about my having a brain. My father was very outspoken. He told me I was out of my mind to go with someone like him. He told me if I married him, he didn't think it would last six months."

"Did it?"

"Just to spite him, I stayed married for eight months."

"Your father must have been a great judge of character. What did he do for a living? Did he work on Wall Street?"

"No, he was a college professor at UCLA."

"No kidding? I graduated from UCLA. What classes did he teach?"

Her voice went down to a whisper as she said, "He was the dean of the Economics Department."

"Dean? Was your dad Garret Williams?"

She nodded. "Did you know him?"

"Know him? I practically spent every waking hour reading his books and attending his lectures. He was a Nobel Prize winner. What is he doing now?"

"He died of a heart attack five months after I got married four and a half years ago."

"I'm sorry. I didn't know."

"That's all right. Let's talk about you. Jerry told me most of the basics, but not about your likes or dislikes. I see you like fish, but you're not eating your vegetables, so I guess that moves to the dislike side." Her voice had an inflection that made the statement a question.

"I've told you how I met my ex, how did you meet your wife?"

Chapter 18

That question came right out of left field. I wasn't sure how to begin.

She continued, "I'm sorry. I shouldn't have asked. You belong to a club, so I guess you like golf."

"I do like golf, but I haven't played in a while."

"What's your handicap?" she asked.

"I'm listed as a fifteen, but I am probably a twenty or twenty-one."

She again smiled, "I guess that means you're a hustler."

I don't know why, maybe it was the tone of her voice that forced me to smile and say, "I met my wife in Vietnam."

She put down her fork. "You don't have to say anything if you don't want to."

"I don't mind, it's just knowing where to begin."

I began the story with our moving into the jungle after we heard the back door blow up.

"We walked for three days and nights. At times, we saw troops wearing uniforms that didn't belong to anyone we knew and avoided them. One of the two Vietnamese walking out with us was called Min. He continued to tell me stories he had heard from his grandfather and legends that came from God knows where. He was a fascinating storyteller with a wealth of knowledge about the history of his country.

"Vietnam's early chronicle like its recent history was and is characterized by a continuous struggle for autonomy. First came the Chinese domination. That was overthrown in the ninth century and replaced by what we today call feudal warlords. After ten centuries, the French moved in and took over. French rule only lasted until the Second World War when the Japanese tried their hand in running the country. Although the Chinese, French, and Japanese ran the country, they didn't run the people. When the Communists under Ho Chi Min helped throw out the Japanese, they declared independence, which started the French Indo China War. In 1954, the French threw in the towel and the Americans became the primary sponsor of the anti-communist struggle."

She interrupted, "This Min sounds like a very colorful person."

"He is. During the journey I found out he was a graduate of the French University. Listening to his stories kept my mind occupied. During the late afternoon on the fourth day, we spotted a little village at the foot of the mountain we were on. I sent Tom, who is still one of my closest friends, and Giac, the other Vietnamese man, ahead to take a closer look. We followed ten minutes later, coming in from both sides of the village. Tom met us at the start of the hamlet's main street.

"Giac was meeting with the elders. The day before, some troops came through from what used to be called Saigon and was now Ho Chi Min City. They were looking for the Americans who were responsible for the deaths of ten or fifteen people at the rear of what used to be the American embassy. We were to be considered bandits and shown no mercy. Anyone helping us would be punished."

I took a sip of water as Karen commented, "This is some story. You must have been scared stiff."

"It's funny, but I still remember like it was yesterday. Min came out from behind one of the buildings. Someone said, 'Lieutenant, you have a problem.'

"He was followed by Giac and the village chief. 'What's this problem I have?'

"'I am.'

"I turned towards the response that came from the shadows. Out stepped a woman about five feet, six inches tall with long, black hair dressed in traditional Vietnamese clothing. 'My name is Marcia Kellog. I am a captain in the U.S. Army Nursing Corp. I was here delivering the chief's first son when the hospital unit I was attached to bugged out. They've been hiding me from the North Vietnamese for the last five days. Do you guys have any idea what's going on?'"

Karen's eyes were wide as saucers. "Don't tell me they left your wife behind also?"

I nodded.

"What happened next?" she asked, sounding like she was holding her breath.

"I told her quickly of our predicament and asked when was the last time the enemy had been through the village."

"That was the first time you met her?" Karen mumbled the words.

I paused and looked out the window. "Yes it was."

After a few seconds I continued, "She listened to our story and then said, 'Lieutenant, they came through yesterday and told the chief they were headed towards the border, which is only twenty miles away. Get your men together and let's get a move on. We don't want to be here when they return.'

"I smiled and held out my hand. 'Marcia,' I said, 'my name is Aaron. Change into something comfortable while we negotiate with the chief and please leave your captain bars in your pocket. I am in command of this detail and will expect you to follow my orders.'"

"Did she?" Karen asked.

"She didn't even shake my hand. She answered with two words: 'We'll see.'"

Chapter 19

I rubbed my eyes. I could feel moisture building up in them. Karen must have noticed because she looked out the window towards the course and said, "Before you ask, I belong to the Carlsbad Country Club and I'm a fourteen. I love the game and I carry my clubs with me wherever I go."

A few other musicians joined the piano player and were playing "Little Things Mean a Lot," the song I believed Patti Page made famous. I started to hum the song as I watched some of the people get up to dance. I looked back at Karen and asked, "Would you like to dance?"

"I'd love to, but I am a bit rusty."

"That makes two of us." I rose and held out my hand.

As we reached the dance floor, I again noticed that everyone was staring. Karen noticed it also and asked, "I didn't look, but is your zipper open or something?"

I started laughing. "I hope not." She came into my arms like we had attended Arthur Murray's and graduated at the top of the class. As I held her, I thought to myself, *She is fun to be with.* Her hair moved in front of my face as the words to the song came to mind, "Touch my hair as you pass my chair, little things mean a lot." The song ended and we started back towards the table.

Karen hesitated and then asked, "Can you tell me where the restroom is?"

"I'll show you," I replied. I took her hand and headed down the hall past the bar. "It's right over there." I pointed at the door that had a picture of a woman on it.

I stood by the bar waiting for her return when I heard the announcer on the television say, "This has been one great fight, folks." I looked up at the forty-eight inch screen as the boxers stood waiting for the results to be tabulated. The camera zoomed in on the fighter in the white shorts as he clenched and unclenched his fists. The announcer continued, "Perez looks a little uptight. He's won twelve straight bouts, but this is by far his toughest."

The referee signaled for the bell to be rung and in a loud voice shouted over the noise of the crowd. "The winner is Tony Perez." The camera again zoomed in on Perez as he stopped clenching his fists and raised them in triumph.

Karen walked up behind me and asked, "Do you like the fights?"

"Not really. I know who the heavyweight champion is, but not much past that."

"I didn't think you did from the expression on your face."

"It's not the fight, it's something the fighter was doing."

Karen looked back at the screen. "What was he doing?"

"He was clenching and unclenching his fists."

I held the chair for Karen as the waiter arrived to take our dessert order.

"Nothing for me," said Karen. "I've had a long day and I'm exhausted."

I looked at my watch. "Jesus, it's after 10 P.M. It's time for us to go." We reached the car and as I opened the door, I exclaimed, "I remember now!"

"Remember what?"

"Something has been bothering me for two days and I just remembered what it was."

"Anything important?"

I hesitated. "I think so, but regardless, it can't be as important as tonight."

"That's very nice."

The ride back to the hotel took almost no time at all.

I wished I had gone to a restaurant further away. I didn't want this night to end. When I pulled up in front of the hotel, the same two valets were there. I threw them the keys and said, "Don't lose it."

I walked Karen into the elevator and asked, "What floor?"

"Four."

"I had a great time tonight. I would love to do it again sometime soon."

"So would I. It's been fun. I don't remember the last time I had such a good time."

The elevator stopped on the fourth floor and Karen led the way.

"What time do you expect to head south tomorrow?"

Karen thought for a few seconds. "I'm in no hurry, probably around 10 A.M. or so." She stopped in front of room 426.

"How about having breakfast with me?"

I heard myself ask the question. It was not something I had planned, but I knew after the three hours we spent together, I wanted to spend more time with her.

Karen hesitated. It looked like the question had surprised her. She smiled and answered. "I'd love to. I usually get up about 5:30 A.M. and run for about four or five miles. I could be ready about 7:30 A.M." Her voice had risen again as if she was asking a question.

"That's great. How about I pick you up at 6 A.M. and run with you. If you want, you can check out then and change at . . . no, that's not a good idea. I'll pick you up at 6 A.M."

I saw what looked like a look of relief or concern in Karen's eyes.

"Is something wrong?" I asked.

"No," she answered. "Everything's right." She leaned over and kissed me on my cheek. "See you at 6 A.M."

I stood on the other side of the door for a few seconds before I headed toward the elevator. I wonder if I should have invited her back to my house to change. Maybe I should have offered to let her stay at my place for the night. I wonder what the rules are today. All the way down to my car, I kept wondering. "I hope she doesn't think I'm a jerk," I finally said aloud.

As I drove away, I smiled and said to myself, *I did have a good time and tomorrow is another day.* I almost forgot about the fighter.

Chapter 20

I was leaning against my car door looking up at the sky when I heard the hotel's automatic door open. I turned and watched Karen look around before she spotted me. She walked toward me and smiled.

"Good morning. It looks like it's going to be a lovely day."

She was wearing a charcoal San Diego State sweatshirt and a pair of white shorts. Her legs were tan, long and healthy looking.

"I can't believe how wide awake you look after only six or seven hours of sleep."

She smiled and said, "Thank you kind sir, but if you think that kind of talk is going to get you out of running, think again."

This time it was my turn to smile. I held the car door open. "They have a park about five or six miles from here that has a jogging path."

"That sounds great," she replied.

I put the car in motion and looked over at her long legs. "I hope it's not too cold. You might be sorry that you didn't wear sweats."

She looked at her legs and then at the sky through the glass sunroof. "The sun is starting to rise. It'll probably be too warm by the time we're finished. Anyway, I'm looking forward to the breakfast you promised me."

Pink azaleas bordered the park just a few miles from the hotel. After a few minutes of stretching, we took off. In the stillness of the morning, you could hear the leaves in the trees waving with the slight wind.

At first, Karen took the lead, but soon after, my longer legs moved me out in front. Karen pulled alongside of me and said, "It's time to start moving it out."

I had already started working up a sweat and just nodded my head. The next twenty minutes I spent looking at Karen's butt. Every time I tried to pass her, she stepped it up another notch. We approached the sign that said one more mile. I watched Karen slow down. As I came alongside, she asked, "Is this where we turn around and head back or is there another path back to the car?"

Before I could answer, Karen tripped over a branch that was lying on the path. She fell sideways right in front of me. I tried to maintain my balance and stop her from falling at the same time. I found myself with an arm around her waist and my hand cupping her breast.

"Shit," I said as I let go of her and landed on the grass with her landing on top of me. "Are you all right?"

She was sitting on the grass rubbing her ankle. "I think so. The ankle feels a little sore and I scraped my knee. Are you all right? For a second, I thought we weren't going to fall, but you let go of me and down we went."

I felt myself blushing. "Sorry, I didn't have a good grip and before I could get another one, we were on the grass." I stood and held out my hands.

Karen rubbed her breast. "It certainly feels like you had a good grip."

For the second time, I felt my face grow warm.

She grabbed my hands and lifted herself to a standing position. "Let's walk back. I want to talk to you about some thoughts I had about last night's conversation."

I became conscious of her hand not leaving mine as we started back along the path.

"After you left, I was thinking about that little book you have. I pulled up the symbols that I remembered on my computer. Yesterday's closing price is approximately the same as listed. Either someone is clairvoyant or there is one huge fraud being perpetrated. I would suggest that you contact someone at the Securities and Exchange Commission and ask them to investigate."

I let her words sink in before I replied, "I feel responsible for some people dying. I also believe there is more to this than I can see right now and would like to give it some thought before I turn loose." I paused.

"The lady from the accident and one of the police."

I had answered her unspoken question.

"The lady cop?" she asked.

I nodded. "She was found dead a short time after I left her. I know there is nothing I could have done, but there is something inside of me that wants to get even."

"Is it some macho thing that says you have to kill them?"

"No, I don't think so. It's just . . . " I hesitated, "It's just that I can't stand by and do nothing. Thanks to you, I now have an idea about what they're doing. I just don't know who they are, and how I do something about it. I don't want to turn this over to someone and never get to see the guilty people punished."

We continued to walk hand in hand in silence. As we reached the car, I asked, "Do I sound foolish?"

"A little, I'm afraid. If these people are responsible for six deaths, I don't think you should get involved."

I put the car in gear and started back to the hotel.

After a few minutes, Karen asked, "You're not thinking of doing something to prove to your friends that you're not afraid." She paused. "Or to impress them, are you?"

"The people that care know that I'm not afraid and as far as impressing anyone, you're the only one that I've met that I think I would like to impress, but maybe not that way." I smiled as I looked at Karen to see her reaction.

"How long will it take you to get ready?" I asked as the car stopped in front of the hotel.

"Give me forty-five minutes," Karen replied as she looked at her watch. "It's 7:10 A.M. Let's say 8 A.M."

I felt myself grimacing. "We better make it around 8:30 A.M. I live about twenty minutes from here. I figure that it will take a round trip and about the same amount of time to get ready."

"I'm sorry, I wasn't thinking. Why don't you just give me directions to the restaurant and I'll meet you there."

"I'm not good at directions. I'll be back around 8:30 A.M. or 9 A.M."

"It's too bad you didn't bring your clothes with you. You could have changed here," Karen said as she got out of the car.

"You know, you could check out and change at my place. I have three full bathrooms and I can bring you back here after breakfast for your car."

"That sounds like a deal. Give me ten minutes to get my clothes together. Are you sure it's not an imposition?" The door closed before I could get a word out of my mouth.

True to her word, she was back down in ten minutes. She hadn't changed her clothes, but had added some lipstick. The bellhop took her bags and put them in the trunk.

"What's the name of the place we're having breakfast? I hate to say this, but I am starving."

"It's called The Outside Inn. It's located on the Pacific Coast Highway a little north of Malibu. If it's okay with you, we can go right now dressed the way we are. They have no dress code, only great food."

"Go for it," she exclaimed.

In some ways, she seemed to have the same sense of adventure as Marcia, always ready to say, "Let's go."

"The landscape is beautiful. I've always wondered how the pioneers found their way through these mountains. It's not like they had a paved road."

I smiled. I always asked the same question when Marcia and I drove through the canyons.

"If it's too cold, I can close the windows."

"No, it's fine. This is one of those days that reminds everyone why they live in Southern California." She opened her purse and took out a pair of sunglasses. "I hope you don't think I'm a busybody, but I keep thinking about the book you have."

I glanced at her face. The glasses hid her eyes and for a second I thought that she had put them on for exactly that reason.

"What were you thinking?"

"If what you want to do is make them pay in some way other than your getting a gun and shooting them, I have an idea." Karen paused as if waiting for an answer of some kind.

"I don't want . . ." I started to say as the mobile phone rang.

"Aaron," I called out over the sound of the wind after I pushed the receive button.

"Good morning, Aaron. It is my wish that I have not interrupted anything important."

"Good morning, Min. I'm on my way to breakfast in Malibu, but I always have time for a friend."

"You are with a lovely lady, I hope."

"She's very lovely and very intelligent."

"Apologize to the lady for this interruption, but it is important that I meet with you as soon as possible."

I now wished that I had picked up the phone instead of using the hands-free button. I could not ask Min what was so important without having Karen hear the answer. As if reading my thoughts, Karen leaned across and released the phone from the cradle.

"This sounds like a confidential business call."

"Thank you." I spoke into the mouthpiece, "Min, it's Saturday. Are you sure that this can't wait until Monday?"

"I am sure."

I looked over at Karen. This was going to ruin my whole day. "Well, how about this afternoon?"

Min replied, "Will you be able to get Tom and Scott to attend this meeting?"

"Tom and Scott? This must be important. I will have to call you back. Give me about thirty minutes."

"Tell your lovely lady friend that I am sorry to intrude and look forward to the day that I will meet her. I will await your call." The phone went dead and I put the receiver back into the cradle.

"Min said to tell you he is sorry to intrude and looks forward to meeting you."

"He sounds like someone I would like to meet. Is he a customer?"

"No, he is one of my closest friends."

"You've told me how you met. Someday you'll have to tell me how you became friends. Every minute with you becomes more and more interesting."

I smiled. "I've told you that the story is boring. We met in Vietnam and have remained friends ever since."

"That's only the beginning of the story, but you have some important calls to make. Someday I'll talk you into telling me the whole thing from beginning to end."

"I bet you will." I looked up and said, "Tom" into the little microphone.

"Do you want to take him off the speaker?" asked Karen.

"No need. Min sometimes gets paranoid. I don't have to worry about Tom."

"Hello," came Tom's voice over the speaker.

"Tom, its Aaron. I have to . . ."

"Aaron," Tom interrupted, "How was your date last night?"

"It was great, the reason I'm calling is . . ."

"So tell me, did you get laid?"

"Jesus!" I grabbed for the phone. "Karen is sitting beside me."

"Why didn't you?"

I lifted the phone to my ear.

I glanced at Karen. She was sitting like she hadn't heard a word that was said. "Min called and wants to meet today as soon as we can get together. I am on my way to breakfast and should be able to make it sometime after 1 P.M. He didn't say what he wanted, but it must have something to do with the bugs we found. Can you call Scott? Set up a time and leave the message on my machine at home." After a slight pause I continued, "Thanks, I'll tell her."

The car glided to a stop on the Pacific Coast Highway. I turned to Karen and said, "Can you do me a favor and take off your glasses?"

Karen hesitated a few seconds and then lifted them away from her face. "How's this?" she asked.

"That's fine. I just wanted to see your eyes when I apologized for Tom."

Her lips curled upward as she asked. "What did Tom do?" Her eyes sparkled and I knew that she was playing with me. Before I could answer, a horn sounded from behind us. The light had turned green. I forced my foot down on the gas pedal and burned rubber, leaving the car behind me at the intersection as the light turned red again.

Karen was laughing out loud. "The next thing I know is you'll be apologizing for the guy that blew his horn."

I started to laugh. "This morning is not going as I planned."

We were seated immediately at a table facing the ocean.

"This is beautiful," said Karen.

I looked around. It was difficult not comparing Karen to Marcia. I took a sip of juice and responded quietly, "Yes it is."

We ordered breakfast and I said, "Before I started with the phone calls, you said you had an idea about the book."

"I do, as long as what you want to accomplish doesn't involved someone getting shot or some other type of bodily harm."

"Truthfully," I replied, "I'm not sure exactly what I want. I want them punished, but I'm still not sure how. I know if what I'm hearing from the tone of your voice means getting you involved, I don't want that. If I thought I was going to do something that could get you hurt, I might even be able to walk away and do nothing." I stopped for a few seconds. "No that's not true. I couldn't walk away and do nothing."

"You don't seem like the kind of person that could walk away . . . from anything."

"What does that mean?" I responded.

"Just from what I know of you and what you have told me. The last time you walked away from anything was in Vietnam. How about finishing the story? If I remember you found a village somewhere in Cambodia."

I again reflected back to eight years ago.

Chapter 21

Just before we reached the border, Min reported seeing a camp where none should be. American soldiers manned it with Vietnamese as backup. The camp held about three hundred workers who looked like Montagnards, except there were no women or children. The mountain people always kept their families with them. We decided not to approach it at night, but wait for the next morning.

Early the next morning, I took Marcia and Giac into the camp below. I had Scott and Tom station the men around the camp at two-hundred-yard intervals. As we entered the encampment, attracting everyone's attention, Min sneaked in and joined the men who were working inside the camp. We presented ourselves to the major who walked us over to the other two officers. I had Marcia wear her bars and act every inch an officer.

She told them we were from Koh Tang and when the Cong had overridden the base, we escaped into the night. We had been walking for nine days trying to hook up with our troops. We were told by some South Viet troops that the war was over and the Americans were gone. We weren't sure they were telling the truth and we didn't have the slightest idea where we were.

The colonel asked the name of my outfit and I told him the truth. He motioned at Giac and I told him I thought he was an officer, but wasn't sure since his English wasn't so good. He turned to one of his men and told him to ask the gook where he was from and where he thought he was going.

They spoke back and forth for two or three minutes, and his man turned back and said, "He's a South Viet regular trying to get himself a ticket back to the States."

The general then joined the conversation. "Did you promise him a ticket?"

Marcia said, "I did. I thought it was a good idea."

The general laughed. "Join us for breakfast. Your man can eat at the mess tent."

"His invitation sounded like a command and we took it as such. "By the way," he added, "leave your weapons here. We don't like them being brought into the compound." As he spoke, the men around us listening moved ever so slightly. These were trained men. If we had any intention of not leaving the weapons, we wouldn't have had time to take them off of our arms.

As Marcia walked away, the man with the colonel's insignia stated the obvious. "She's a good-looking woman. Have you tried to get a piece of that on your trip?"

I looked at him. He gave the impression of being tall, but was really an inch or two shorter than me. He was thin and his hands never stopped opening and closing. His accent was pure Southern, or maybe Texan, I wasn't quite sure which.

"I wish," I replied. "But she is one tough bitch." We started toward the mess tent and I asked him, "What are you guys doing here?"

He waited a few seconds, clenching and unclenching his fists, and then answered, "We're waiting on and helping our people get out of the country. You three are a surprise. We usually get advance notice."

"Unfortunately, we don't have a radio or we would have called. How do you get us out? Do planes fly in?"

"There are no planes. We give you a guide and he walks you to the Gulf."

I thought that over and casually asked, "How far are we from the Gulf? Giac told us to head towards Phum Tani and from there to Malaysia."

"I guess you could try it that way, but we haven't lost anyone yet," he answered in his Texan drawl.

I walked over to the tables that were set up buffet style and gazed at the food. "Can I help myself? I'm starved."

He smiled and said, "Go ahead." The hairs on my neck stood straight up. I had the feeling I was being given my last meal.

"The gook has to eat outside," he continued. I turned facing him. "I thought they were our friends."

He smiled. "Were is the operative word around here. Do you have any objections?"

I now looked him straight in the eye and my stomach tightened. "Absolutely not, but I owe him something for getting me this far. I promised I would try to get him to the States."

"He's not going to make it. The real question is, will you?" His eyes never left mine and his smile never left his lips.

I shifted my eyes to Giac and nodded my head. From thin air, Giac produced a .45-caliber pistol. He aimed it at the Texan's head and in almost flawless English said, "Make my day, Pilgrim."

I smiled and told Giac, "You mixed up two pictures."

Giac smiled for the first time since I met him and said, "I just wanted to make sure he understood his options."

The Texan had stopped smiling. "You're crazy. You'll never get out of this camp alive."

I shrugged my shoulders. "Nothing has changed from two minutes ago, has it?"

A shot from somewhere outside turned all of our heads.

"You're finished," the Texan shouted with a sneer on his face.

"Maybe, but if I am, guess who's checking out right before me?"

His face tightened. "Don't be a fool." His voice started to take on a pleading tone. "This operation will make us all rich beyond belief."

"Says who?" I asked.

"It's a CIA operation. This operation has ties throughout the Pentagon." Before he could say anything else, the tent flap flew open and in walked Scott and Min.

"The camp is ours," Scott said triumphantly. "Min found out the people working the fields were Montagnards and South Viet troops. They helped us take over. The major tried to fight and was the recipient of that shot you heard. That's a real shame. I was starting to like him."

"How's Marcia?" I asked.

"I was wondering if you'd ask," she said as she entered the tent. Tom walked in right behind her and reported that we had taken thirty prisoners including three Vietnamese who were working with the general.

"They're processing some of the finest coke I have ever seen. Are you listening?" he asked.

I jerked my head towards him. I had been staring at Marcia and felt foolish. I wondered how they were going to get it out. Almost like she was reading my mind, Marcia said, "They must have a plane!"

"A plane? Of course they must. Has anyone seen it?" I asked as I looked around. "Have any of you guys seen it?"

"It's not here," Min interrupted. "It comes in every week to pick up the drugs."

We had moved outside the tent to the dirt street. Our men had the former guards lined up and seated on the ground. As I looked around, I saw at least fifteen men that I presumed were dead, but I had only heard one shot. I pointed at one of the bodies and asked no one in particular, "Friend or foe?"

"We didn't lose any of our boys," Scott answered. "One of the Montagnards got hurt and they lost about thirty in all. It seems that when they took the Montagnards as prisoners, they had families with them. The women were raped and then put on a plane to be delivered with the kids to God knows where. The men were forced to watch what took place to their women and as close as I can determine, a woman to these animals also included girls down to the age of five or six. As they were being loaded on the plane, every fourth or fifth male child was held back and beheaded as a show of strength or superiority; I'm not sure which. When we freed them, the first thing they did was to get a little bit even."

"How many prisoners did we take?" I asked.

"We have forty-five Vietnamese and seven Americans including the three officers."

I turned to the American wearing the general's uniform, "How could you allow this to happen?"

He smiled and turned his back on me. I crossed over to where he was standing, put my arm on his shoulder and turned him around facing me.

"I was talking to you," I shouted.

"I heard you," he sneered. "You can play at being in charge for today, but tomorrow is my turn."

I heard one of my men ask, "What the hell does that mean?"

He turned away from me and looked at my men.

"I can promise each of you over one hundred thousand dollars and a ride back home. Your other option is to start running now. We have more than two hundred men out recruiting. They are expected back within the next twenty-four hours. We also have men stationed at listening posts every four or five miles. I am really surprised that you didn't run into one of them on your way in here," he mused. "The war is over. There is no reason for you to take a chance with your life any longer. Now is the time to get rich. This war was started by the fat cats back in the States and we want our share."

"How will you get us home?" Tom asked.

"The plane is due in here tomorrow at 8 A.M. It flies from here to Malaysia. From there, it's a hop, skip and a jump to Singapore."

"What about the money?" Tom continued.

"I have it here. Each of you gets one hundred thousand dollars before you get on the plane." He looked around at the men and then at Marcia. "I'll tell you what, make it one hundred and fifty thousand each and I keep the bitch."

"Your offer is tempting," Tom said, "but how about you giving us the money now and we take off. When your men come back or the plane lands, your people will set you free and we both forget you're here."

"What about the bitch and Prince Valiant?" the general asked.

"I can't answer for all the men, but let's suppose that Aaron comes with us and you get to keep Marcia, but we still get the extra fifty thousand dollars."

I was looking incredulously at Tom when Scott jumped into the conversation.

"My vote is to let him have them both, but I would like two hundred thousand dollars."

The Texan that had brought me into the mess tent stood up and calmly told everyone that they had a deal. He looked over at the general and said, "That's enough of this talk. Give them two hundred thousand dollars each and guarantee them at least a three-hour head start after we are released. The only thing I want is some sort of show of good faith."

"Like what?" Scott asked.

"Leave a knife somewhere that we can reach it and tie up those two along with us."

Scott walked over to where I was standing and took the .45 out from under my jacket. He turned to the Texan and said, "If you have the authority to deal, lead us to the money." He motioned to Tom to cut the Texan loose and asked, "Who am I dealing with?"

"My name is Brigadier General Edward Waldman." He said this with an arrogance that almost turned my stomach.

"And whom do I have the pleasure of dealing with?" he continued.

"My name is Colonel Scott Miller and my friend here is Major Tom Greenberg."

"If I had known you were both Jews I would have started at seventy-five thousand and negotiated, but a deal is a deal. What do you plan on doing with the two Vietnamese?"

Marcia looked at him. "You're a disgrace to our country." If she had a weapon, I was sure she would have used it.

"Little lady, I am certainly going to have a great time with you before I turn you over to my men." He turned and started walking with Tom about three steps behind him. After he had taken two or three steps, he turned and walked back to Marcia. He stared at her and then smiled as his eyes went from the top of her head to her toes. "Yes, we will enjoy ourselves," he said aloud as he reached out his left hand and lightly touched her breast. He then backhanded her across the mouth. Every eye was on him as he quickly turned marched by and disappeared into the second building on the right. I felt a tug on my jacket as Scott slipped my gun back into my pocket. When I turned, and looked into his eyes, he winked at me. I almost felt like letting out a winning yell, but I quickly realized that this was not a game. I walked over to Marcia and helped her up from the ground where she had fallen. There were tears in her eyes, but she wasn't crying.

As I lifted her, I whispered, "Don't worry, our turn is coming."

I wasn't sure if Tom had told the truth about his rank. In fact, I wasn't sure about anything that was going on. The only thing I was certain of was that I would get even with that strutting son of a bitch. I had never met any of these men until a short time ago. My gut told me that I could trust Scott and Tom and I knew that I would give my life to save Marcia, but the rest of these guys I wasn't sure about. We stood there for less than a minute when Tom came walking back down the street with the general, if that was his true rank. The "general" now had a pearl-handled .45 in his holster and a smirk on his face.

"I gave him back his gun as a show of good faith," Tom said as they got close. "I have the money, almost two million in American greenbacks, so let's get the show on the road."

My hand was getting cramped curled around the butt of the pistol in my pocket as I was trying to figure out what to do next, when the "general" pulled his pearl handled revolver and aimed it at Tom.

"You son of a bitch," he yelled. "Did you really think I would let you take our money and walk out of here alive?"

Without even realizing what I was doing, I pulled the .45 out of my pocket and fired. The bullet hit him in the left shoulder, picked him up, spun him around and deposited him about fifteen feet from where he was standing. As quick as I thought that happened, both Scott and Tom raised their carbines and Scott announced to no one in particular, but to everyone looking on, "Don't anyone get nervous."

The confusion on the faces of our men was evident. They weren't sure whose side they were on or on whose side they wanted to be on. They were Marines, but they were also men and the two hundred thousand dollars certainly looked good.

"I really am a colonel. I was given a field promotion three days before we left Saigon. I was supposed to be on the last 'copter out, but when that didn't work, I decided to tag along with Lieutenant Carlyle. As far as I'm concerned, he is still running this outfit." With that, he glanced in my direction and asked, "What next, Lieutenant?"

I looked at Marcia. "Captain, see to the wounded man." I turned to Giac and asked, "How far do we have to go to reach the ocean?"

Before he could answer, Marcia yelled over, "His shoulder is busted, he's lost some blood, but the bullet passed through."

"Throw some kind of bandage around it and get him ready for travel."

Giac, after a brief conversation with the locals, said, "If we leave now, it will take three nights and two days."

I looked at my watch. It was 3 P.M. I wasn't happy with our prospects as I looked at Scott and Tom. "Do either of you guys know how to fly a plane?"

They both shook their heads no.

"I do," said Marcia. "I took lessons in a Cessna and got my license in a single-engine plane."

I shook my head in disbelief. "You never cease to amaze me. Do you think you could fly that plane coming in?"

"Probably," she answered, "as long as it's not some kind of jet."

"Okay, we wait. By we, I mean the Captain, Giac, Min and myself. Colonel, you take the rest of the men and the money and start walking. I'll use the Montagnards to keep everything under control and meet up with you back in the States."

Scott motioned for me to walk with him. When we were out of earshot of the men he asked, "What the hell do you think you are doing?"

"Someone has to stay behind to insure the escape of the others. Since Marcia is the only pilot, I get along pretty good with the two Vietnamese and they are the only ones that can understand the Montagnards, it seems logical that the four of us should stay behind."

"I don't like it." He kicked his feet in the dirt.

"I'm not sure I like it either, but it makes sense. At the same time, getting the money out of the line of sight of everyone concerned should take some of the pressure off the men."

"What do you expect me to do with the money?" Scott asked.

"Divide it up between the men when you get out. It doesn't belong to anyone that I know, unless you have some other idea."

Scott motioned for Tom to come over and explained what I wanted to do.

"This is pure bullshit," Tom hissed between clenched teeth. "We should stay together."

"Think it through," I replied. "Hanging around for two or three days could become dangerous for all of us. If it starts to turn ugly, Marcia and I along with Min and Giac stand a better chance of getting through the jungle than all of us together." I looked up and noticed that Min had moved closer to us. He raised his hand and asked if he could be heard. I waved him closer and asked him what he wanted.

"I could not help but overhear what you were talking about and I have a suggestion. Have Giac go with the main group. This will ensure that they make the best time and don't get lost. Another minor thought would be that every man be given some amount of money to carry, with the balance to be given them when the destination is reached."

"It sounds like a good idea," offered Tom. "But I'm not sure if the government would consider the money ours to give away."

"Let's cross that bridge when we come to it," I replied.

They left at dawn. As it turned out, we waited less than a day to follow them. During that time, I started to really get to know Marcia. Inside a jungle clearing in the middle of Vietnam we walked, talked and exchanged remembrances of a home that was ten thousand miles away. Marcia was an only child who had one relative, an aunt living in Connecticut. She attended college on a full scholarship and joined the Army as a protest against the war. She believed that if you wanted to change the system, you had to work from within. Her voice had a magic lilt to it. She spoke with an ardor that made you want to be a part of whatever cause she embraced. The time flew by.

When I heard the plane, I wasn't sure if I was happy or sad. The aircraft was a DC-3, piloted by two men in civilian clothes who claimed to be with the CIA. As we prepared to load the seven Americans and three of the Vietnamese who swore they were officers into the plane, Min asked me, "What should we do with the other prisoners?"

I understood the implication of his question. Freeing them before we took off could jeopardize our getting out and leaving them behind was like handing down a death sentence. I felt myself staring into space; I didn't want to be judge and jury over forty people.

"Sir, you must decide, or perhaps you would like me to give the order," Min said.

"No, it's my job," I replied. "Tell the Montagnards when they can no longer see the plane the camp belongs to them. They can continue to live here and keep the prisoners as workers or burn the camp to the ground and deal with them as they would any murderers."

This answer, when relayed to the leader of the hill people, was greeted with smiles, and to this day, I don't know what they decided to do.

At gunpoint, we had the pilot fly us towards Malaysia where we knew there was an Air Force base that didn't exist on any maps. It was one of the jumping off spots that the military swore wasn't there. The trip took less than three hours and as we approached, I used the radio to alert the people on the ground to our situation. I was starting to get a funny feeling in the pit of my stomach. This was too easy. An unmarked plane flying into a secret base with some cockamamie story about a slave labor camp with a wounded general on board was missing only James Bond to make it believable. I put my gun against the head of the pilot and told him not to land. I had Marcia do some quick calculations and told him to head towards Singapore. When this plane came down, I wanted a crowd of people around.

Chapter 22

"Is it that difficult?" Karen asked.

I sat up. I had been staring at the water and hadn't said a word. "No, I don't think so. We were sworn to secrecy and my sense of loyalty, which sometimes I think is misguided, jumps up and gets in the way."

Karen didn't say a word for what seemed like minutes.

"Let me tell you my thoughts," Karen began. "This whole thing smells of money. Whoever these people are, they're investing large sums of money in low-priced stocks, pushing the market up and leaving the rest of the world holding worthless pieces of paper five or six days later. If we run the numbers based on the information we have, one person investing a quarter of a million dollars in a stock which is two dollars and fifty cents and goes up to eight-fifty six days later, has made six hundred thousand dollars. If there are four or five other people doing the same thing at approximately the same time, they now have three million dollars."

Our food came and my stomach growled in response. "Let's eat before it gets cold, but don't lose that thought."

Karen had already started eating. She looked at me and said, "What thought?"

"The one about the stocks."

"Oh that one," she teased.

"What thought did you think I meant?"

Karen smiled, "I'll hold that one also."

I continued eating as Karen poured more coffee into my cup along with hers. We ate in silence and I realized that every minute I spent with this woman, the more comfortable I became.

"These pancakes are delicious, or maybe I should say were delicious."

I looked up from the plate I was staring at and said, "I'm glad you liked them. I've been thinking of what we were talking about before and . . ."

Karen held up her hand. "Hold that thought. I have to use the ladies' room."

"What thought?" I responded.

"The one—" she smiled at my impish grin. "Smart ass, I'll be right back."

When she returned, she passed by the back of my chair and slightly touched my shoulder. I felt her fingers as they seemed to dance across my back. As we walked to the car, I had a feeling that something was going to happen. All the conversation, the back and forth banter, the pouring of the coffee and Karen's touching my shoulder had raised this day to a higher level.

We drove through the pass that led from Malibu to the valley without saying a word. After two or three minutes, I started with the questions that were building up inside me.

"Okay, they now have three million dollars, what happens next?"

Karen pulled a piece of paper out of her pocket. "The second stock on the list is SCOA. It stands for Specialty Corporation of America. Your book says that on next Thursday the stock will be at five dollars and twenty-five cents a share. Three million profit dollars will buy about five hundred thousand shares. If they include the money they started with, you can add another two hundred thousand shares. The following Tuesday the book says to sell. It has no price next to the sell, just the date. I would guess that they would expect the stock to rise four to five dollars per share, which means they would have about six million in profit and a bankroll of eight to nine million.

"The third stock on the list is NOME, which stands for National Organization of Medical Electronics. They sell SCOA on Tuesday and buy NOME on Thursday. Nome is listed at seven. Using my numbers, they could purchase up to one million shares. If it only goes up five dollars, they have another five million. Now they're up to twelve million. Three trades and they're plus ten million. Twenty-four trades and they could have over three hundred million. The reason for the increase is that the profits will go up faster as they have more money to invest."

I looked at my watch. We had been driving for about fifteen minutes.

"We're only about ten minutes from my place. Would you mind hanging around for a while? I would like to introduce you to my friends."

"I'd love to meet them as long as you don't think I would be intruding. Just remember, I have to pick up my car and I do have a three-hour ride to get home."

"I'll explain why I want you at the meeting and I promise to get you back to the hotel by 4 P.M."

We pulled into the driveway. "Here's my house." I hit the button on the visor and the garage door opened.

"I don't remember the last time I saw such a clean garage," Karen joked.

"It's not used for anything but parking the car," I answered somewhat defensively. I got out of the car and asked, "Which of these bags have the things you need to shower and change?"

"As long as I can dress casually, the small one will do."

She answered the question in the form of another question. It was almost as if she was asking me how I wanted her to dress to meet my friends.

"Casual is fine. Tom and Scott never dress up on the weekends and Min, well he's just Min."

Karen bit her lower lip as if in thought and then decided. "I think I'll need both bags."

I lifted both bags out of the trunk and started towards the door. I pushed a button on my key ring and the door to the house swung open.

"Very clever," Karen whispered. "Does your magic key ring do any other tricks or open any other doors in this house?"

"Only a couple of tricks, and only to one other door inside the house."

"Which one is that?"

"I'll never tell," I replied, laughing.

Entering through the garage, we passed through a laundry room into the kitchen.

"Very, very nice." Her eyes seemed to take in the entire room from where she stopped.

"This way," I hollered. "These bags are getting heavy."

"Poor boy, do you need some help?"

"No thank you. The other bedroom is just down this hall. I'll put the bags on the bed and give you a quick tour."

"I suggest that you check your phone and find out what time your friends are arriving and then I can take the tour."

"Good idea. I almost forgot about them."

I called my message center and told her, "Tom said they would all be here between 12:30 and 1:00. He also said, again, I should apologize for him."

Karen's eyes twinkled, "I'm sorry, I wasn't listening when you were on the car phone. What was it he said that you are going to say you're sorry for?"

"Never mind. We have about two hours, so let me show you the house. I have to check and make sure I have some soft drinks and some tea for the guys."

I walked Karen through the house. It was a sprawling fifty-four hundred square foot ranch style home. Aside from the master bedroom, there were three other bedrooms, each with its own bathroom. There were formal dining and living rooms and a very large den. I became conscious of how much space there was for one person. We finished the tour back in the kitchen area, which aside from having a granite-topped center island also had a table with six chairs that faced the backyard and the mountains beyond that.

"I am impressed. Whoever decorated it did an excellent job. It's so neat and clean that it doesn't even look lived in."

I looked around. "My wife did most of the decorating. She really enjoyed doing the shopping and laying out where everything would go. As far as being neat and clean, I have a woman come in twice a week to dust. I haven't used this part of the house very often over the past year. I haven't had any visitors until today for about the same period of time." I shrugged my shoulders and said, "Make yourself comfortable while I look around the garage for some soft drinks."

"While you're looking, I'm going to spend some time on my computer so that I can have more facts at my fingertips when your friends arrive. When are you going to tell me what you think?"

"I want my friends to hear what you have to say and then I'll talk about my thoughts."

After a couple of minutes, I came back into the kitchen and said, "I have to run to the store. Is there anything special that you would like to drink?"

"I'd like some Evian, and how about something to nibble on for your friends?"

"Good idea. I'll be back in a few."

It only took me twenty minutes to go the store and return. When I entered the kitchen, Karen wasn't there. I started down the hall calling her name when I heard the shower going in the guest bedroom. I decided that I might as well change while she was getting ready and we could then spend some time going over her notes. I showered quickly. With a large bath towel wrapped around my waist, I entered my walk-in closet to pick out some slacks and a shirt. As I re-entered the room, Karen walked into the bedroom with a hand towel wrapped around her head and nothing else.

"What the hell are you doing here?" she yelled.

"When I got back, I called your name and when I heard the shower I decided that I should get dressed. What are *you* doing here?"

Karen looked down at herself and started to turn away. She looked back and said, "There's no bath towel in that bathroom, so I came in here looking for one. What are you staring at?"

I quickly turned my back on her. I felt like a little kid who got caught staring at a naked woman.

"Turn your back," I said over my shoulder. "I'll throw you my towel and I'll step back into the closet."

Karen started laughing. "Tell you what. Close your eyes and I'll come and take the towel and you can open them after I leave."

Now I started laughing. "Hold on, I'll get you a fresh one." I went back into the bathroom, picked up another towel, and walked back into the bedroom that was now empty.

"Where are you?"

"I'm in the hall, just throw it out."

"Here it comes." I had walked to the door and threw it into the hallway.

"Thanks." She then continued, "Knock, knock."

"Knock, knock?" I thought for a second. "Who's there?"

"Apollo," came the reply.

"Apollo who?" I asked.

"I apologize for yelling at you." Karen then entered the bedroom with the towel wrapped around her. She walked over to where I was standing and kissed me on the cheek.

"Am I forgiven?" she asked.

I reached for her as she stepped away.

"No, you're not forgiven."

"What would I have to do to be forgiven?" She again had that teasing impish grin.

"How about drying my hair with that towel you're wrapped in."

"That's all? You are easy. I'll tell you what. How about I owe you a hair rub. I pick the place and you pick the time. The only caveat is that it's not here and not now."

I looked around. Karen continued, "I've done a bad job hiding that I'm attracted to you. You are honest, you are fun to be with, and I have the feeling that this could be maintained over a longer period of time. I don't think that I can compete with a ghost." She walked over to me, put her arms around my neck and kissed me full on the lips. "Let's see if that can hold us. Now, I have to get dressed."

Chapter 23

The next hour went by very quickly. The only interruption was a phone call from Barry.

"Aaron, this is Barry. We have to talk."

"Okay, talk." I answered.

"Not over the phone. In person."

I sighed, "You might as well come on over and join the party. Tom, Scott and Min will be here around 1 P.M."

"What's going on?"

"If what you want to talk about in person relates to our earlier conversations this week, I guess you should be here."

"Aaron, listen to me. Don't pull any of that macho bullshit. We are talking about some serious people. If you can get some of your people to start watching your building and your house, start doing it now. Don't wait."

"Barry, slow down. Come on over and let's discuss this. We can decide what we should do when you're here."

"Aaron, at least have some of your people watch Tom and Scott's family. Listen to me for once."

"If you're that concerned I'll have someone watching."

"Good, I'll see you soon. There's one more thing. At least take your gun out of the closet and be prepared." The phone went dead.

"Is something wrong?" Karen asked.

"There must be a full moon. Either that or everyone is infected with some strange malady."

"Who's Barry? Or is that another story for a rainy day?"

"Barry is a police captain who believes I saved his life one night and has since become a guardian angel type of person."

"Did you save his life?"

"Well, let's put it this way. There were a lot of shots fired and I ended up with a bullet in my butt."

"My hero," she said sarcastically. "Was anyone else wounded?"

"Barry was a sergeant then and one of his people lost his life. Barry actually killed all three of the crooks, but I still think that he has never forgiven himself for not firing quicker."

"Is he married?"

"No, his wife walked out on him for a dentist. They recently signed the divorce papers and he's been seeing one of the women from my office. Don't say anything because it's supposed to be a secret."

"Don't worry, I won't. What was Barry concerned about?"

"I'm not sure. He wants me to take my gun out of the closet and make sure it's loaded."

"What? Does he think I'm that dangerous?"

"He doesn't even know you're here. Like I said, it's a full moon and I promised to make a call."

The hands on the clock were straight up when there was a knock on the door.

"Someone is a little early," I said as I headed towards the front of the house.

"Are you sure?" asked Karen in a voice that had a sense of urgency to it.

I stopped and walked over to the kitchen cabinet, opened the door and took out my pistol. I checked to make sure it was loaded and continued to the front door. She was making me paranoid.

"Is anyone in there?" Scott's voice came from the other side of the door.

I shook my head. "I'm coming." I opened the door still holding the revolver.

Scott looked at the revolver and asked, "Is it something I said, or did you think it was Tom?"

"Very funny. I guess Tom told you what happened. Come on in and let me introduce you to Karen Williams."

Scott walked into the kitchen holding a box and stopped when Karen stood. "Hi, my name is Scott. I didn't think you would still be here, but let me say it is my pleasure to meet you."

Before Karen could say anything, there was another knock on the door and in walked Tom followed by Min. I was shaking Min's hand when both Min and Tom noticed Karen.

She extended her hand and said, "Aaron asked me to hang around. I'll let him explain and if there is a problem, I can go sit in the backyard until you finish."

Min walked over to Karen and looked at her for a fleeting second before he said, “If Aaron has suggested you stay, I am sure he has good reason.” He extended both of his arms and encircled Karen’s outstretched hand inside them.

“You must be Min. Aaron told me you are one of his closest friends. He said the story of your meeting is very long and not very interesting. I think he is not telling me the exact truth. Someday if you have the time, I would love to hear your side of it.”

“An old man has much time. I would find it an honor.”

Karen then turned to Tom. “You must be the third musketeer. I would recognize your voice almost anywhere.”

Tom shuffled his feet not knowing what to say. “Did Aaron tell you I was sorry?”

“He told me something, but I’m sworn to secrecy about what goes on inside this house. Why don’t we all go into the den and we’ll let Aaron fill you in on why I am still here. If after you hear the story you are still uncomfortable, I will wait outside on the patio until you are finished.”

Before they could move, there was another knock and in walked Barry. I made the introductions.

Karen led the way into the den. She motioned for Min to sit in the recliner that had an ottoman attached to it.

“I think you will find this seat to your liking.” She then turned to Scott and asked, “How would you like to sit on the sofa next to Barry?”

Scott smiled. “I’d love to.”

Karen then turned to Tom. “And you can help me bring in the soft drinks and ice. After that, maybe I’ll forgive you.”

I stood mesmerized as I watched Karen charm my four friends. She bossed them around like she had known them forever. As I watched, I realized that she had dressed semi-formal for this meeting. She was wearing a curve-hugging skirt from a business suit and a silk blouse that was open at the neck. She had changed into shoes that had heels, not the spike kind, but high enough so that they showed off her legs.

As Karen led Tom back into the kitchen, she turned to Min. “Mr. Min, would you rather have some tea? I put up some hot water and I did find some orange pekoe.”

Min had been following her with his eyes. He smiled and said, “I would rather have iced tea if it’s no bother.”

“No bother at all,” she answered. She took Tom by the arm and finished leading him into the kitchen.

"How was the trip out here?" I asked Min.

"The roads were a little crowded with cars, but the trip went fast. My driver is very skillful."

"Is he waiting in the car? I asked.

"My driver has company to sit with. There is not a problem."

Karen and Tom re-entered the room. Tom was holding a tray with soft drinks, bottled water, ice and a tall glass with iced tea in it. Karen lifted the glass of iced tea and handed it to Min. "It has no sugar, but I have a few packets here if you so desire."

Min shook his head in a negative manner.

She motioned for Tom to put the balance of the drinks on the coffee table in the middle of the floor. She then turned to Tom and said, "You are now forgiven." She motioned back to me and said, "You're on."

Scott jumped up. "Hold it, I want to find out how your date went last night." As he said this, he opened the box and took out a machine that looked like a light meter and started pointing it around the room.

I pointed at Karen and started waving my finger in a circular motion. She caught on immediately.

"It was really very nice. He was a perfect gentleman. He had flowers sent to my room. He picked me up right on time and had me back in the hotel early enough for me to get my beauty sleep."

"It's clean."

"What was that all about?" Karen asked.

"Someone has been planting listening devices in our office. We felt it prudent to make sure there were none here," replied Scott.

"Before the conversation starts, might Aaron tell us why he has asked this lovely lady to join us?" Min asked.

Karen smiled, "Thank you for the compliment, Mr. Min."

"Okay, let's get started. As most of you know, last Monday night I was involved in an accident where a woman was killed. She had in her possession two hundred and fifty thousand dollars and a little notebook."

"What little notebook?" interrupted Barry.

"This one. It fell out of her purse when the car blew. I had put it in my jacket and had forgotten all about it until Carol handed it to me. The cleaners had found it and sent it back with my clothes. The book has a date, a series of letters, a three-digit number, and another date. For the life of me, I couldn't figure out what the letters or numbers meant. When I showed it to Karen, she explained that it wasn't in code. It was a date to buy a certain stock and a date to sell it. Karen has printed the first couple on a sheet of paper so that you can follow what I am saying."

I handed the sheets of paper to each of them. "The first one is WWSI or World Wide Services, Inc. Last Monday, the stock was at two dollars and fifty cents. It closed Friday at eight fifty. If the woman in the accident had used the money to purchase one hundred thousand shares, she would've made six hundred thousand by yesterday. Next week's stock is SCOA or Specialty Corporation of America. The stock is at about five dollars. If someone were to use the money they earned and the principal, they could purchase another one hundred and fifty thousand shares and earn, I don't know, another six hundred thousand. The list goes on and on. If there are four or five more people in different parts of the country doing the same thing, they could be talking three million plus a week."

"I know a little about the Securities Exchange Act of 1934. What you're talking about is illegal," said Scott.

"So is killing people. I don't think these people are worried about doing something illegal." I realized that I had raised my voice and stopped talking.

"Where does Karen fit in?" asked Barry.

"She has an idea."

"Can we hear it?" Barry continued.

I looked at Karen and said, "Explain it slowly."

Karen stood. "Aaron has told me that he feels he must get even. Using that as a starting point and understanding that in the getting even, he means not doing some sort of bodily harm, I have formulated a get even plan. This book tells us when the bad guys are going to buy and tells us when they are going to sell. If we started buying in front of them and sold before they do, we would be forcing them to pay more than they wanted or expected and they would be the ones left holding the paper." Karen stopped and looked around the room. "No questions yet?"

"I have one," said Scott. "I understand that you are in the business of buying and selling stocks. Would you be involved in these transactions?"

"That's another part of the plan. I can, if necessary, trade through three or four different brokerage firms. I already have open accounts with them. It would, of course, be better if we were able to use as many different brokers as possible. That would mask our trades, at least for a little while. We should be able to make the money that they intended to make and leave them with the bad paper. We would have to work under the principle that what they are after is money and the loss of that money is what will hurt them the most."

"How much money would we need to do them damage?" asked Min.

Karen looked around the room. "I think we need some more ice. While I am getting some, why don't you decide if I am to stay or go out into the yard to sunbathe."

Karen picked up the ice bucket and left the room.

Everyone noticed that the bucket of ice was more than half full.

"Well guys, if we're going to vote, I vote to keep her," said Tom.

"She is a very interesting person. I think our friend Aaron has found someone he is comfortable with. I think we should ask her to stay at least for today. If things change in future, we can change our minds." Min finished talking and looked around the room.

Barry stood up and looked into the direction of the kitchen. Not seeing Karen, he started, "The reason I came out today is that a body was found early this morning. The dead guy was a private investigator located in Camarillo. He chased husbands, spied on wives and anything else that someone could make a buck doing. His death wouldn't have caused a ripple in a lake except that under a pillow on his sofa they found a computer disk. When they plugged it in, they brought up the last case he was working on. I have a copy of the printout with me, but let me give you the Reader's Digest version. He was hired for one hundred thousand dollars to come up with information on Aaron and Be Safe.

"He turned over to the person or persons that are presently unknown everything you would want to know about Aaron, the company, Tom, Scott, and their families. His report contained the schools your kids go to, where your wives shop, and approximately how much money you have in the bank. The last entry told about how he was getting the last payment and he had to return all documents, notes, et cetera. He decided to keep a copy just in case. He thought he was being paid too much for such an easy job. The people we are dealing with are dangerous. You must take steps to protect your families."

I stepped into the conversation. "Barry called me about a half hour ago and asked me to have your homes and families watched until we had this meeting. I called the duty officer and told him to call in some extra people."

"Everything you said he checked about us could almost be found in the public library. Who would pay that kind of money for shit information?" Tom looked around as he asked the question.

"That was why you had your gun out when I arrived," Scott said as if explaining an answer to everyone.

"You had a gun out?" Min asked.

"Barry asked me to have it nearby when he called. Scott arrived early and Karen was a little nervous."

Everyone turned as Karen returned to the room.

"I wasn't nervous, just a little cautious. It is becoming evident that we must be smarter than they are and precautions about the safety of your families must be taken. Barry, you are a captain of the police." She turned to Aaron, Tom and Scott. "You three own a security firm." She then turned and faced Min. "I am sorry, Mr. Min, for ignoring you. When I suggest that precautions be taken to protect families, I am of course including you. Unless someone has a better idea on how to beat these bastards at their own game, I suggest we get started."

"What makes you think I want you involved?" I asked.

She smiled and looked me straight in the eye, "Don't you?"

I smiled and everyone else, after watching the two of us, started smiling.

"Okay, Karen stays," I said to the group. "I promised her that I would get her back to her car later afternoon. Barry, we'll get back to you in a minute. Min, why did you want to see us?"

"Before I start, may I ask where Miss Karen's car is?"

"I left it at the Hyatt Hotel in Westlake Village when Aaron picked me up for breakfast this morning."

I realized that Min had just asked where Karen had spent the night and she very adroitly answered him.

Min continued, "If you would be so kind as to give me keys, I will have my nephews bring it here."

"That would be very nice. I'll be right back. The keys are in my purse."

When she walked out of the room, Min again started talking, "Aaron, you must be sure that you want her involved. It could be dangerous."

"I know that. There is something about her that makes me want to be with her. I haven't felt this way in over a year."

Karen re-entered and asked, "Did I miss anything?"

"No, we were just talking."

Karen handed the keys to Min. "It's a Cadillac convertible."

Min raised himself off of the recliner and walked to the door. He opened it and said something to one of his nephews in Vietnamese. He then returned to the room and sat back down.

"When Aaron visited my home, he questioned me about the people that were part of the cleaning up crew in the Be Safe building. He believed a Cuban group could have hired one or more of them to spy on you. That same person or persons could also be a danger to me in the future." He looked down at his hands and continued, "I did not believe it possible. The people, I had them looked at again. It did not take long, but we found a person who did not tell the truth when he came to us. I had told Aaron that I did not think any of my people would be working for the Cubans. I was correct about that. In Vietnam, there were some unfinished things that were left behind. There were families that thought they were wronged. Over the past eight years, I have tried to remedy the old problems. A few still remain. This person that did not tell the truth when hired has now told us of his real past. We did not ever consider him or his family as a problem."

He paused and looked at Scott, Tom and myself in that order. "If you remember when we all left Vietnam, we left behind in that camp some Vietnamese guards. There was also a group of these guards that were not in the camp, but out on patrol looking for more workers. They returned soon after we left. They found two of the guards barely alive. From them, they learned of what happened. One of the men on patrol lost his father and a brother. His family believes that they have a debt to be repaid. The one we found working for us was part of plot to get even. He was already in place when he received word from home that he was to help these people. He received his instructions late Wednesday afternoon from the office of the Vietnamese counsel general."

"Jeez Louise," said Scott. "Where is this guy now?"

Min looked at Barry before he answered. "He fell and broke his neck. His body was delivered to the Consulate where he received his instructions for forwarding back to Vietnam."

"I just remembered something." Everyone turned to look at me. "It's been bothering me for two days. Twice I've seen someone outside the house that seemed to be taking a walk. He didn't look familiar, but he opened and closed his fists as he moved. Last night as I watched the television, one of the fighters did the same thing. That reminded me about him. The last time I saw someone doing that was when we were in the camp in Nam. The General who hit Marcia . . ."

"You mean the one you shot?" interrupted Tom.

"Yeah, that son of a bitch."

"Do you think it was him outside your house?" asked Barry.

"I don't know. He didn't look like him, but as I think about it, he had the same body shape and he was always clenching and unclenching his fists. I still have a hard-on for that guy." I turned and looked in Karen's direction, "Sorry, Karen."

"Don't let it bother you. I'm just one of the boys."

There were a few seconds of silence that seemed to stretch for minutes when Scott said, "Okay, let's put it all together." He held up one finger. "Aaron gets involved in an accident on the freeway. The woman in the accident has two hundred and fifty thousand dollars in her purse."

"Don't forget the notebook," I interrupted.

He continued to talk as if I hadn't said a word.

"She also has a notebook with a list of stocks. That list has prices and dates that look like buy and sell instructions. Some section of the federal government gets involved and they all end up dead. Someone working for Min who is trying to settle an old score we were all involved in helps to bug our offices. Aaron believes he sees someone who is also associated with all of us in our past. A private detective who is investigating all of us turns up dead."

"Don't forget," said Karen. "These people have the ability to make close to a half a billion dollars."

Barry stood up and started to pace the floor. "I'm having a little problem here, folks. So far I've heard about someone falling down and breaking his neck." He turned and nodded his head at Min. "A scam to bilk the American public out of a half a billion dollars." He turned and nodded to Karen. "A stalker who may or may not be a murderer." He nodded at me. "A bunch of lesser charges such as breaking and entering, hanging illegal wiretaps and part of a story that happened seven years ago, which I don't think I want to hear. I'm a police captain. My job is to uphold the law and protect against all of these things."

"That is why I asked Karen to stay. Karen, continue where you left off."

Karen stood and walked to the door leading out to the backyard. She turned and faced all of us. "I told you earlier by purchasing the stocks before they do and selling the stocks before they get a chance, we force them to buy at a higher price, which in theory will get us more profit when we sell and force them to take lower-than-anticipated profits. I have three accounts that I can trade through. I will not use any of my clients' money, just my own. I would like each of you to do the same through your own brokers. With buy orders coming from six or seven different brokerage firms, it will become difficult for them to figure out what is going on for the first two or three stocks. Afterward, we may have to change our strategy.

"Since I don't know how liquid each of you are, I would suggest that all profits and losses, if any, be shared equally."

"Just what does that mean?" asked Barry.

"I estimate that it will take at least a half million dollars to have any effect on what they are doing. Regardless of how much each of us can put into the pot, we are partners. If Aaron put in three hundred thousand and we each put in between ten thousand and one hundred thousand and the profits were six hundred thousand, we would each make one hundred thousand dollars."

I immediately realized what she had done. Not knowing how much money each person had, she tied everyone into the plot. I looked at Min and then at Barry. Before he could formulate a question, she continued.

"We are going to need Barry's help to find out who these people are. Once they realize what we are doing, I get the impression that they will not be happy. We must also use some of the security people that you have working for you at Be Safe to watch your wives, children, and Mr. Min. I am assuming, and I know what that gets me, that you three and Barry can handle yourselves."

She paused, I thought, for effect. "I believe that we can earn over a million dollars by using the first three stocks on the list." She let that number sink in and then continued. "At the same time, we will be putting a world of hurt on whoever they are. This would also give Barry two and a half weeks to find them. Any questions?"

"I have one," said Min. "When we, I mean Captain Barry, identifies these people, what will we do with them?"

"I thought we would turn them over to Barry or the government for their disposition."

"That's what I thought also," chimed in Barry.

Min took a long sigh. "You were not with us in Vietnam. If these are the same people, they raped eight and nine year old girls before they sold them into slavery. They cut off the head of every fourth boy child as a show of strength. They whipped, starved and who knows what else to those people. We can not let them go free."

I jumped in. "Why don't we find out who they are before we decide what we are going to do with them?" I looked straight at Min. Our eyes locked for a few seconds and then Min nodded his head in agreement to the unspoken thought passing between us.

Min stood, "I must be leaving. Monday morning brokerage firms in New York, Colorado, San Francisco and Hong Kong will start purchasing five hundred thousand shares of this SCOA stock."

Karen said, "I don't think you understand. The stock is five dollars. I was thinking more in line with a hundred thousand shares."

"That is fine. You purchase one hundred thousand from smaller firms. It will confuse them more."

"But that will be over two and a half million dollars."

"Probably three and half before it's over. If you are correct, they will have no way of stopping their people from purchasing. Their people will only be able to buy at seven or higher. When we sell at eight and a half or nine, stock should go back to four or five, costing them hundreds of thousands of profits. The one after that is only listed at three dollars and change. We should be able to make much more. Here is my card. Call me with instructions as to when to sell." He turned to the rest of us. "It was very nice seeing you all again. Next time we meet we will be dividing much money between us. You lovely lady, it has been a pleasure. Watch over my young friend. I owe him my life."

He turned and started towards the door. He turned back to Karen and said, "The next time we meet, please call me Uncle Min." Before the front door closed, his niece entered and gave Karen, whose face was still flushed, her keys.

"Is he serious?" asked Karen. "He has three or four million dollars to invest? Today is Saturday. Where will he get the cash on the weekend?"

"If Min says he is going to do it, he will," I said.

"Let's figure out how we're going to do our part. Barry, if we go under the assumption that these people are the ones that we met in Vietnam, can you get any information on them through any sources you have over at the Federal Building?"

Barry was deep in thought. "I can ask the questions, but I think I have another problem. If Min catches up with these people before us, he will not turn them in."

"You're not sure of that," I said.

"Are you?" responded Barry. "You don't think that guy they caught bugging your office fell, do you?"

Scott stood up. "Let's worry about that later. I think I could probably raise about one hundred thousand to buy the stock. How about you guys?"

"I have almost that much around," continued Tom. "I could have my broker sell another fifty or so on the opening."

"That's a good idea," said Scott as he re-entered the conversation. "I could probably do the same."

"I don't even have a broker," said Barry. "I have about thirty thousand in the bank and another hundred and fifty in a 401(K) plan. I'm not even sure I know how to get it out in a hurry."

"I have some forms in my car that will allow me to open an account for you. If you sign the papers and give me a check for twenty-five thousand dollars, SEC rules allow me to trade stocks for you through my firm."

Barry looked at Karen and said, "I guess I'm in. I owe Aaron my life." He thought for a second and then asked, "How do I cash in my 401(K) and add it to the pot?"

"That would probably take a week. A better way would be to take out a loan against it. You could probably have the money in a couple of days and whatever interest they charged would be tax-deductible. In reality, we will be selling the stock for a profit before more money is needed." Karen got up and said, "I'm going to the car to get the forms for Barry to sign. If I can believe what has happened here, Min will purchase five hundred thousand shares, Tom and Scott will buy about sixty thousand shares, I will purchase through my company about fifty thousand, which means that the stock should be at about eight or nine by Wednesday."

She was walking towards the door when I stopped her and said, "Hold it. Just what do you think you're all doing? I somewhat understand Min. Someone is on his blood trail and he has to fix it, but you guys are crazy. I'm the one that saw the accident. I'm the one that has this feeling that I have to save the world. Not you people. Barry, if you remember correctly, maybe you saved my life. Tom, Scott, you guys got me out of Nam, and Karen, we really just met. This isn't your fight. Weren't you the one that said you couldn't or wouldn't invest your clients' money? We now know most of what has been going on over the past week. There is no reason for you people to get involved. Let's just let Barry find these people and take care of the punishment. I will buy stock along with Min and when the shit hits the fan, they'll come after me and I'll be ready."

"As far as I'm concerned, the three of us walked out of Nam together," Scott answered.

"Just what the hell do you think partners are for?" Tom raised his voice as he spoke. "We're here to share the good times. If my wife ever found out I didn't join you guys and let a fortune get away, she'd kill me."

"Especially after I tell her about Karen," Scott rejoined the conversation.

Both of them spoke lightly about what was going on, but their eyes had turned to steel.

"Are you finished?" asked Karen. She looked at Tom and Scott. "I'm going out to get the forms for Barry to fill out. You try and talk some sense into him while I'm gone."

Chapter 24

"Hold it," I yelled. "Didn't you hear what I said?"

"I heard you and I'm sure your friends heard you." She stared straight at me. She took a deep breath, threw back her shoulders and continued, "Your expertise is not in the buying of stocks and bonds. Mine is. What you are good at, along with Tom and Scott, is security. What Barry is good at is law enforcement. What Min is good at would probably scare the hell out of me, but together we can kick the stuffing out of these people. While we're teaching them a lesson, you and I can find out if we are compatible. If we're not, we'll both have a bunch of money to show for our efforts. If we are, we can decide together what to do with all of our ill-gotten gains, maybe a vacation to Hawaii. I'll find out at the same time about your friends and they can find out about me. I'm not Marcia, and you're not Terry, which is probably the good news from my end. We've only known each other for one week. We've spent very little time together, but it's been a fun time. Don't become a male chauvinist. It doesn't suit you. I'll be right back."

Karen left the room and I looked at my friends.

"I'm glad that's settled," Barry exhaled.

"Aaron, tell me again where you found her," Scott said.

Tom chipped in, "I vote yes. I'm almost afraid to say no." They all started to laugh. A tension that had been building had been released.

Karen walked back into the room. "What did I miss?" That started another round of laughter.

"Let's get serious," I continued. "Karen will call the shots as far as the buying and selling stock. If I know Min, he has already placed orders for his half-million shares. How should the rest of us proceed?"

"Each of you should contact your broker before the market opens in the morning. Make sure your orders are placed by dollars instead of shares. We don't know how the stock will react to Min's purchases. Call me when your broker has executed the trade. I'll keep track of our positions and come Tuesday, I'll start tracking the competition."

I jumped in and continued, "Tom, you arrange for surveillance of both your wives and children around the clock. Scott, you take care of the building. Barry, I'll give you the name of the son of a bitch from Vietnam. We all had to sign a piece of paper that swore us to secrecy under some dire threat to life and limb, but I think I have a copy of a diary that Marcia kept. You see if you can find out what happened to that guy. Unless any of you have something else to say, let's break it up. I promised Karen I would have her on the road soon."

Karen said, "Meeting you has been a pleasure. Before this is over, I think we'll be close friends. Barry, please come into the kitchen for a minute and we'll fill out these forms."

"See you in the office tomorrow," Scott said as he headed towards the door. "I can't wait to get home and tell Constance all about Karen."

"Mary will be on the phone ten seconds after I get finished telling her the story," said Tom. "Tell Constance to expect the call."

Barry came walking out of the room. "That was painless."

The three men left together as I went looking for Karen.

"Karen," I yelled. "Karen," I yelled for a second time.

"What are you yelling for?" she called back to me. "I'm putting the glasses in the dishwasher."

"I thought you might be taking another shower," I answered back, trying to put a leer on my face.

"I don't think your heart could handle it."

I put a smile on my face. "Listen carefully. If these are the people that I think they are, they are not nice. If this thing we're doing starts to go wrong, I want you to get out of San Diego quickly. Call me and then go somewhere and hide until I can get down there."

"Don't worry. I'm a big girl. It's going to take them at least two trades to know that they're in trouble and at least another two weeks to identify where the trades are coming from. By that time, you and Barry will have them identified and in custody."

I shrugged. "Maybe, but don't take any chances."

"I won't, but tell me, do you really think that Mr. Min has that kind of money?"

"If Min says that he does, you can go to the bank on it."

"It's going to mess up how we were planning on splitting the profits. I had assumed approximately equal amounts from everyone. If he buys one half a million shares, he will have three or four times as much as the rest of us combined."

"We can worry about the profits later. First, let's get out of this with our skins intact."

Karen looked at her watch. "I have to get on the road. I must tell you, this has been the most exciting two days of my life."

"I'll get your bags and meet you by the car."

"Pop the trunk." Karen pressed her key ring and the latch opened. "Anything you need to have in the front?"

"No, I'm set."

I slammed the trunk closed and walked to where Karen was standing. I put my arms around her shoulders and pulled her close. "I had a great two days myself. Don't worry about ghosts. I think I am very close to them being a thing in the past. I will never forget Marcia, but I . . ."

Karen put the tips of her fingers on my lips.

"I know. Let's take the days and weeks as they come."

She entered her car, turned the key and said, "It looks like they filled my car up with gas."

"You must have made a great impression upon Min. Maybe not that great," as I stepped back a few feet. "They didn't wash it."

"That's another story you'll have to tell me someday."

She pulled out of the driveway waving her arm good-bye. I walked back into the house, picked up the phone and dialed Tom. "It's me. She just left. Starting Monday, make sure that we have around-the-clock on her." I listened and then continued. "Sure, those two would be great. Can we spare them? You're right; she is a very interesting person. I'll see you on Monday. Enjoy the balance of the weekend." I took three steps away from the phone and it rang.

"Hello? Hi Barry. Yeah, I trust her . . . I'm not sure I can keep Min under control. We're going to have to find them first. His name was Brigadier General Waldman. That's all I know. I'll start looking for Marcia's diary tonight and get back to you as soon as I find it . . . Yes, we are having them watched. I'll keep in touch."

I hung up the phone and walked into the bedroom. There was a picture of Marcia on the nightstand. I picked it up and sat on the bed staring.

"It's been over a year," I said aloud. I fell asleep with the picture still in my hands. I woke around 8:30 P.M. It was dark outside and there were no lights on inside of the house. I had slept for about five hours and hadn't dreamt once.

Chapter 25

Sunday just flew. I contacted Carl Hewlett, my broker, and arranged for the buying of the stock. It was like playing twenty questions. Was I out of my mind? Did I have a tip? If so who from? Was there any insider trading involved? He went on and on. He gave me the distinct impression that he didn't want me to do this. I finally asked the question, "Carl, is there something about this trade that bothers you?"

"Now that you're asking the question, yes there is. You have never gotten involved in the buying of stocks other than to say yes or no to my suggestions. You have never ever bought a piece of crap like this one. In fact, I don't ever remember you asking about something like this. If you said you heard a story and want to invest five or six thousand dollars, and take a flyer, I wouldn't say a word. But to buy fifty thousand shares or a quarter of a million dollars worth is insane."

"Okay, if it will make you feel any better, I got a tip. It's not insider trading because I don't even know what they make."

"That's because they don't make anything. Specialty Corporation of America. They could be a Mafia front company for all we know."

"Carl, listen to me. I have to get this done and done early Monday morning."

"Aaron, I don't know what's driving this, but I will fax you an authorization letter now. Sign it and fax it back. I'll get it done."

"Thanks, Carl. Don't worry, I think I know what I'm doing." Under my breath I said, "I hope I know what I'm doing."

I called Karen a little after noon. "Explain to me again how this works," I said as she answered the phone.

"Whatever happened to asking me how my trip was?" She asked.

"Hi Karen. How was the trip back home?"

"Is there anything else that you would like to know?"

"Yeah, explain to me again how this is going to work."

"Well, I guess half a loaf is better than none. We start buying at about five dollars a share. We should be complete around six and a half or seven. On Tuesday, they should get in around that number and finish at about eight or so. We start unloading at eight and a half, which should drive the stock down into the four-dollar range. At that point, our friends would be losing two to three dollars for every share they bought. They could end up losing as much as four hundred thousand dollars."

"And there's no way they can trace where the sales are coming from?" I asked.

"They can eventually, but it will take at least three weeks. If you and Barry are as good as you think, you'll have them before then. Have you made your arrangements yet?"

"Yes, I made them this morning. My broker wasn't happy."

"I can understand that. What are you doing all day?" she continued.

"I'm cleaning out closets. There are a lot of clothes here that aren't being used and I'm packing them up to send over to the Salvation Army."

"Have you lost or gained weight?" Karen asked.

"They're not mine," I answered.

Karen went silent.

"Are you still there?" I asked.

Her voice was soft. "Are you sure you're ready?"

"I'm sure," I answered simply.

There was nothing else to say, so I hung up the phone.

Chapter 26

I pulled into the parking lot at 5:45 Monday morning. Both Tom and Scott were already there. We walked into the conference room and I dialed Karen's office number.

"K. W. Securities."

"Can I please talk to Karen Williams?" asked Tom on the speakerphone.

"Miss Williams is on the phone. Can you hold?"

"Yes I can," replied Tom

"Who should I say is calling?"

"Please tell her that Tom and Scott are here."

The phone went quiet and then Karen answered. "Good morning. Where's your friend?"

"I'm here."

"Good morning, Aaron."

"Morning. What does it look like?"

"The indication is that the stock will open up about fifty cents. There was a huge trade at four and seven-eighths outside the country."

"When does the market open?" asked Scott.

"It opens in about ten minutes, but there are markets open all night. I can't tell where this transaction took place, but it looks like maybe Europe."

"That must be Min," said Scott.

"Probably," answered Karen. "Guys, I hate to be a pain in the butt, but I must get on the phones. I'll update you as you call in the trades that your brokers are making."

"So long Karen," I said.

"So long Aaron."

I pressed the button breaking the connection and turned to Scott and Tom. "I'm headed down to San Diego. I feel wasted standing here."

"Don't forget to take your pistol and keep checking in."

I nodded agreement to Tom and walked out.

My phone was ringing off the hook as I passed my office. "Aaron here."

"Aaron, the first ten thousand went off at five and a quarter and the second ten thousand went off at five and a half. This stock is going ape shit. We're going to be close to six any minute now. Do you want to keep buying or should I hold up?"

It was Carl with my first trades of the day.

"Keep buying. I want fifty thousand shares by the end of the day."

"I hope you know what you're doing," he replied as he hung up the phone.

I headed out the door to my car. I had put a couple of changes of clothes in the trunk just in case and I was now glad that I did. I checked the glove compartment to make sure that my gun was still there and then started towards the freeway.

As I passed the Sunset Boulevard exit, the phone rang.

"Aaron, its Tom."

"Anything wrong?"

"No, I just wanted to tell you that Scott's last trade went off at five and three-quarters. I'm done at five and a half. Carl called and it looks like your trade will go off in the six-dollar range. He asked if I knew what was going on and I played dumb. To tell the truth, it was pretty easy. We've been calling the trades as they occur into Karen and she sounds pretty happy. I didn't tell her you were on the way down. Don't you think you should call? She may have a business lunch or dinner already set up."

"Don't worry. I'll be fine. Talk to you later."

Three hours later, I arrived at Karen's office. I parked the car and walked up to the directory in front of the building. Karen was in office numbers 102 and 103. I walked down the hall and entered without knocking.

"Good morning. How may I be of assistance?" asked the receptionist.

"I'm looking for Karen Williams."

"Miss Williams is in conference right now. Was she expecting you?"

"I don't think so. I can wait until she's free."

"Perhaps one of our other people can help you. If you could give me your name I'll check."

"No thanks. I'll wait."

She stood and pointed to a magazine rack.

"We have many books over there and if you like I can get you some coffee or a soft drink, Mr. . . ."

"My name is Aaron Carlyle. A cup of black coffee would be fine."

I could tell by the look on her face that my name rang a bell. She walked down the hall and returned carrying a china cup and saucer with coffee in it. She put the cup down on the table in front of me. "You may have a long wait. Miss Williams has given me instructions not to disturb her this morning. I will try and get a message to her within the next half hour."

"That would be nice," I replied.

From where I sat, I could hear what sounded like at least three other people working in the office. Somewhere behind the partitions phones rang and were answered and life went on, but not on the woman's desk in front of me. It was as if that desk was outside of the daily goings on. No one else came through the door until 11:30 A.M. when a UPS man entered with two packages. If the faceless people inside did anything but sit at their desk and answer phones, I couldn't tell from where I sat. As if by magic, the door to Karen's office opened. Karen walked out and picked up the two packages, looked up at me and said, "What are you doing here?"

I looked at her and responded, "I'm visiting a friend and thought you might do me a favor and suggest a place to eat."

"I would ask you to join me for lunch, but I'm taking my mother."

"Are you ashamed or afraid to introduce me?" I prodded.

She smiled. "Lunch is at 1:30 P.M." She turned to the secretary and said, "Call Patti's and change the reservation from two to three people." Turning back to me she said, "You might as well come on in and see where we are. I'm trying to set up a conference call for 3 P.M. this afternoon so that I can brief everyone at the same time."

I followed Karen into her office. In many ways it was just like her. Everything was very functional and very attractive.

"Have a seat at the conference table. I'll use the hook up from the PC to the projector and show you where we stand."

Karen picked up what looked like a television clicker except she used it to lower the lights. As the lights dimmed, she hit the projector's ON button and a set of numbers appeared on the wall.

"For purposes of keeping track of all the buy and sells, I have divided the grouping into six parts. I am calling the groups by each of our first names. They are Barry, which includes Tom, Scott, Mr. Min, Aaron, others and me.

What you will see are the names of the people, the amount of each purchase, the price paid for that particular purchase, and what the total cost was. The others are purchases that are not ours, but part of the everyday thirty to fifty thousand-dollar shares that are normally traded.

"By tracking these, tomorrow I should be able to tell when they are getting in and what price they are paying. Now take a look at the wall."

Name	Quantity	Price	Total Cost
Barry	25,000	5.125	$128,125
Barry	30,000	5.25	$157,500
Barry	20,000	5.75	$115,000
Tom	15,000	5.50	$82,500
Scott	5,000	5.125	$26,625
Scott	10,000	5.39	$53,900
Scott	5,000	5.75	$28,750
Aaron	10,000	5.25	$52,500
Aaron	10,000	5.50	$55,000
Aaron	20,000	5.75	$115,000
Aaron	10,000	6.00	$60,000
Min	200,000	4.88	$976,000
Min	125,000	5.75	$718,750
Min	100,000	6.00	$600,000
Min	75,000	6.25	$468,750

Our Total Investment: $3,648,400

Other Trades:

2,000 @ 5.50
6,000 @ 6.00
5,000 @ 6.39
2,000 @ 6.50
400 @ 6.50
500 @ 6.75
1,000 @ 7.00
3,000 @ 7.25

"What you are looking at is a chart that shows we have purchased six hundred and sixty thousand shares of stock. We ended up spending almost four million dollars. Of that money, over two and a half million came from Min, I think. Looking at the reaction from other sources, the stock will probably end up very close to seven. That would give us over a six hundred thousand dollar profit. Here's where the fun starts. Tomorrow they will start buying. They could drive the price up to high eights. When we start selling, we could have another million in profits. When they start selling, there shouldn't be any support, which will take the price back into the five-dollar range. Their loss will be in the area of two to three dollars per share for every share of stock they purchased. Because of all the trades from overseas and the smaller amount from at least a dozen brokers here in the states, they won't be able to trace anything until the second time we do it."

I looked at the figures on the wall. "Is there any chance that the stock will go down before we start selling?"

"Very little. For the stock to go down there has to be someone selling the stock. As long as we hold on to the stock, it'll only go where we want it to."

"When does the government get involved?"

"A flag has probably already gone up. They will be checking with the company to find out if anything is happening and then they will be checking to see if any person or firm has purchased more than five percent."

"Haven't we done that?"

"Technically we have. The overriding factor is that none of us individually has, except for Min. Since his trades have come from outside the country, it will make it a little tougher. By the time they get an answer from Hong Kong or wherever, we'll be out and on to the next stock."

I looked at my watch. "Isn't it time we went to lunch?"

Karen looked at hers and said, "Sorry I got so wound up. Let's go."

I held the door for Karen and as she entered the front office she turned and asked, "Did I introduce you to my mother earlier?"

"Was she here?" I answered.

"Mom, meet Aaron Carlyle. Remember I told you about him. He tripped me when I was running in a park."

I turned as the secretary rose from her chair and extended her hand.

"Hi Aaron. My name is Dorothy. Don't let my daughter get under your skin. She told me she had a wonderful weekend."

"How come you didn't say hello or something when I came in?" I asked.

"She told me she got word through the grapevine you were coming and wanted to teach you a lesson. I think she was trying to decide how to act when you got here."

"Has she always been this way?" I asked.

"Only since she was a little girl."

"Come on you two. This is a busy day."

I held open the door and as Karen passed me, she poked me in the ribs.

"Smart ass," she mumbled.

Her mother turned and asked, "Did you say something?"

"She said I have a nice . . . "

"Stop it you two. Keep this up and you'll have to eat by yourselves."

At lunch, Karen's mother talked about her husband.

"I understand that you met my husband when you went to college."

"Yes I did. I loved his classes."

She didn't answer for a few minutes. I looked at Karen and she shook her head slightly, telling me not to say anything.

She then continued, "He was a very intelligent person. I always wished that he could communicate with Karen as well as he seemed to transmit his thoughts to his pupils. He loved her almost more than life, but he couldn't tell her that."

Before she could go on, Karen interrupted, "Time to go. The conference call will be set up in about thirty minutes."

Karen's mother told me about how hard she worked and about how little time Karen had for fun.

Karen's only comment was, "Mom, Aaron's not interested."

To which I replied, "Mrs. Williams, I am interested. In fact, if you have any baby pictures of Karen on a rug, I would love to see them." When we exited the car I whispered to Karen, "I missed that view."

She smiled as we entered her office. She pushed some buttons and the picture came up again on the wall.

"Take a look," she said. "There have been another sixteen trades while we were gone. None of them are over three thousand, but they have driven the stock up over seven-fifty."

There was a buzz on the phone and a voice said, "Karen, your conference call is ready."

"Thanks," said Karen. "Put it through."

"Whom do I have?" she asked.

"This is Tom. I have Barry and Scott with me."

"This is also Min, but I am not with them."

"If anyone is interested or cares, Aaron is with me in San Diego," said Karen as she stuck out her tongue. She continued, "Each of you was faxed a copy of today's transactions. Collectively, we purchased over six hundred thousand shares of the stock. We averaged five dollars and fifty-two cents a share. There were another fifty-four thousand shares purchased by people that either follow the stock or noticed the trend. The last trades of the day were made at between seven-fifty and eight dollars. We have a paper profit of over one point five million dollars."

Karen let that sink in for a few seconds and then continued, "Most of that is due to what I believe were Mr. Min's trades. Since most of them came from offshore brokers, it is a little difficult to trace. My original plan was to have the five of us split the profits equally, but now I think we should re-think our position. I don't want or need an answer now, but think about it."

"This is Min speaking. Please do not anyone think about changing original plan. This campaign is not of my doing, but of Miss Williams. Without her, it would be very much different. Leave plan as stated when we started."

No one else entered the conversation. Karen cleared her throat and continued.

"I want to make sure that everyone understands what we are doing, so that no one gets nervous. We have collectively, but independently, pushed up the price of a stock by purchasing more than is normally bought in a short period of time. We have done this with the belief that someone else will be doing the same thing tomorrow with the same stock. The day after the other people buy, we are going to sell what we have purchased. We could have as much as three dollars profit on each of the six hundred thousand shares we purchased. After we sell, there will be no one left to buy the stock, which should take the price back down to its original price. That should create a loss of three dollars a share on every share that they purchased."

She paused and waited to see if anyone had any comments. When no one spoke she continued, "Tomorrow I will orchestrate the sale of between fifty and one hundred thousand shares to ensure that there is a supply for our friends to purchase. The market should kick in with another couple of hundred thousand shares as some profit-taking develops. After today, the buying should be hectic and we could see prices in the nine dollar range."

"Everyone get a good night sleep and I will start contacting you at about 5:45 A.M. tomorrow. If there are any questions, now is the time."

"This is Min. I have a small one. Has Captain Barry had any success in finding out where these people are?"

"The government suits are stalling. Maybe tomorrow, but I doubt it. If I had to guess, I would think by Thursday."

There was no reply from Min.

"Did you hear me?" Barry asked.

"Yes, I am sorry. My thoughts wandered. I will hang up now. I will talk to everyone again tomorrow."

Karen said her goodbyes and the connection was broken.

"That was an odd conversation at the end of the call. Is something going on that I'm not aware of?" she asked me.

"There is a dramatic difference between how Min and Barry want to handle these people. Barry will not be forthcoming with information, but when he gets it we will know what is going on, even if it's a day later. Min will not share his thoughts under any circumstances."

Karen shut off her computer and started walking towards the door. "Where are you staying tonight?" she asked.

"I haven't figured that out yet," I replied.

"You can stay at my place. I'm sure my mother wouldn't mind."

"If you have enough room, I'd love to." We walked outside of her office as her mother was walking out the front door.

"I'm glad you're finished. I was going to leave you a note. I'm meeting Jo-Anne for dinner and a movie. I'll be staying at her house tonight. See you tomorrow. It was very nice to meet you, Aaron. I'm sure I'll see you again."

It was 3:30 P.M. The stock market had been closed for a couple of hours.

Chapter 27

I asked Karen, "Should I follow you home?"

"I get into the office before 6 A.M. If you think you can be up and ready by that time, hop into my car and I'll drive."

I took the clothes out of the trunk of my car and transferred them into Karen's. She was driving a Cadillac convertible. While I was getting my clothes, she put the top down.

"Very nice looking car. How does it handle?" I asked.

"Like a dream. Get in, I'm about thirty minutes from home." We took off down the San Diego Freeway like we didn't have a care in the world.

Las Vegas

"Tell me again what went on with the stock today!" yelled ex-Brigadier General Waldman.

"You knew this could happen," stammered the thin man with glasses. "Sometime yesterday some people over in Asia started buying the stock. Maybe they see it as a good takeover company or something. Today when the market opened and the buy orders kicked in, people around the country started jumping on the bandwagon. It looks like there were over fifty trades, which could mean fifty different people buying in. There were four large trades of over one hundred and fifty thousand shares and the rest were anywhere from four hundred to ten thousand. Some of the big trades were over six dollars and some of the two, three, four and five thousand blocks were going as high as seven-fifty."

Waldman looked around the suite they were meeting in and in a low whisper asked, "Do you think anyone is fucking with us?"

"I don't know. If I had to guess, I would think not. Whoever is buying in to SCOA has invested over four million dollars. We're buying about four hundred thousand shares, or about three million dollars worth. They've invested more than we have. If they're investors, it's good for us. The stock will go over eleven dollars in a short period of time."

Sweat was running down his forehead causing his glasses to slide down the bridge of his nose. Waldman stared at him without saying a word. Finally he spoke, "Listen carefully, shit for brains. If it turns out that you screwed this operation up, I will personally deliver to your wife parts of you she has never seen before. Now get the hell out of here and make sure you do tomorrow what we hired you for."

Waldman waited until the door closed before he turned to the other men sitting in the room.

"He could be right, but just in case, one of you keep an eye on him. I don't want him turning rabbit if it goes down wrong."

One of the men stood. "I'll watch him, General. If he starts to run, what would you like me to do?"

"Follow him and call me. I'll let you know what to do if and when. Keep in touch."

"I'll call in every four hours." He looked at his watch and walked out without saying another word.

"We cleared over three million on last week's buy and with four and a half million going into play tomorrow, we should clear two and a half more by Thursday night."

He looked around the room. "Let's enjoy ourselves while we're in Vegas. Friday, we move to San Francisco and they don't have all the pleasures that Vegas does."

Carlsbad

"One of the greatest pleasures I get out of life is being able to leave work in the afternoon and just kick back and relax."

Karen was sitting on her patio in a pair of white shorts and a light blue golf shirt, explaining to me why she picked this particular house to live in.

I was sitting on a chaise lounge and nodded my head in agreement. "I've got to admit that I could get to like this type of life. I don't know why, but I always felt I had to live closer to a major city. How long have you lived here?"

"It came on the market about four years ago. I thought it was overpriced, but it had everything I wanted: a pool, a view of the ocean, proximity to a country club, not too far from the freeway, and large enough to accommodate my mother, but giving each of us our own space. You probably noticed that my mother has the master bedroom downstairs.

It's the largest of the four bedrooms in the house and allows her to come and go as she wants. These stairs lead to mine." She motioned to a staircase behind me that led to the second floor.

"I leave for work early and because of the layout, I never have to bother her."

"She doesn't work with you every day?" I asked.

Karen started laughing. "No, she hardly ever comes to the office, but when she heard you were on your way down, she couldn't resist coming over to meet you. She spent all day yesterday asking questions about Friday night and Saturday."

"Talking about Friday night and Saturday, when you came up to L.A., I fed you. When are you going to feed me?"

"You have a choice, I can make an omelette or there is a great Italian restaurant I just love down on the beach about a half mile from here."

"What kind of omelettes do you make best?"

"Did I tell you this restaurant makes their own pasta and bakes their own bread?"

"I like omelettes with onions, peppers and American cheese."

"Did I tell you I don't have any eggs?"

"Is that true?"

"No, but I love this little restaurant."

"Well, why don't we go out for some Italian food then."

Las Vegas

"I'll have a steak, medium rare, with a baked potato. Make sure you serve it hot." Waldman spit out his order like a general talking to a private. "Bring another round of drinks for all of us and make it quick."

Waldman surveyed the table. Five of the six men who always accompanied him were seated with an empty chair next to each of them.

"What time are the broads expected?"

"I told them to get here at 9:30 P.M.," answered the man closest to him. "I figured they could have dessert before we had dessert."

The men laughed.

Waldman looked at his watch. "It's 8:45 P.M. Has anyone heard from Paul?"

"He called in earlier. He was parked across the street from the house that Carson went to. It wasn't his house, so Paul thinks he has a skirt on the side. He gave me the address and I'll check it out tomorrow."

"The next time he calls in, tell him when the lights go out to come on back."

A busboy appeared with a tray full of drinks and started handing them out.

Waldman looked at him and said, "Hey you. What's your name?"

The busboy answered, "Dennis, sir."

"Let me see your wallet."

"My wallet?"

"Are you deaf? I said let me see your wallet."

The busboy put down the last drink and reached for his back pocket. He took out his wallet and handed it to Waldman.

"What's your last name?" Waldman asked.

"Carter, sir."

"Where do you live?"

"1725 Ocean Avenue."

"Are you married?"

"No, what's with all the questions?"

"Just answer them. Who's the girl?"

"She's my girlfriend."

Waldman took a hundred dollar bill out of his pocket and handed it to the busboy.

"I see you bet a C-note on the Lakers. This should cover the bet. They won't win. Sorry for all the questions, but we're talking about some very serious business and I had to make sure you weren't spying on us."

The busboy looked at the hundred and said, "For this kind of money, you can ask questions all night long. I think the Lakers can pull it off."

"Go tell the waiter I would like our food now."

The busboy left and the five men just sat around the table saying nothing. They had been through this before.

Two waiters appeared. They placed the trays down and started handing out the food. When they finished, the waiter who took the order asked, "Will there be anything else, sir?"

"Yes there is. What's the name of the busboy who delivered our drinks?"

The waiter looked over towards the bar.

"I think they sent over Dennis. Was there a problem?"

Waldman didn't answer. He asked another question.

"How long has he worked here?"

"I'm not sure. Maybe two months. Maybe a little longer."

"Is he married?"

"I don't think so. I've heard him talking about a girlfriend."

"Okay. Thanks for the info. We're having some guests join us for dessert. When they get here, make sure we get some good service." Waldman raised his shoulder in a circular motion. "Eight years later and it still bothers me. Does anyone know the line on the Lakers game tonight?"

Carlsbad

"Miss Williams, how nice to see you again," said the waiter at the Bella Piaty. "I have a table overlooking the ocean." The waiter held the chair for Karen as Aaron sat down next to her facing the ocean.

"May I get you a glass of wine?"

"I'll have a glass of Merlot," said Karen.

"I'll have the same," I said.

"We have some specials tonight. While I get your wine, look at the menu. Aside from the specials, the menu has many other interesting choices."

I looked at the ocean. "The water is beautiful. If the food is as good as the view, this will be one hell of a meal."

The waiter returned with the wine and we both ordered the special.

After he left, Karen asked, "What makes this person you think might be involved invoke such animosity? I saw the look that you and Mr. Min exchanged. It wasn't pretty."

"It goes back to Vietnam. I told you part of the story. Scott, Tom, and myself were left behind when the United States pulled up stakes. We hooked up with some Marines and started walking out. After we found Marcia, we came upon a rogue CIA operation just over the border in Cambodia. An Army general called Waldman had taken as slaves two or three hundred local tribesmen. They raped the women, some as young as six or seven years old and then sold them to houses of pleasure throughout Southeast Asia. They lined up all the male children and cut off the head of every fourth child to prove how strong they were. When we stumbled across their camp, they tried to negotiate a deal to keep Marcia as a toy."

"As a toy?"

"I guess they were going to pass her around."

"What ended up happening?" Karen asked almost in awe.

"I ended up shooting a general and we took over the camp. We flew out to Singapore in a plane they had and the rest is history."

"You ended up shooting a general and the rest is history? What type of history books are you reading?" She gazed out at the ocean, deep in thought. "I guess he didn't die if you think he's involved in this . . . this, I don't even know what to call it."

"No, he didn't die. We turned him over to the CIA in Singapore and they arrested us. After a couple of days, a Marine colonel found us and brought us back to the States. Part of the deal was that we never talk about what happened. Marcia kept a diary she had everyone sign. Marcia gave the diary to a lawyer. If anything happened to either of us, he could release the information. It's now back in my house. They have no way of punishing Marcia."

While I had been telling the story, the waiter had brought our food. We finished in silence, each with our own thoughts.

"We can have coffee back at my place."

I motioned for the waiter. "The food was spectacular. I don't remember having swordfish that tasted this good."

The sun was going down as we arrived back at Karen's.

"If it's all right with you, I'd just as soon skip the coffee. I just recently started sleeping through the night."

"It's fine by me. I have to get up early. I go running at 4:45 A.M." Karen picked up the remote and turned on the television.

"The Lakers are playing Chicago tonight. It should be a good game." She kicked off her shoes and sat down next to me on the sofa. "I think the Lakers will kick their butts tonight."

"I don't think so," I replied.

"How about I bet you a dollar? The paper says the Lakers are a four-point underdog."

I looked at her. "Are you trying to hustle me?"

"Is it a bet or not?"

"I'll tell you what," I said. "Let's bet it even. The winner sleeps in and the loser does the five miles."

"Done," she said as we both settled back to watch the game.

Chapter 28

I opened my eyes to the sounds of the cavalry charging across some river in black and white. Karen was asleep in the crook of my arm. I lifted my other arm and looked at my watch. It was 4:15 A.M.

She started to stir and I was afraid to move. She felt like she belonged there. Her eyes opened and she looked at the television. "Who won?"

"I don't know. I just woke up."

"What time is it?"

"4:15 A.M."

"I get to sleep another thirty minutes." She closed her eyes and as far as I could tell, she was out like a light. After a couple of minutes, she turned over and looked up at me.

"You have a bony lap. I'm surprised I was able to get any sleep." She sat up, stretched and then stood.

"I'm going to change into my running clothes. Do you feel up to giving it a try?"

"Sure, why not?"

After two or three minutes of stretching exercises, we were off.

This day I was able to keep up with her. We ran in the street where there were lights to see by and as the hands on my watch reached 5 A.M., the sun was beginning to rise. We ran for twenty-five minutes up and down streets that led back to her house. When we entered, I could smell the coffee brewing.

"Your mom came home last night?"

"I don't think so."

"I smell coffee."

"I have an automatic brewer set to start at 5 A.M. each morning."

"Smells great."

"Why don't you have some? I have to shower and get ready. I'll be out in ten minutes."

Ten minutes later, she came back out wearing a bathrobe. "That does smell good. Would you like some toast or cereal?"

"No thanks. Coffee is fine."

She walked to the refrigerator, opened the door and took out a loaf of bread. As she closed the door and turned, she dropped the bread on the floor. I bent over to pick it up at the same time that she did. Our heads collided. I fell back into the chair and she fell onto the floor. I bent over to pick her up and the chair slid out from under me. I ended up in a heap next to her. She was rubbing her head and I was rubbing my butt.

"That hurt," she said.

"You're telling me," I answered

I stood and held out my hands.

She reached out and pulled herself up to a standing position.

"Thank you," she said.

"You're welcome," I replied.

"I have to finish getting dressed," she murmured.

"And I have to shower."

Neither of us moved. I exerted some pressure and drew her closer to me. My arms went around her waist. Her arms somehow ended up around my neck. I leaned forward and kissed her lightly on the lips. She put her cheek next to mine and we stood holding each other.

"I must get dressed," she said as she pulled herself out of my arms.

"Can't you be a little late this morning?"

"You know better than that. Today's the day they start buying. We must monitor the transactions. If you're going with me, you better hurry." She turned and started out of the kitchen. When she reached the door she turned back.

"Don't worry, we'll get there one of these days."

Las Vegas

"Hey Paul, what time did you get here?" asked Waldman.

Looking at his watch, Paul answered, "About fifteen minutes ago. The lights didn't go out until after he left around 11:30 P.M. last night. I followed him to his house and decided to see what was going on. His wife came out with his two kids at 1:10 A.M. I called in, but no one answered the phone. He came out at 5:15 A.M. and went to his office. I called in again and Hal answered the phone, so I had him get over there to watch him. I'm beat."

Waldman looked at Paul and asked, "What do you think is going on?"

"I think he told his family to get lost. You probably scared the hell out of him yesterday and he's not taking any chances."

"Go get some sleep. If you need to take an edge off, we have plenty of desserts from last night still hanging around. By the way, you did a nice job."

As Paul walked into the bedroom, Waldman's face grew dark. He picked up the phone and started dialing other rooms in the hotel. The message was the same with each room that answered.

"Get up here in a hurry. Something's not right."

Within twenty minutes, the four other men were in the suite.

"Where are Hal and Paul?" One of the men asked.

"Paul is inside sleeping and Hal is watching the would-be rabbit. It looks like he sent his wife into hiding. He's at his office now, but if it doesn't go right, I think he's getting ready to run. I want to find out where his wife is. I want to find out who the girlfriend is and I want to find out if he has tickets to somewhere. The market is due to open in about five minutes and our people should start buying. I want the information by noon."

He pointed at one of the men. "You stay with me. Hal's going to need some relief and I want us to be mobile. Let's start moving."

Carlsbad

Karen was pointing at the monitor. "I have the computer set so that a bell will ring every time there is a trade on SCOA. It will also give me a hard copy for future reference."

"That's a neat program. Did you design it yourself or have someone do it for you?"

"It was part of the program I purchased. It allows me to keep track of up to twelve selected stocks as they . . . " She stopped as the bell rang.

"Look at that," I said.

"It's one of theirs. One hundred and ten thousand shares at seven-fifty."

The bell rang again. "That's not them. It's only six thousand at seven and five-eighths." The bell rang again and again. Karen staring at the screen said, "Fifty thousand at eight, sixty thousand at eight." There was another ring. "Another forty thousand at eight." The bell started ringing almost every minute or so. Karen continued calling out the trades.

"Four thousand at eight and a quarter. Forty-eight thousand at eight fifty. Two thousand at fifty, three thousand at fifty, two thousand at seventy-five. It's starting to stall."

Karen picked up the phone.

"Sell another twenty five thousand at eight and a quarter."

A minute later, the trade came through. I looked at the paper I had from yesterday.

"We made over seventy-five thousand dollars on that twenty-five thousand shares." Karen smiled and shook her head. "There's a lot more where that came from."

The bell rang again.

"Bingo. Sixty-eight thousand shares at eight dollars and seventy-five cents." She handed me a piece of paper

"Look at this. As close as I can figure, they have purchased over four hundred thousand shares at about three point two million dollars. There have been thirty other trades that have driven the stock up over nine and a half dollars."

I looked at the clock on the wall. It was almost 11:15 A.M.

"Where in the world has the morning gone?"

"It sometimes gets pretty hectic."

"What did you mean when you told the person on the phone to sell another twenty-five thousand?" I asked.

"Our plan was never to hurt the little guy if possible. We had to seed the market early on to keep the stock from going over ten in the first hour. We sold back one hundred and fifty thousand shares at a profit of about one half a million and kept the market somewhat stable. The bad guys have bought four hundred thousand at an average cost of eight dollars. The market is now at . . ." She looked at the screen ". . . Nine-fifty. They're up six hundred thousand right now and will probably be up over a million by the time the market closes today. While they're counting their money, tomorrow we'll be selling and pushing the stock down below the seven dollar level."

Las Vegas

"What's happening?" Waldman asked quietly into the phone.

"It's reacting just like it's supposed to. Your people are placing their orders and getting filled at reasonable levels."

"What do you consider reasonable?"

"The last sixty-eight thousand went off at eight seventy-five. As close as I can figure without putting it down on paper, your people have purchased four hundred thousand shares at an average price of a little over eight dollars."

"You're telling me that they spent over three point two million."

"Somewhere around that." His voice was getting a nervous sound to it.

"I thought it was only going to cost us two million one to two million three."

"We didn't know about this other group getting in before us."

The silence was deafening. Finally Waldman asked, "Who is this other group?"

"I don't know."

"What are we paying you for? I can get 'I don't knows' from people I don't pay. By the way, where is your wife?"

The question thrown into the middle of the conversation threw his mind into a panic.

"She must be at home or maybe she's visiting her mother."

Waldman let his answer hang there for a few seconds and then he replied, "I guess she must be at her mother's. I don't think she's at home." He then hung up the phone without waiting for any other comments.

Waldman turned to Paul who had just re-entered the room. "He's lying. Get someone over to help Hal. I don't want this guy to get away."

When Paul left the room, Waldman picked up the phone and dialed a nine to get long distance. After the connection was made, he punched in a set of numbers and then hung up. Five minutes later his cell phone rang.

"Hello. I think we may have a problem. Our people bought four hundred thousand today, but we averaged about eight bucks a share." He listened and then continued, "I know we were supposed to average around six, but there was a lot of buy orders yesterday. This idiot in Vegas that's monitoring it said the buys came from overseas."

"No, I don't know where from overseas. This broker you suggested. . . Yeah we have a different one for every other week . . . I have the boys watching him. He looks like he's getting ready to run. Maybe he decided to take a piece of the action on his own. . . . Says you, there's a lot of money involved . . . The reason I called, how about checking with your friends at the SEC. Maybe they can tell us where the trades are coming from. I'm due to leave here after we sell on Thursday. I'll contact you from San Francisco on Friday . . . I know you're not supposed to get involved, just get me an answer." He slammed down the phone. "Asshole . . ."

Standing across the street from the Lincoln Memorial in Washington D.C., the person that Waldman referred to as "asshole" closed the lid on his cell phone. He turned and walked towards the Vietnam Memorial. He stopped at one of the kiosks and looked at the medals and other memorabilia that were on display. He lifted one of the ribbons and held it up to the sun.

"It's a Special Forces ribbon," said the youngster sitting behind the display.

"Actually, it's a copy of one," he replied as he put it back down. He continued walking in the general direction of the "wall." He knew that he would go over and look at his name. Every time he passed close by, he went over and looked. It was scary seeing his name listed as one of the men that had lost their lives in that God-forsaken place. He walked up close and ran his finger across the raised letters.

"Did you know him?" An elderly lady standing a few feet away asked.

"I thought I did." He replied as he walked away.

Chapter 29

Tuesday afternoon. I had been reading periodicals for most of the day. Karen had had lunch brought in and aside from a couple of "look at this" comments, she had stayed glued to her monitor. She had been taking calls from other clients, but she never strayed far from whatever the screens were telling her about SCOA.

"Well the markets finally closed," I heard Karen say to herself. I looked at my watch and it was 1:10 P.M.

"How did we make out?" I asked.

"I'm calling your office, Barry and Uncle Min. We'll all go through it together."

"Karen, this is Scott. I've got Barry and Tom with me."

"I'm expecting Uncle Min to join us in a second. Aaron is with me in my office."

"Sorry that I am late," came the voice of Min. He continued, "I see that the stock market was down, but that our stock closed at nine dollars."

"You're right. Actually, it closed at nine to nine-fifty. Let me tell you where we stand. I have segregated those trades that were made for twenty -five thousand shares or more, from the ones in the five hundred to ten thousand variety."

"Why those quantities?" asked Tom.

"I believe that they would try and buy larger quantities so that they could avoid having a lot of trades. They would have a better chance of buying low. We did much the same thing yesterday."

"How many shares did they buy?" asked Scott.

"I think they purchased four hundred and one thousand shares at a total cost of a little over three point two million."

"When we were talking Sunday, I thought the number that we expected them to spend was about two and a half million," I interjected.

"That's the good part," Karen answered. "We forced them to come up with more cash than I think they expected to use. Their average cost is a little over eight."

“With the market closing at close to nine-fifty, they’re up over six hundred thousand,” sated Tom.

“If I were them, I would now be expecting the stock to rise over ten some time tomorrow. Originally, they anticipated that they would be buying in at the five to a half level. This extra three dollars a share was going to be their profit.”

“What would you want us to do tomorrow?” asked Min.

“I would like Tom to call his broker tonight and place a sell order for all fifteen thousand at the opening. Those sales should go off in the nine to nine-fifty range. Min, you’re second. As soon as the first fifteen thousand shares are traded, have your broker sell two hundred and fifty thousand. Scott, tell your broker to start selling at 10:15 A.M. and Aaron, you tell yours to start at 11 A.M. Min, at thirty minutes before closing, sell whatever you have left.”

“What about you and me?” asked Barry.

“I will use our stock to try and keep the market orderly.”

“What does ‘orderly’ mean?” he responded.

“When these sales start appearing, the price of the stock could drop like a rock. If it does, someone has to be there to buy some to stop the free fall. I will be selling and if necessary, buying until all of us are out of the stock.”

“How bad are the regular people going to get hurt?” asked Barry.

“A little, maybe. In going over the trades, I have a feeling that many of the sell orders were of the short variety.”

“What does that mean?” Barry interrupted.

“That means that the stock that was sold to us wasn’t owned by the people that sold it. They ‘borrowed’ the stock and will buy it when they have to deliver it. As the stock starts to come down, these are the people that are going to jump in to buy what they shorted. The only other option is for our friends to step in and buy more to keep the price up, but that would be suicide.”

“How so?” I asked

“This stock has no base. The company isn’t strong enough to support a price in the ten-dollar range. At fifteen times earnings, the price of the stock should be right around five or six dollars. For someone to keep buying at a nine-or ten-dollar number, it would be tantamount to throwing money down a sewer.”

“Do you think they would do that?” Min asked.

"I wouldn't. What they would do is anyone's guess. I would hope they wouldn't. I have been working under the assumption that we are dealing with bright people. If they start doing dumb things, our strategy would have to change."

No one said a word. Then Karen asked, "Are there any more questions?" Everyone answered no.

"Everyone understands what they have to do?" This time everyone answered yes.

"We'll talk again tomorrow, same time, same station." She hung up and looked over at me.

"Tonight, I am making dinner."

"What are we having?"

"It's a surprise. Let's go."

Thirty minutes later, we were at her house and ten minutes after that, I was sitting in the Jacuzzi. I had a glass of wine in one hand and some Ritz crackers with cheese in the other. Karen had moved the television to where I could see it from where I was sitting and I was watching a re-run of "Spenser for Hire." I called out to Karen, "Are you going to join me?"

"I told you I was cooking dinner."

"It's only after 4 P.M. Dinner can wait."

"I need another fifteen minutes to get everything started and then I'll join you."

I was watching "Hawk" driving his BMW around the streets of Boston when Karen came out. She had on a San Diego Charger jacket over a green bathing suit. She poured herself a glass of wine and leaned over to refill my glass.

"Another cracker?" she asked.

"No thanks, it might ruin my appetite."

She placed her glass on the floor, took off the jacket and slid into the swirling water.

"That feels good," she whispered. She continued, "The muscles on my back and shoulders seem to tighten up after a full day of sitting at the desk."

"Turn around. I used to be pretty good at loosening up tired muscles."

She turned her back to me and I moved across the spa.

I put my hands on her shoulders at the base of her neck. Her skin was as smooth as the proverbial baby's butt. Her muscles were taut. She stretched her arms out in front of her as I moved my hands from her neck down her spine to the point where her bathing suit covered her backside.

I raised my hands back up to her neck and repeated the procedure. As I continued the process, the straps that started out on her shoulders somehow slipped down onto her arms. The next time my hands started at her neck, they continued down her upper arm to her elbow at which point she moved her hands and freed the straps from her body. She turned to face me. Her breasts were rubbing against my chest right below the bubbling water. My hands framed her face as my lips moved from her closed eyes, to her nose, to her lips. My arms encircled her and she raised hers and put them around my neck. Her tongue flickered over my lips and the bubbles stopped. The silence was deafening. We parted and looked around as I heard a shotgun blast. Karen jumped and I threw my body over hers. We heard the voices at the same time. It was the television, Spenser said to Hawk, "You have to learn to be careful when you use one of those."

Hawk answered, "I missed you, didn't I?"

We both started laughing. The straps were back in place and I asked, "Where were we?"

"I think we were about to have one of those magic moments."

"Shall we continue?" I asked.

With that, the phone rang.

"It's a private line. I have to answer it." She stepped out of the spa and walked over to the phone.

"Karen here . . . What did you tell them? . . . Did you get a name and phone number? . . . No, everything is fine. You did the right thing. I'll see you in the morning." She hung up the phone.

"Something wrong?" I asked.

"I don't know. That was my office. They received a call from the Securities and Exchange Commission wanting to know how many shares of SCOA we purchased and who it was for."

"What did your office tell them?"

"The only thing they could. We do not buy per client request. We are a one hundred percent discretionary firm and they would have to call back in the morning and talk to me."

"Did they leave a name and a number to contact?" I asked.

"No. They said they would call back in the morning."

I got out of the spa and picked up my cell phone from the table. I dialed my office.

"Be Safe Security," intoned Carol.

"Carol, this is Aaron. Please get me Tom or Scott."

"Mr. Miller's office."

"Please connect me with Scott."

"Sure thing, Aaron. Hold for a sec."

"Hey Aaron, when are you coming back to work?" Scott asked.

"Karen got a call from the SEC or someone claiming to be from the SEC."

"They certainly worked fast," replied Scott. "What do we do now?"

"You tell Tom, then get in touch with Barry and bring him up to date. Call your brokers and tell them to duck the question and call you if they get a call. I'll call Min and bring him up to date. We proceed as Karen outlined this afternoon. Make sure everyone understands that there are no changes."

"Sure thing. Keep in touch." Scott hung up and I placed a call to Min.

"Min please."

"Who is calling Min?" It sounded like his granddaughter, but I wasn't sure.

"This is Aaron Carlyle."

"Mr. Carlyle, Uncle Min thought you might be calling. He left a message for you. He said that if there are no changes to your schedule that there is no reason to call back. If there are to be changes, you are to call a number that I have."

"There are no changes."

"Then I am to tell you that he expects to arrive at the place you are at no later than 8:30 tonight."

"He knows where I am?"

"He must or else he would not have left this message."

"Thank you for the message. One question: Is he by himself?"

She hesitated and then answered, "No. He has some of the family with him. Good-bye."

She hung up on me like she had given out some information she wasn't supposed to. I turned to Karen.

"Company is coming. I don't know how or why, but Min is on his way down here."

Las Vegas

The cellular phone rang once before Waldman picked it up. "I'm by myself. What have you found out? . . . Fifty-seven different brokerage firms and how many trades? . . . One hundred and eighty three different trades. Where are most of them coming from? . . . Hong Kong, Singapore and Germany? Any big action from the states? Well, we'll see what happens tomorrow." Before he could say anything else, there was a click.

That son of a bitch never stays on the phone for longer than fifty-five seconds. Talk about being paranoid.

As Waldman was talking aloud to himself, one of his men entered.

"Who are you talking to?"

"No one. I wasn't talking to anyone. What did you hear?"

"Just something about fifty-five seconds."

"Forget you even heard that."

"It's forgotten. The reason I came in was to tell you that we got some tickets to Siegfried and Roy, those two magicians. Do you want to come?"

"I might as well. There's nothing I can do here."

Chapter 30

"Uncle Min, welcome to my home. I'm surprised you know where I live."

Min had arrived within five minutes of the time his granddaughter had told me to expect him. Three cars had pulled up at the front door, but only one other person got out.

"Can I get you something to eat or to drink?" Karen continued.

"Thank you, but no. I come on extremely urgent business." Min entered the room, looked around, closed the blinds and sat down on the sofa.

I looked at Min and saw he was upset and asked, "What is this urgent business?"

"You called my home earlier and had a message relayed to me that we were proceeding as planned. The only reason you would have called is that something had changed. Is it your SEC that has gotten involved quicker than we thought possible?"

"How did you know?" asked Karen.

"My brokers also received calls."

"Did they leave numbers where they could be called back?" I asked.

"No, they did not. In fact, at one of the numbers they called a . . . I don't know what they call it, a machine told us the number they were calling from."

"A caller I.D.," interjected Karen.

"Yes, that is it."

"And?" I asked.

"The call was made from the Vietnamese Consulate in San Francisco. They of course did not get any information, but as they call other brokers that we used, we may not be so lucky. It is my thought that they will only call today those firms that purchased more than twenty-five or fifty thousand shares. After tomorrow, that number will drop to the five or ten thousand level. This organization we are against has many friends in high places. It only took twenty-four hours to learn the names of the brokers we used. We must make sure that our people are protected and it is my thought that we go on the offensive."

"Just what does that mean?" asked Karen

"When they lose their money tomorrow, they will start checking everyone that purchased this stock on Monday. Some of the names, of course, will be familiar to them. They will send people to ask questions. These people must be identified quickly and not allowed to report back to their leader."

"How do you propose we do that?" Karen continued.

Min looked at me and I answered for him.

"We can have our brokers ask for identification. Those people that we find not to be telling the truth we turn over to Barry or the FBI."

"If I may add to the plan, I would suggest we take them prisoner and hold them for some time to make the people in charge very nervous. We will also be able to find out information about their organization."

As he spoke, Min's eyes never left Karen's face. She stared at me and said, "When I said that this was going to give me a chance to see if you and I were compatible and at the same time find out if I liked your friends and if they liked me, I didn't understand what that meant. This is going beyond anything that I could have contemplated."

I asked, "What does that mean? I told you people had been killed and these were not nice people. I asked you more than once not to get involved. Did you think this was some kind of game?"

She looked at me and then turned to look at Min.

"Will you please tell your friend to stop yelling? You can also tell him that I think I may be falling in love with him. If he thinks for one second that either one of you are going to scare me out of being part of this, you are both crazy." She turned to look at me. "I know you think this isn't a game, but it is. The only problem I am having is learning the rules. I understand what Min suggested. These people might never again show up anywhere. What you two are overlooking is that there are six of us on this side and when strategy is discussed we should all have some input."

"The less people accountable the better," I said to Karen and Min.

"Why don't we talk to the others before a decision is reached. You can always go off and do what you want, but at least the rules are being followed."

I looked at Min. I knew she was right.

He nodded his head and asked, "When should we have this meeting? It should be face to face and must be before tomorrow night."

Karen said, "I could probably be out of here by 1:15 P.M. tomorrow. What's two hours north of here?"

"We could meet at 4 P.M. at my house. Barry, Tom and Scott would have only an hour and maybe a half to travel, but it is somewhat central," Min replied.

"Leave me directions and I will be there," Karen said softly.

"We could go up together."

"No, Aaron. You have to go up tonight. You must talk to the three of them before the meeting. This is too important to just spring on them."

"I could speak to them on the phone." Even as I said the words, I realized I had to talk to them in person. They were my friends.

"You're right," I said with some regret. "I can be home by midnight. I'll call from the car and meet with them in the morning. We'll all meet at Min's tomorrow afternoon."

Min said, "I am now leaving. Drive carefully, Aaron. I will see you tomorrow." He bowed at Karen and walked out.

She turned to me. She had what can be best described as an unhappy smile on her face. "This romance isn't working like I thought it would."

I walked closer to her and held out my arms. She let me encircle her and give her a hug. I stepped back a half step so that I could look at her face and I answered, "I think it's going better than either of us could have hoped for."

She looked up at me and said, "I'm not like this. I'm really a conservative person. I don't get involved in anything risky. That's why my clients like me. I may never forgive Jerry and Susan for inviting me to dinner. Meeting you has changed my way of thinking about my life."

"That means I owe them something big for Christmas."

We both jumped at the sound of the voice. It was Karen's mom.

"What are you doing here?" Karen yelled.

"Don't yell at me. I'm your mother. I saw three strange cars parked out in front and I decided to take a look. I came in the back as they pulled away and all I heard was your last statement and all I can say is I like the new you. Since you came home last Saturday, you've been a changed person and the change is for the better."

As she finished her statement, Min's granddaughter stepped out from behind her. In her hand was a small pistol.

"It is okay for her to be here Mr. Carlyle?"

Both Karen and her mother jumped.

"Who are you?" stammered Karen's mom. Her eyes never left the pistol.

I stepped in, "This is Min's granddaughter."

"My name is Soo Kim, or Sookie to my friends."

"What are you doing here?" asked Karen.

"As we pulled away, your mother was spotted coming in through the back door. We weren't sure who she was and I was asked to insure your safety. Grandfather said to tell you that you are getting careless."

"Not so, little cousin."

Soo Kim jumped and turned to see Tuloc standing behind her. "Where did you come from?" she asked.

Tuloc grinned, "I will tell you over dinner the first chance I get."

"What makes you think I would go to dinner with someone that sneaks up like a snake in the night?"

"I think you would rather have dinner with me than let me have nothing to do except to have dinner with Uncle Min and discuss my day."

"You loathsome, blackmailing, snake in the grass, have dinner with you. I would rather eat with a, a . . ."

"How about next Saturday night?" Tuloc interrupted.

She turned and headed out the door. Tuloc yelled after her, "I'll pick you up at 7 P.M." He turned and the grin on his face was as big as the Cheshire cat's.

"Who are you?" asked Karen.

"Let me make the introductions. Tuloc is a 'nephew' of Min's who works for Be Safe. On Saturday, I made arrangements for some of our men to watch your home. Tuloc is the head of that team of men. He is also apparently a little sweet on Min's granddaughter. Tuloc, say hello to Karen and her mother, Mrs. Williams."

"Karen, Mrs. Williams, it is my pleasure. I was a student of your husband's at UCLA."

"It's very nice to meet you. It's amazing how many of my husband's students I've met lately."

"Tuloc, I guess I should be thanking you for scaring the hell out of me, but I really can take care of myself. I think I've proven to Aaron that I'm in pretty good shape," said Karen as she shook his hand.

"I am sure you are. In fact, I never would have come in except I was showing off for Soo Kim. My instructions are to watch the house. I suppose whoever passed down the instructions wasn't worried about you."

The lie was so glib I almost believed it. Karen looked at him and then at me. She looked back at him and said, "Thank you." He turned and left the way he came in.

Karen's mother said, "Someone has got to explain to me what is going on here."

I looked at Karen and then turned to her mother.

"I was just leaving. Karen can explain after I'm gone. I have a three-hour drive."

Karen started walking me to the door. I stopped and said, "I forgot my clothes. I'll be back in a second."

"Hold it!" she said. "You leave them right where they are. I'll have them cleaned and pressed. I want you to have a reason to come back."

I looked over at her mother and said to Karen, "I have a reason, I never got my hair dried."

"Why don't you kiss her good-bye? I promise not to look." She turned her back to Karen and myself and said, "Take your time. I'm not going anywhere."

We kissed. I could feel the promise of things to come.

She whispered in my ear, "You be careful and call me when you get home. No stopping for some good-looking policewoman."

I left and drove about a half block when a car behind me raised its high beams. I pulled over and Tuloc got out of the passenger side and walked over to my window.

"Is everything okay, Mr. Carlyle?"

"Everything is fine. I'm not sure she believed you, but I'm also not sure she didn't. Take care of her."

"I will, don't worry."

Chapter 31

I arrived home at midnight. I had called my friends from the car and told them we needed to meet early in the morning. Barry was expecting a call at 7 A.M., so we decided on 7:30 A.M. at Barry's condo. I called Karen from about five minutes away from my house. It was getting late and I didn't want her waiting up for the call. She answered on the fourth ring.

"Hello."

"Hello yourself," I answered.

"Aaron, what time is it?"

"It's almost midnight. Did I wake you?"

"Wake me? No, I was enjoying a movie and didn't hear the phone ring."

"What movie?" I asked.

"What do you mean what movie?"

"I just wondered what type of movies you enjoyed."

"The kind that you can close your eyes and sleep through."

"And I thought you would wait up until I got home."

"Whatever gave you that impression?" she asked innocently.

"Probably something you said."

"Men. They only hear what they want to hear."

"Sleep tight," I said

"I will." She didn't hang up, but she didn't say anything more. I called, "Karen, are you there?"

"I'm here. Aaron, take care of yourself."

With that, the phone went dead. I entered my house, put on the television, crawled into bed, and hit the sleep button for ten minutes. I didn't remember the set going off.

I arrived at Barry's early. After one knock, Carol opened the door.

"You're early," she stated as if I had done something wrong.

"Sorry, but I thought I might help Barry make some coffee."

"Where are Tom and Scott?"

Shrugging my shoulders, I answered, "They'll probably be here in a couple of minutes."

She turned and called into the bedroom,

"Aaron is here and I'm leaving." She headed towards the door and said to me, "I put up a pot of coffee, it should be ready, and Aaron, go slow, he's not in a good mood. The call from Washington wasn't what he wanted."

I stood in the doorway and watched her pull away. Barry came out of the bedroom trying to fix his tie.

"It either comes out too long or too short. It's a pain in the ass wearing ties. Like a cup of coffee?"

I walked over and poured myself a cup and asked, "Do you have any milk or cream?" Before he could answer there was a knock on the door.

"It's open," he shouted.

In came Tom and Scott with Scott carrying a box of donuts.

"We figured you'd have coffee without something to go with it."

Barry waited until we all poured some coffee and then he said, "I have some bad news."

"How bad?" asked Scott.

"That guy Waldman is a really bad penny. The people I know at State tell me his record is clean."

"How can that be?" I asked. "The shit he was pulling in Nam should have put him away for life."

"The people I talked to said there is nothing in his file about Vietnam. On top of that, he was given an honorable discharge with all the rights that go with it."

"What made you think he was a bad penny?" asked Scott.

"That's the call I was waiting for this morning. I know a guy, not real well, but well enough so that he would talk to me off the record. It seems that this Waldman had a history of heaping physical abuse upon his men that may have cost some of them their lives. Right before the Vietnamese war started, he was a colonel slated to undergo a series of tests to determine if he was insane. When the war began, he was in the Philippines waiting for transportation home. At the last second, he was transferred to Vietnam on special assignment. The records get a little squirrely around that time, but he ran a group called The Specter Group. They were responsible for taking out whole villages that someone thought liked the Cong better than us." He paused and took a sip of coffee.

"All his previous records were destroyed and they were replaced with glowing reports. He was promoted to general, but the other officers stayed away from him. There was a story going around that he shot and killed a captain and a major because they wouldn't have a drink with him. Everyone believed he was part of the Company, which is why he seemed to walk on water."

"That fucking CIA. Everything and anything they touch turns to shit," Tom blurted out from the kitchen where he was refilling his coffee cup.

"This friend," I continued. "Where does he get all his information?"

"I don't know," he continued. "It's a funny thing, I only met him, well I didn't even meet him. He called me last Wednesday morning after we had that fracas on the freeway. He said he was checking up on what happened since a government person was involved. He told me if I ever needed help to call him. After all my sources came up dry, I gave him a try."

"How do you get in touch with him?" I asked.

"I called an 800 number, left a message and he called back twenty minutes later."

"Did you ever check him out?" I questioned.

"When he called last Wednesday, I told him I didn't give interviews over the phone. He asked me to call the local office of the U.S. Attorney General and ask for him. Leave a number and he would call that number back. The return call took less than ten minutes."

"What's his name?" asked Scott.

"Webster, Daniel A."

I picked up the phone and dialed information in New York.

"U.S. Attorney General's office in Manhattan, please."

I dialed the number. After two rings, a machine answered it. I put the call on hands-free so that everyone could listen.

"If you know your party's extension, please dial it now. If you wish to speak to an operator, please stay on the line." The message was repeated in two other languages. "Thank you. Your call is important, please stay on the line. Some one will be . . ." A real voice broke in.

"This is the operator, how may I help you?"

"I'm trying to locate Daniel A. Webster. He told me to call the Attorney General's office and you would connect me."

"Did he say what department he was with?" she asked.

I looked at Barry; he shook his head no.

"I'm sorry, but he didn't. This is very important. Can you look up his name in your directory?"

"Let me transfer you to my supervisor. Please hold."

"This is Carolyn Rush, how may I help you?"

I motioned to Barry to ask the question.

"This is Captain Barry Sands of the Ventura California Police Department. I am trying to locate a Daniel A. Webster. I spoke to him yesterday and I have something else to discuss with him."

"Can you confirm who you are, Captain?"

"I can give you my badge number and the number of my office. They can give you my home phone number, which is where I am now."

"Please let me have your badge number and I will . . . I'm sorry, Captain. While we were talking, I ran up the computer and we have no one by that name listed."

"Are you sure?"

"I'm not, but the computer is. I tried to pull up Daniel Webster without the A, and that didn't work either."

I looked at Barry and shrugged my shoulders. He continued with the operator. "Am I correct that you have my phone number?"

"Yes I do."

"Please give that number to the agent in charge. Give him my name, Barry Sands, and ask him to call me when he gets a chance. My office number is 805-555-2000. I am at one place or the other."

"I will, Captain."

Barry hung up the phone and looked at the rest of us. "Now what?" he said with a sigh.

"Call the 800 number he gave you and ask the same questions," I replied.

"What good will that do?" asked Scott.

"Maybe none, but give it a try."

Barry picked up the phone and went through the same scenario, except this time the person on the other end told him he would get the message delivered. We sat back and waited. I poured another cup of coffee and turned to my three friends. "We have a little problem." I looked around and saw that I had everyone's attention. "Like I told Tom yesterday, Karen's office received a call yesterday afternoon from the Securities and Exchange Commission. Min's brokers overseas also received some calls. These people we are dealing with have some very high connections."

"What were they told?" asked Tom.

"They were both in essence told the same thing. In Karen's case, they were told that no sales were ever made to a client's request and in Min's situation, they were told they were bought for a numbered account. Min drove down to Karen's last night and laid some other bad news on us. The brokers he bought through used caller I.D. and traced the call back to the Vietnamese Consulate in San Francisco."

"No shit!" exclaimed Barry.

"No shit," I continued. "Furthermore, Min believes that they only checked out those transactions that were more than twenty-five thousand share blocks. Karen's estimate of their losses now stands at over two million dollars, which Min also believes will cause them to step up their scrutiny of smaller transactions."

"What does he think we should be doing, getting out?" asked Tom.

"Just the opposite," I continued. "What he would like us to do is have people waiting at our brokers' offices and grab the people that come asking the questions. He would like us to take them somewhere to be questioned, held and then turned over to the proper authorities when this is over."

Barry erupted. "Is he out of his ever loving mind?" He shook his head. "They call that kidnapping!"

Scott asked quietly, "What type of questions does he think we should be asking?"

Barry turned to Scott. "Don't tell me you're even considering this dumb proposal!"

"Does anyone think these people would be or could be real SEC people?" interjected Tom.

"Karen has suggested that we all meet this afternoon and formulate a game plan. She is leaving Carlsbad at about 1:15 and Min has said we can use his house for a meeting. It's not halfway, but as close as any I could get in the short period of time."

"What time?" asked Barry.

"4 P.M." I replied.

"I have to tell you I don't like it. I have a feeling someone is going to get hurt," Barry said.

"Better someone else than one of us," answered Tom. He looked at me and asked, "What do you think, Aaron?"

"I don't know. I would like everyone's input and then we can decide together."

"Decide what?" Barry asked.

"I guess what to do if they start going to visit our brokers." I paused and then continued, "Another thing would be what do we do if they start calling on our families."

No one said a word until Scott spoke up. "We let that son of a bitch live once before. I vote we don't let that happen again."

"I knew you guys were crazy. Let me handle it. That's what I do for a living."

I interjected, "Maybe Barry's right."

Scott replied, "Let's not decide now. Let's think it over and at the meeting we can decide what the best way to proceed is."

Everyone turned as the phone rang. Barry picked it up on the second ring. "Hello . . . Yes this is Captain Sands. Thanks for returning my call so quickly. My friend Aaron Carlyle is here and wanted to ask you a question. Hold on, I'll put him on."

"Hi, this is Aaron Carlyle. I have a question about this general you told Barry about. Is it possible he has had some face surgery?" After listening for a few seconds I continued, "I thought I saw someone that had the same general shape, but with a different face . . . Thanks, you can get back to Barry with the answer. By the way, what department of the Attorney General's office do you work in? . . . Is that headquartered in New York or Washington? . . . How's the weather there today? . . . You should move to Los Angeles, it's eighty-five out here. Thanks for your help." I turned to my friends, "He's a phony. It's pouring and sixty-five in New York. He said it was clear and cold."

"Maybe he's not in New York."

"Maybe you're right, except he said his department was headquartered in Washington, but he was in the New York office."

"That's another part of the equation we'll have to talk about this afternoon," said Tom.

"We'll all ride down together," I said.

Everyone nodded in agreement. "If we leave the office by 3 p.m., we should get there in plenty of time," Scott added.

The man who said he was with the Attorney General's office smiled as he ran his thumb down the side of his face over a thin white scar. He looked at the phone in his hand as he said aloud, "Aaron, you always were a pain in the ass."

Chapter 32

"This car rides as smooth as glass," said Barry from the back seat of Tom's luxury sedan.

"I thought you were asleep," Tom replied.

"I think I was. Did I miss any interesting conversation?"

"No, I don't think so," said Scott who was sitting next to Barry in the back seat. "We were just talking business. Pilferage seems to be down at most of our clients. We were talking about how to best present this information in our annual report."

"Here we are," said Tom.

"I've never been here before. Is there any protocol to follow?" asked Barry.

"Not really," I replied. "The only thing to remember is there are relatives all over the place."

"Are some of them in the parked cars?" he asked.

"You guessed it," I answered.

Scott stopped the car in front of Min's house. The front door opened and out walked Min's granddaughter and another man. He walked up to Tom and said, "I will park the car for you."

Tom handed him the keys and followed us up the stairs.

"Hi Soo Kim," I said.

"My friends call me Sookie." She smiled.

"Sookie, let me introduce my friends. This is Tom, Scott and Barry."

"I have seen Tom and Scott before. I doubt if they would remember me. I was very young. Barry I have only heard about." She held out her hand. "All very good things." She added with a smile, "My grandfather is waiting inside, please enter."

"Good afternoon, gentlemen. Welcome to my home. Please have a seat while we wait for Miss Williams."

"Excuse me," I muttered as I reached for my cell phone. "Aaron . . . thank you." I put the phone back in my pocket and turned to the group. "Karen will be here in about ten minutes."

"While we are waiting, would anyone like some liquid refreshment?" Min asked the question as his granddaughter entered the room with some hot towels on a silver plate.

"I'll have iced tea, please," I replied.

"If you have a light beer, that would be nice." Barry looked up.

Tom and Scott both asked for an iced tea.

"I assume that everyone saw the closing price of SCOA today." We all turned to look at Min. We had not discussed the stock or its price earlier. I was sure we had all been following the price of the stock, but with Karen out of pocket, we had no way of knowing which trades were ours.

There was a slight knock on the door and we turned in unison as Karen entered.

"Sorry I'm late. There was a little more traffic than I expected." She glided into the room. Her first stop was by Min. "Uncle Min, it is a pleasure to see you again." She turned to Tom and Scott. "How's my friend behaving?" She touched each of them on the shoulder as she walked up to Barry. "Since you are my only client in the room, let me say how nice it is to see you again."

Barry smiled. "I'm waiting on pins and needles to find out how we made out," he replied.

"Let's say a little short of great," she answered.

"Hi Aaron." She waved her hand in my direction and winked. "Are we ready to start the meeting?"

Sookie entered the room and walked over to Karen with a hot towel. "For your face after a long journey. Would you like something to drink?"

Karen looked around the room. "I'll have what Aaron is having. Thank you."

"I will bring your drink into the dining room. My grandfather had us set up the room so that you could eat while you discuss business."

Min rose and walked into the dining room. Everyone followed behind. "Please sit at the head of the table," he said to Karen.

"Suppose you sit at the head and I sit at the opposite end," she countered. Min smiled and took his seat.

I was amazed. She had done her homework well. She continued to say all the right things to Min and to captivate my friends.

After we were seated, I looked at Karen and said, "You're on."

She started, "Just to bring you all up to date: Two days ago we purchased six hundred and sixty-five thousand shares at an average price of about five dollars and fifty cents each. Our total investment was three million, six hundred and forty-eight thousand dollars. Yesterday, when our competition was finished buying, the price of the stock was over nine dollars and a half. Someone who I believe was with them entered the market today at the bell and purchased another twenty-five thousand shares at over ten dollars."

"Why do you think it was them?" asked Min.

"Please let's hold all the questions until I'm finished so that we can talk about the transaction in its entirety."

Min nodded his agreement.

Karen continued, "At about this time, our first sales started to appear. Tom's stock was gobbled up at ten dollars and twenty-five cents. Min's two hundred thousand were picked up at between ten dollars and nine fifty. Let's assume nine and five-eighths. Scott's twenty thousand drove the price down to nine dollars. The sales by Aaron, Barry and myself took the price down to eight and a quarter. At about this time, panic started to set in. Someone, and again, I think it was them, purchased another twenty-five thousand shares to shore up the stock. When Min started unloading, it was all over. His broker unloaded the three hundred thousand shares at an average price of six-fifty. When I say the average is six-fifty, you must understand that tomorrow you could buy the stock for four and a half-dollars. Our profit on the total transaction is one million six hundred and twenty-seven thousand dollars. Each one of us has an extra two hundred and seventy-one thousand dollars that we didn't have on Monday."

We sat there stunned. Everyone started looking around the room at each other.

"Can we now ask some questions?" asked Min.

"Sure thing," she answered

"Why do you think that they purchased more stock today?"

"I have been tracking the firms that the trades are made through. Today's trades came from the same firms as the other day. It might not be them, but I doubt that the firm would put any of its other customers into this type of stock."

Tom asked, "How much money do you think those sons of bitches lost?"

"I can't tell until they finally start selling tomorrow, but if I had to guess, I would think close to two and a half million dollars."

Again the room went silent.

"I thought they only invested three point two million," said Tom.

"They started with about three point two and added another million today. That's four point two million for five hundred thousand shares. They averaged almost eight dollars and a half per share. I think they'll be lucky to get back four dollars by the time they're finished."

"Which now brings us to the bigger problem," I said aloud. "These people are not going to be happy campers. We know they have connections of some kind. Yesterday's phone calls were only the beginning. I think we can start expecting visits from their people."

"What makes you think regular agents of the Securities and Exchange Commission won't be making the calls?" asked Barry.

Karen jumped in, "Regular SEC people would do a due diligence first. I believe the brokers will start receiving registered letters some time next week asking for information. The letters will probably ask for answers within two weeks. Any time after that, the brokers can expect either phone calls or visits."

"So you are saying if we are visited tomorrow or the next day, the people would not be SEC agents." Min was pushing hard for Karen to say what he wanted.

She replied, "No one but a broker will be visited. The broker would have to give up the name of his clients over the phone and he would be a fool to do that."

"Even if he is threatened?" Min pursued.

"I don't know," Karen answered.

"What are you suggesting?" interjected Barry. "It sounds like you are trying to put words in her mouth."

"I am trying to show all possibilities," Min shot back.

"You know we can't have people at every brokerage house in the country to check these people out. What you're aiming for is for us to have people from Be Safe picking these people up and God knows what."

"What I am attempting to do is solve a problem." Min's voice had risen. As he took a breath, the door opened. In walked Soo Kim with two other women. They each laid bowls of food on a smaller table that was placed up against the wall. Soo Kim gave instructions as she pointed to where each bowl was to be situated. I didn't take my eyes off of Min. I knew he was upset, I just wasn't sure yet whom he was upset with.

Karen asked, "Is there something I can do to help?"

"No thank you. I along with my sisters can handle everything."

"How many sisters do you have?" I asked.

"There are only the three of us," Soo Kim replied.

"Please help yourself to some food," Min interrupted.

I got the distinct impression that Min did not want this conversation to go any further.

"I think I will. Karen, would you like something?" I asked.

"Thanks," she replied. "Everything looks scrumptious. I think I'll have a little of everything." With that, everyone rose and started helping themselves to what could be described as a feast to end all feasts. After thirty minutes of small talk and in most cases three or four helpings of food, Soo Kim came back in and cleaned away the dishes. As the door closed behind her and before anyone else could start the conversation, I stood and started talking.

"Let me list our options as I see them. This General Waldman is back in our lives. He definitely has help from someone high up inside the government. This same person may be trying to distance himself by helping us, through Barry. Waldman is a sadistic killer and, if he is running true to form, is associating with the same type of people. He had expected to make over half a billion dollars, which he would have done, except that by a stroke of misfortune, he ran afoul of us. He will try and get even. We can't sit around waiting for him. We owe it to our families and the people that work for us to make sure nothing happens. We have discussed the issues with each other all day. Here is my suggestion. We don't worry about brokers all over the country. We cover Karen and our three brokers. The rest of them don't know anything anyway. Anyone that comes around asking questions has got to be held until we find out where Waldman is hiding. That information should be turned over to Barry so that he can act on it. None of the brokers are located in Barry's sphere of influence, so we have to use our people for the start. Once we have Waldman's location, if Barry can handle it, he handles it. If he can't, we handle it."

"What does that mean?" asked Barry.

"I guess that means we do what we have to do."

I looked around the room.

Tom nodded yes.

Scott said, "I was with you then and I'm with you now."

I looked at Min.

He whispered, "There is a saying among my people." He stopped and looked around the table. "Aaron believes that I make up all the sayings.

I will hold this one until everything is over." He smiled and added, "I of course go with the majority."

I looked at Karen. Her face was still as stone. Her fingers gripping the table were the only indication of agitation. The only things that moved were her eyes.

"I am a little afraid to ask the next question. I'm also afraid not to."

"Ask it," I said. "If we are afraid to talk between ourselves, we shouldn't proceed."

"If I vote no, does that mean we don't go forward?"

"I think what that would mean is we would have to come up with a plan that you would say yes to. Are you voting no?"

She looked around the table as if looking for help. Her eyes landed on Barry.

"Barry? What I am hearing is that we as a group will have men stationed at my office and the offices of the three other brokers that were used to purchase stocks. When someone other than a legitimate SEC agent comes to those offices, he will be detained and questioned. When we find out where this General Waldman is, you will be notified and you will make arrangements for him to be arrested."

Barry answered, "That is the plan, but I think we can improve on it a little. Instead of taking the impersonators at the brokerage houses, I suggest we have them followed. We really don't want anyone to see us take them out. I believe they will all end up in the same place where we can get them all in one fell swoop."

"That makes sense," said Tom.

"Even if we can't, we would have a little advantage of knowing where they live for future use."

"Karen," I said. "The logistics of how this goes down will be worked out later. Right now, we have to decide whether to proceed."

"I vote yes," she said.

"Barry, that leaves you."

"I have some reservations, but I don't see any other way out. Let's go ahead with it."

I turned to Min. "We will need some of your closest relatives. One of our people will head up each team with your people as backups."

"Are you afraid my people are not up to the task alone?" Min asked.

"No," I replied. "My people all have licenses to carry firearms. I will have Scott send letters to each of the firms involved." I turned to Karen, "Including yours." I looked straight at her eyes to make sure there was no argument forthcoming. "The letter will offer a free evaluation of the security of each of their offices. It will tell them that the appraisal will take two to three days. That should be enough time to complete what we are after." I looked around the room to see if there were any questions.

Chapter 33

Las Vegas

"The price is where?" Waldman screamed into the phone.

"When our people start to sell tomorrow, they'll be lucky to get four dollars . . . What do you mean it's not your fault? Who's fucking fault do you think it is? Tell you what, come on over here and we'll discuss it. What do you mean you're too busy? . . . Okay, when you get a chance, come on over." Waldman slammed down the phone and picked up his cell phone. He dialed a number and said, "I think he'll be out in a minute or so. Pick him up and bring him in." He dialed another number and said, "Is his girlfriend still in the house? Good, bring her over."

Thirty minutes later, the door to the suite opened and in came the stockbroker, stumbling as he was pushed by one of the general's men. His glasses sat crooked on his face.

"You can't do this to me," he stammered.

The general smiled. "I can't do what to you?"

"This is kidnapping." His voice was trying to show a bravado that his demeanor showed as a lie.

"This isn't kidnapping. This is a business meeting. I just have to ask you a few questions." The general's voice was quiet and had a gentleness to it that the stockbroker had not heard before. He started feeling a little better.

"What happened to the stock today?" The general asked.

"That other group sold everything that they purchased the other day. They did exactly what you were planning on doing."

"Who do you think the other group is?" The general again asked in his sotto sounding voice.

"I don't know. Most of the buys came from outside the country. I can't trace them."

"I think you are lying." The general said these words very quietly.

"I'm sorry, I didn't hear you."

"I said, I think you are lying." This time his voice sounded like thunder.

"I'm not. I swear on my mother's grave that I'm telling the truth."

"Forget your mother's grave. How about swearing on . . . " he motioned his head and one of the men opened the door to the bedroom. The broker looked towards the door as a woman was literally dragged in by her hair.

"Oh my God," he said as his voice shook.

"Wrong words. What I want to hear is who are the people that purchased the stock."

The broker looked at the woman. She was only wearing a bra and panties. Her mouth was taped shut and her hair was a mess falling down around her shoulders.

"Please don't do this," he cried.

"Do what?" asked the general. "Do you know this hooker?" he continued.

The woman's eyes were wide. She had been crying and her mascara had started to run down her cheeks.

The general again nodded to one of the men who proceeded to tie her hands behind her back. When he was finished, he reached across her body and ripped the tape away from her mouth. He pushed her into one of the chairs that had been around the desk in the suite.

"Don't talk unless I ask you a question," the general said to the woman. He turned to the broker. "Let me ask the question again. Who are these other people that bought stock?"

"I keep telling you, I don't know."

The General turned to one of his men and said, "Hal I don't think he's being cooperative, do you?"

"It doesn't sound like it to me." Hal very quickly stuffed a napkin in the woman's mouth. He then very slowly took a knife from his pocket. He stared at it for a second and then pushed a button on the side. The blade appeared as if by magic. He walked purposefully in front of the woman, grabbed a handful of her hair and sliced it from her head. The broker who was now sweating profusely jumped up.

Waldman backhanded him across the face, knocking him to the floor.

"Let me ask you another question. Did you or any of your friends invest in this stock yesterday?"

The broker's eyes turned wild. "No. I swear we didn't!"

"Who is we?"

"I didn't mean we. I meant me. I didn't . . ."

The general nodded at Hal.

"Don't move, Sweetheart. I would hate to have to hurt you." The knife cut through one of the straps.

Waldman again asked, "Who's we?"

"There isn't any we." Tears were now streaming down the broker's face. Waldman again nodded at Hal.

"This is starting to be fun," Hal said as he sliced the other strap.

Waldman looked at the broker who was now crumpled on the floor. "I will now explain the rules. I will ask a question. You will answer the question. If you do not, Hal will slice pieces of the bra and panties your girlfriend is wearing. When there are no clothes left he will start to slice little pieces of her. Do you understand?"

"I don't know anything."

"Wrong answer." He nodded again at Hal who proceeded to slice the bra in half exposing the woman's breast.

Hal took the tip of the knife and started drawing little lines on the woman's torso without breaking the skin.

She whimpered softly.

"Please stop. I'll tell you what you want to know."

The general smiled. "Go ahead."

"I purchased twenty-five thousand shares at six and a quarter yesterday."

"When did you sell them?"

"I sold them this morning for nine-fifty."

"That's a profit of over eighty-one thousand dollars. Weren't we paying you enough?" the general again in a friendly-type voice asked.

"Yes you are. It was a dumb thing to do."

"I can't imagine you buying stock in your name. You must have bought it under someone else's. Whose name did you use?"

Gathering up what little courage he had left, the stockbroker asked. "Is that important?"

"Wrong answer," yelled the general. He nodded at Hal who sliced the rope holding the petrified woman's hands, lifted her and threw her down on the sofa. She landed face down, but quickly turned over and pulled up her knees to her chest to try and cover her nakedness.

"One more wrong answer and each man takes her once before we put the knife to her face."

The woman screamed, "Tell him. For God's sake, tell him."

The accountant took a deep breath. "The account is in her name." He was starting to babble. "I was trying to put some money aside so that my wife wouldn't be suspicious when we went on vacations." Tears were streaming down his face as he looked at the general.

"I just wanted to find out what was going on," stated the general. He hesitated and then continued, "We're not bad people. We paid a lot of money so that you would do a job for us and until today, we didn't have a complaint. You still have to finish the job tomorrow. I can't let you get away clean, but after looking at your girlfriend, I can understand the pressures that you were under."

The look on the broker's face was one of apprehension. He was going to get away from these animals. He didn't see Hal walk up behind him, grab his hands and lay them flat on the tabletop. He looked at the general who smiled just before he brought a full bottle of beer down on his fingers. He opened his mouth to scream but a towel was shoved in his mouth. The bottle was brought down a second time. He almost passed out from the pain. The general opened the bottle and poured its contents over the obviously busted fingers.

"Sorry for that, but like I said, I can't let you get away with that type of independent action. Take your girlfriend, get your hand fixed and make sure you do a good job for us tomorrow. By the way, you can deduct the eighty grand from what you thought you were getting."

The stockbroker, holding his crippled fingers gingerly in front of him, walked over to his girlfriend. She had hardly uttered a word since she was thrown into the room. He held out his good hand and said, "Let's get your clothes and get out of here."

"Sorry about that," said the general. "The hooker either stays with us or leaves the way she is, without her clothes."

"You can't do . . ." The bespectacled man stopped. "I guess you can." He looked at the woman and shrugged his shoulders. Together with as much dignity as a man with a busted hand and a woman without any clothes could muster, they walked out of the suite.

As he started laughing, the general said, "A week from now, one of you guys will have to come back here and make sure neither of them ever speaks to anyone again."

"How about I hang back a day or two and do it this week?" asked Hal.

"Sometimes I worry about you," said the general. "The money won't clear until Monday or Tuesday. You can come back the day after we get notification. You'll have to find some other way to enjoy yourself."

"Karen, is there any way for you to identify the office that's directing the trades for them?" Barry asked.

"I don't think so. The trades I think are theirs are coming from four different brokerage firms. There are a couple of other strange trades, but I couldn't be sure."

Tom looked at me and said, "It's your show, call it."

I had been making notes on a scratch pad. I took a deep breath and started, "Tom, you assign two of our senior men to each brokerage firm. Min, if you could, I would like two of your men outside of each of these firms. When we identify any of the opposition, I want two chase cars ready to go. Tell our men if they cross into Ventura County to make sure that Barry is notified at once. Scott, you get around-the-clock protection for Karen, Mary, Constance and the kids. Talk to them so that they don't get too worried stiff."

"Wait a second. I don't need any protection," interjected Karen.

"I know you don't, but I'm supplying it anyway."

"What about Tuloc? He's still watching the house, isn't he?"

"He should be," I answered.

"Well, then that's enough, and I don't want any men hanging around my office."

"If I may," interrupted Min. "My granddaughter Soo Kim has always fancied herself as an independent person. Would you allow her to spend time with you?"

Karen looked around the room. She could sense that she didn't have much room to maneuver. "I would love to have Soo Kim be my house guest and show her how Wall Street works."

"That's settled," I said aloud. "Now let's get back to what we do when we find out where they are located. There are three things that could happen." I held one finger in the air. "We follow them to their headquarters or wherever they're staying. If that happens, we contact Barry and let him lead us into action. We only use our licensed operatives with Barry." I held up a second finger. "We are forced to take them off the street. In that case, we have to bring them somewhere close to where they are taken. Tell our men to drive either to our office or to the closest motel where they can get a room."

Scott held up his hand. "I have a suggestion. Why don't we have our men take a room somewhere close to the office they are working at and go straight there?"

"That's a good idea," I replied as I made a notation on the pad. I held up three fingers. "The final scenario is they never show up. This would leave them out there and us having no idea knowing when they decide to get even."

"Do you think that's possible?" asked Karen.

"I think that they'll come after us. Maybe not within the first three to four days, but they'll come."

"We have to find them first," said Barry. He continued, "I wonder if we can find out about Daniel Webster."

"You're right. We have to find them first and we have to find out about Daniel Webster," I commented.

"Let me work on that," Barry replied.

"Okay, everyone knows what they have to do, let's get at it. Keep in touch. Use Be Safe as a central point and be careful."

Chapter 34

Las Vegas

"That show was pretty good." The general was holding court in the lounge of the hotel in which they were registered. "We could learn something from those guys. They are masters at having you look one way while they do something in another direction."

"I still don't see how they move those big cats around," said one of the men.

"I think they use mirrors," said Paul.

Karen was staring into the mirror, ostensibly touching up her lipstick. Her eyes were watching everyone saying goodnight. I knew she had wanted to spend a little time with me, but it didn't look like it was going to be possible. She had glanced at me when I told Min I didn't have a car and that meant I was leaving when the others left. She watched me approach through the mirror.

"Hey, I got a deal for you," I said.

She smiled, "And what is that?"

"Soo Kim can't leave for about two hours. How about you and I go somewhere for a cup of coffee or something and when I bring you back, you let her drive you home. I'll keep the car and drive it down Friday afternoon."

"What are you planning for Friday afternoon?" she replied.

"I was hoping that Friday I could relax in your Jacuzzi and maybe Saturday see if you're as good as you think you are on the golf course."

"How did you do with cleaning out your closets?"

"Not bad. I got the stuff from the closet into the garage. Hopefully the Salvation Army will bc by tomorrow to pick it up."

"Then I have a better idea."

"What's that?" I asked.

"Why don't we just go and park somewhere for a couple of hours. When we come back, I'll go home with Sookie and Friday afternoon I'll come back with her. You pick me up and after that, everything will be the same except it's your house instead of mine. I don't want you claiming home court advantage."

I turned to Tom who was standing by the door. "Go ahead without me. I'm going to take Karen's car home."

"Drive safe." He waved good-bye.

"Let's go," I whispered.

Just as we reached the door, Min called. "Aaron, please stay for a few minutes so that we may talk."

I looked at Karen. She mouthed, "Someday."

"Is it important?" I asked Min.

"I think so," he replied. He looked at Karen and said, "My granddaughter finds herself ready to leave. Would you like her to follow you home?"

"No," Karen answered. "I would like to travel with her. I am leaving Aaron my car and this way I can get to know her better."

"Soo Kim," he called.

"I am here, grandfather. Is there something you need?"

"Miss Williams is ready to leave. She wishes to travel with you in your car. Drive carefully. There is no need to prove you know how to drive fast. The amount of speeding tickets you have received proves that."

Soo Kim bowed her head and said. "Grandfather, how many times have I told you the police always stop single women and give them tickets? They wish to get their phone numbers and ask them out for dinner."

"I know how many times you have told me that. I would just like you to be careful."

She smiled and said, "I will be careful."

"Your talk about police asking you out for dinner brings up interesting question. I asked Tuloc to join us for dinner this Saturday and he said he expects to be busy. Do you think he is seeing someone?"

"I do not know what that person who is like a snake in the grass would be seeing."

"So it will be just you and I?" he queried.

Soo Kim hesitated, "Grandfather, I have made other plans for Saturday night. I will not be able to join you for dinner."

"Other plans? What does this mean? Where do you expect to be?"

Soo Kim looked up at the ceiling. It was obvious to me that she was looking for some divine intervention.

"I think it is getting late," Karen spoke up. "I would like to get on the road and get home as soon possible. There is some work I still have to do tonight." She looked at Soo Kim and winked before she continued. "Thank you very much for inviting me to your home. It is very beautiful and the food was superb."

Min looked at Karen and then at Soo Kim. "I leave my granddaughter in your hands. I think she will listen to you. You could be the friend she needs. Please ask her to be careful and make sure she does not speed."

Karen's face reacted with a touch of blush.

"I will." She turned and gave me a peck on the cheek and called to Soo Kim, "Let's get the show on the road."

They walked out together and as the door closed Min said, "She has no mother or settling influence to watch over her. I think your Miss Williams will be good for her. Come back inside, we must talk."

I sat down at the dining room table with Min sitting opposite me.

"Aaron, you are by nature a romantic. In the jungle, you defended your lady fair. You weren't afraid to fight, but you didn't finish the job. Here we are eight years later and we are faced with the same problem. This animal is capable of killing your wonderful Karen, yet we sit around talking about how he should be handled. Unless we look forward to eliminating him from our lives, he could do us all damage. I for one will not allow him to hurt anyone in my family and I would ask for your support in this goal. I have seen both Tom and Scott at work in difficult situations. They are both good men, but they lack what you would call a killer instinct."

I hesitated before answering. "Min, I am not a killer. I have killed and I have a feeling that before this is over I may kill again, but only to protect the people I love. That includes Scott, Tom, their families, you and Karen. If I am given the choice of killing or capturing, I hope I am strong enough to capture. Saying all of that, I am prepared to do what has to be done. What did you have in mind?"

"My concern is the involvement of the Vietnamese government. They of course know my name. I am going to contact them and explain that this fight is between this ex-general Waldman and us. If they insist upon joining in, I will see to it that their names will appear upon a wall where their relatives can grieve for them."

"You can't start a war with the Vietnamese government."

"I would not be the one starting the war."

I looked into his eyes. "You're serious."

Without blinking he replied, "Like you, I have killed in the past. Like you, I would rather live in peace, but I will not live my life looking over my shoulder."

"How do you plan on setting up this contact?" I asked the question before I realized that by doing so I was committing myself to this cause.

"There are people who can set up a meeting. After we get our initial response from Waldman, I will make the call."

"Min, there is a story about a man called Don Quixote who fought windmills. I will not lead my friends into this type of battle. If I agree, it is you and I. The others must be protected."

He smiled. " I'm sure that you won't believe me, but we have a story about a man called Sung Han. He fought the same battles."

I smiled. "You're right, I don't, but I do remember one of the stories that you told me in the jungle. When one starts on the road to revenge, he should first dig two graves."

His smile never left his face, but his eyes changed. "You remember well. It is one of the reasons our friendship has flourished."

Chapter 35

Las Vegas

"The market's been open for over two hours. What do you mean we haven't been able to sell any of the stock?"

The wary broker, with his hand in a cast, cringed as he listened to Waldman rant and rave over the phone.

"I purchased fifteen thousand shares at five dollars this morning for my own account and that's not even helping."

Waldman took a deep breath and quietly asked, "What's the stock at right now?"

"Four and a half."

"How many shares have we unloaded?"

"Maybe fifty thousand."

"What price have we gotten?"

"Including the ones that I purchased, a little less than five dollars a share." Before Waldman could say anything, the broker continued, "We have lost three dollars a share on the fifty thousand we sold. My suggestion is that we take our beating and get out. We might be able to average four dollars if we act fast."

"That's a loss of over a million and a half dollars." Waldman's voice was starting to show his anger.

"If you wait, the price could drop to three dollars."

"You're enjoying this, you rotten bastard. I should have broken your fucking head." Waldman was now screaming into the phone.

The broker looked at his hand and smiled. He was petrified about what would happen in the future, but he was enjoying the discomfiture of his tormentor.

"I don't know why you are saying that. I put seventy-five thousand of my own money into the game."

"That was the seventy-five that you ripped off from me the other day."

"Just tell me what you want me to do." He was resigned to his fate, whatever it might be, and decided to try and be a man. There was no answer. He looked at the phone and asked, "Are you there?"

"Yeah, I'm here. Sell it for whatever you can. I'm leaving for San Francisco this afternoon. I want a total before I leave."

"I'll have it for you by 2 P.M."

"Have it ready by 1:45 P.M." Waldman slammed down the phone. He walked over to the window and looked down at the strip. The men in the room had seen this look before. Very quietly, they stood up and left the room. Hal, who was the last one to leave, turned and asked, "General, is there anything you would like me to do?"

The general shook his head. "Not now. Maybe later."

The door closed and the general walked over to the phone and dialed the 800 number that he knew by heart. Five minutes later his cell phone rang.

"We have to have a meeting," he said before even saying hello. "What do you mean what for? Haven't you been watching the stock market?" He listened to the reply and before he could say anything else, the phone went dead.

"Son of a bitch. Someday I'm going to get even."

"I can't believe they let that happen to themselves."

"Let what happen?" Soo Kim looked up.

"They averaged less than four dollars a share when they sold their stocks."

"What does that mean in dollars and cents?"

"I don't have an exact amount in cents, but the dollars amount to over one point four million in losses."

The intercom interrupted their conversation.

"Aaron Carlyle on line one, Karen."

"Thank you." Karen picked up the phone.

"Aaron, you're not going to believe how they ended up. They did some things I would never have done and it ended up costing them. As close as I can figure, they lost over a million and a half dollars . . . You're right, they will not be happy campers."

"That's great, Karen, and yes I am ready for Friday night. Now let me ask you a question. Were you able to determine where they were being directed from?"

"It's funny that you should ask. I told you they did some things I wouldn't have done. Well, this morning someone tried to drive the price back up by putting in a buy order at higher than the market price. It didn't work, of course, but I was able to pinpoint the brokerage house that did it."

"That's great. Where and who are they?"

"It's a small one man shop located in Vegas. I'll fax you the name, address and phone number after I hang up. It's in the other room."

"Karen, be careful," I whispered into the phone.

"Don't worry about me. I have Sookie here to watch over me. See you Friday night."

Las Vegas Airport
2:15 P.M.

"General Waldman, please pick up the white courtesy phone."

"Anyone see one of those white phones?" Waldman looked around.

"Over there, next to the water fountain," pointed one of the men.

The general walked over and picked the phone up off the wall. "This is General Waldman. Please put the call through."

"Sorry I'm late."

Waldman clenched his teeth. "I thought I told you to bring the information to me at the airport." This broker was becoming a pain in the butt.

"I know what you told me, but I decided it wasn't such a good idea."

"You decided! Who told you to decide anything?"

"No one, but I thought it would be better if I gave you this information over the phone."

"What's the information?" snapped the general.

"Your losses are a little over one and a half million dollars."

"Were you able to figure out who the other people were that bought the stock before us?"

"No. The trades were from too many different places."

"It was nice doing business with you." The general hung up the phone. He walked over to the group of men waiting to board the plane for San Francisco.

"Hal. Take one of the guys and fly to San Diego. Here is the name and address of some woman that owns a firm that was trading in the stock. She only traded about sixty or seventy thousand shares, but she was in early and out even earlier. Find out the name of her client or why she decided to get involved. After you finish there, meet us in Northern California. I'm calling all the boys in to have a sit down next Tuesday. I think it's time to get even."

The general wasn't sure the woman knew anything, but it was a place to start. This name, Karen Williams, was in fact the only lead he had. The phone call produced only her name. There were other brokerage firms, but the quantities were wrong. He would have his friends at the Vietnamese Consulate look into the other brokers overseas.

"Where did you go to school?" Karen asked Sookie.

"My grandfather insisted that I graduate from Stanford. It was his desire that I would become Americanized and he believed that was the place to be. I had wanted to go to Berkeley, but he said that it was too radical to get a good education."

"Stanford wasn't a bad place to send you." Karen started to get up as the doorbell rang.

"I'll get it," Sookie stopped her as she walked towards the front door.

"Don't forget to ask who it is before you open it," Karen yelled after her.

"You worry too much," she called back as she opened the door. Two men stood in the doorway.

"Miss Karen Williams?" one of the men asked.

"I'm sorry, Karen is inside. Who should I say is calling?"

One of the men took his wallet out of his breast pocket and flipped it open.

"We're from the Securities and Exchange Commission. We're here to see Miss Williams regarding some transactions she made."

Soo Kim smiled and turned towards the kitchen.

"Karen, there are a couple of men here from the Securities and Exchange Commission." Karen came out of the kitchen and asked, "Could I please see some identification?"

The same man again opened his wallet and flashed his credentials.

"Could you please take it out of the wallet and hand it to me?" Karen asked.

The man started to take it out of his wallet when the second man produced a gun. He slammed the door shut and asked.

"Is there anyone else here?"

"No. My mother is out tonight. Who are you?"

"I'll ask the questions. We're here to check up on some trades you made the other day."

"I'll tell you nothing," Karen said calmly.

Out of nowhere, his hand appeared and knocked her to the floor. Soo Kim started to move towards Karen when the second man grabbed her by the hair and pulled her back. She turned in his direction as he pulled a knife and said, "Move again and I'll slice you up so that your mother will have to use you for sushi."

She started to put her hands on her hips when he slashed her across the arm. She refused to make a sound.

Karen staggered up. "Stop that. What do you want to know?"

"That's better. You purchased and then sold a bunch of SCOA stock this week."

"That's right. I purchased about sixty thousand shares."

"Why did you sell them two days later?"

"The stock almost doubled. That's what I do for a living. I buy and sell stock for clients on a discretionary basis. Let me get a towel or something for Soo Kim's arm."

"Not yet, I have a few more questions. How come you bought that stock in the first place?"

"It was listed in the Wall Street Journal's 'Heard on the Street' column."

"When?"

"Last Sunday."

Thc man turned to his friend that was holding the knife. "Hal, is there anything else we need to know?"

"Yeah, find out the last time either one of them had a real man."

"You heard my friend. When was the last time you had a real man?"

Karen became alarmed. She had thought the man who was asking the questions was in charge. All of a sudden, he was listening to the man with the knife. "You boys got the information you came after. Why don't you leave before somconc rcally gets hurt?"

Both of the men smiled. The one called Hal looked at the second man and smirked. "Which one do you want, Tommie?"

The one called Tommie pulled a gun and said, "I'll take the Chinese lady. You can have the mouthy one."

"Suits me." Tommie pointed the gun at Soo Kim.

"Start taking off your clothes and do it slow." He pointed the gun at Karen and snarled. "You sit on the floor and don't move."

Karen looked at Soo Kim. "They can't make us do this." She got no further as Tommie swung the gun against the side of her head.

"Start stripping!" He yelled at Soo Kim.

"You will have to shoot me." Soo Kim stood tall.

"How about I shoot your friend?"

Soo Kim looked at Karen leaning on the floor. She wasn't sure what she should do when she heard a shot. She jumped back and looked at Tommie who was holding the gun. There was a hole right above his nose.

"Don't move." It was Tuloc standing in the doorway.

"Drop the knife. Don't make me say it twice."

Hal turned towards the front door as it opened.

"You heard my friend. Drop the knife or you can join your friend."

Without warning, Tuloc fired his pistol again. This time the bullet hit Hal right below the kneecap.

He fell to the floor and the knife fell out of his hand.

Michael Harran was on him like a cat. He searched him and took away two guns.

"I need a doctor," Hal cried from the floor.

Michael turned and kicked him on the wounded leg.

"Open your mouth again and I'll put a bullet in your other leg.

Tuloc had gone over to Soo Kim and gently said, "Let me see your arm." She held it out and he said, "It'll be fine by Saturday night."

Karen was standing, holding her head and looking around the room.

"Should we call the police?"

"Mr. Carlyle first." Tuloc took out his cell phone.

"Mr. Carlyle, Tuloc here. Two men forced their way into Miss Williams's home. . . . She's fine. Soo Kim got a scratch, but she'll be ready for our date on Saturday night." He smiled at Soo Kim as he said this. She stuck out her tongue in return. "One of them is dead, the other has a bullet in his leg. . . . Hold on, I'll put her on. Miss Williams, Mr. Carlyle would like to talk to you."

"Aaron, they killed one of the men. The other one is bleeding on my floor. We've got to call an ambulance and the police . . . Yes, I'm fine. My ears are still ringing, but what are we going to do? . . . Tuloc, he wants to talk to you."

Tuloc listened intently as I gave him instructions.

"Three of your uncle's men from the cleaning service are leaving as we speak. Before they get there, I want you to get the ladies and the one that is alive out of there. Your uncle owns a warehouse in Long Beach. He says you know where it is. Take the three of them there. We will have a doctor waiting. Leave Michael at the house. The cleaning service will put the house back in order and put the body where it can be found. They have been given instructions, so tell Michael that there is no reason to talk to them. Do you have any questions?"

"I have one. Shall I have Miss Williams pack clothes and if so, for how long?"

"That's a good question. Ask her to pack for three days. I'll put her up at my house."

Tuloc replied, "I will see you in about two hours."

He hung up the phone and turned to Karen.

"Miss Williams, Aaron asked that you pack for three days and we leave as soon as you are ready."

Karen, who was still in shock, just nodded her head.

Chapter 36

It had taken a little less than two hours for Tuloc and Soo Kim to get to the warehouse in Long Beach. When the car approached, the front gate swung open as if by magic.

I came running out of the building and opened the rear door of the car.

"I've been worried stiff about you. Come on inside and tell me what happened."

Tuloc had gotten out of the driver's side and opened the rear door. He held out his arm to Soo Kim and said, "You said there would be a doctor."

Soo Kim exited and said, "I am not a child. I do not need your help. I can take care of myself." She took two steps and collapsed in his arms.

He lifted her as if she weighed no more than a child did. He shouted to one of the men, "Please lead the way to the doctor."

Both Karen and I watched as Soo Kim put her arm around his neck and made herself comfortable.

Min, standing at the door, raised his voice and said one word, "Hurry."

San Francisco

"Has anyone heard from Hal?" General Waldman asked the group of men sitting around the table playing cards.

"I've heard from Vic in Colorado and Tony in Chicago. They'll both be here before morning."

Another one of the men replied, "John called and said that he was flying to New York from Boston to meet up with Richard. They were going to fly together and would be here about 11:30 A.M. tomorrow."

"That's ten of us accounted for. Remind me to kick his ass. He should have called in after the job was finished."

"What are we going to do with the loose end in Vegas?" asked Paul.

"You go back down there Saturday morning. Take one of the other guys with you and clean it up."

"Does that include the wife and girlfriend?" Paul inquired.

"Just the girlfriend, if you find her. My guess would be that she's miles away from there by now."

One of the men laughed and said, "If I was him, I would be miles away from there by now."

"Tell you what," said the general. "I'll call him tomorrow and tell him we're going to let him make amends and handle our next deal. That way we'll be sure he's still in Vegas."

"You told me you would have the doctor look at my leg!" screamed Hal from the corner where he had been thrown.

"The doctor looked at it. He decided that unless it gets some attention soon, they may have to amputate it."

"I don't want to lose my leg. Ask me some questions. I'll tell you anything you want to know."

I looked around the room. Aside from myself there was Min, Barry and three of Min's "nephews."

Barry asked the first question. "What's your name?"

"Hal."

"Hal what?"

"Hal Carter."

"Where is your boss tonight?"

"San Francisco. Everyone went there this afternoon."

"Where in San Francisco?"

"I don't know. We never know where we are staying until we get there."

"Where did you stay in Vegas?"

"At the Rio."

"How many men does the general have?"

"What general?" asked Hal. Barry turned and walked away.

"Where are you going? I need a doctor."

"When you decide to answer all of our questions, I'll see about the doctor."

"Eight. There are eight of us besides the general. How did you know he was a general?"

"There's a lot we know. I'll be asking some questions that we already know the answers to. I would suggest you don't try and lie." Barry walked back to him. "Let's start again. Why did you go to Miss Williams's home?"

Hal thought this one over. He finally shrugged his shoulders and answered. “At the airport, the general pulled a piece of paper out of his pocket. He handed it to me and told me to check out who she bought the stock for.”

“Who gave him Miss Williams’s name and address?”

“I don’t know.”

Barry nodded his head at one of Min’s nephews. The nephew proceeded to kick Hal’s wounded leg twice.

“I don’t think you were telling me the truth.”

“It is the truth, I swear it,” he screamed.

“Like I said, I don’t believe you.” Barry nodded again at one of the nephews.

“Don’t kick me again. No one knows where he gets his information. Every once in a while, his cell phone rings and he tells us to get lost.”

This time Min asked the question. “Does your general speak any other language?”

A strange look came over Hal’s face. “He sometimes speaks Chinese or Korean. I don’t know the difference.”

Min signaled me to proceed.

“What was the name of the man in Vegas your boss was dealing with?”

“Some guy named Lundin. He’s the head of a fund. I’m not sure of the exact name.”

“How is he involved?”

“I don’t know.” This time I nodded to the nephew who promptly kicked Hal’s bleeding foot.

He screamed and then started groaning. “He keeps track of all the buys and sells. It’s his job to make sure everything goes according to plan.”

“What did your boss say when he lost the million and a half?”

“It was that much? I knew he wasn’t happy. He had us bring in the broker and his girlfriend for a . . . talk.”

“What did they talk about?”

He had a smirk on his face as he continued, “He had us strip the broad and put a knife to her as he asked the broker some questions. When he was finished, he broke Lundin’s left hand by slamming a bottle of beer down on it twice. He then told them to get out of the room and finish the job he was hired to do. He made the girlfriend walk out naked.”

“It sounds to me as if he got off easy.”

Hal laughed. "He's not finished with him yet. Someone will probably be up there by Monday. The general doesn't like to leave any loose ends lying around."

Barry stepped forward. "Would you be willing to testify against the general when we bring him to trial?"

"You'll never bring him to trial. He's got friends all over the world and in high places in the States."

"Like where?" Min asked.

Hal looked into the shadows where Min was standing.

"Is this some kind of setup?"

"Why are you asking that?" Min replied.

"He has friends that look like you."

"Do they have names?"

"None that I remember."

"You also said high places."

Hal turned to Barry. "I heard him once talking to someone in Washington. This guy he talked to was connected to the CIA or to the FBI. One or the other, I'm not sure which."

"You never answered my other question. Would you be willing to testify?"

He looked at Barry. "I thought I told you that he would never come to trial. If you bring him to trial, I will testify."

The lie was so apparent that not even Barry was willing to believe it and he wanted to.

"How about fixing my leg? You promised."

Min stepped forward. "We will have the doctor look at your leg. We will then move you to somewhere else. As long as you are helpful, we will take care of you."

"When are you turning me over to the police?"

"After we find your boss."

"I could be here for a long time."

Min spoke Vietnamese to his nephews and we all turned to leave. I looked up and saw that Karen was standing in the back of the room.

"When did you come in?" I asked her.

"I think about halfway through the questioning. I'm very proud of you."

"Of me? Why?"

"You didn't let Min bully you into doing something that you felt was wrong."

"It may end up the way Min wants it to anyway."

"I know, but you had the courage to bring in Barry, probably over Min's objections."

"It was no big deal, but I have another question for you."

"At this particular minute I would say yes to anything you asked, including drying your hair."

I smiled. "How about going over to Vegas with me this weekend?"

"Is this for pleasure or does it have something to do with this general?"

"Actually, it has something to do with the general. The broker he used is named Lundin."

"That's the name of the firm that had the odd transaction," Karen interrupted.

"That figures. I don't know if you heard it or not, but the general broke this guy's hand with a beer bottle."

"I heard. You were right. These are not nice people."

"How about Vegas?"

"I would love to go to Vegas with you. Just make sure the room has a king-size bed. I'm staying with Soo Kim tonight and I don't know what the sleeping arrangements are. Don't give me that hangdog look, Sookie needs someone and this way you can dream about tomorrow. Is that when we are going?"

"Tomorrow afternoon. I'll make arrangements and pick you up around 3 P.M."

Las Vegas

"Honey, it's going to be all right. I just received a call from the general. They don't hold anything against me. They want me to handle their next deal . . . No, he's not letting us have the money back. He said I was stupid and had to pay for it. You'll see, we'll make a ton of money on the next deal. Meanwhile, my wife is visiting her parents. Let's get together tomorrow night." He smiled and adjusted his glasses with his good hand after he replaced the receiver.

San Francisco

"I told you it would be easy. Fly over tomorrow afternoon, take care of the shithead and take the late plane back." Waldman smiled to himself. He loved to give orders.

Be Safe

Las Vegas

I held Karen's hand as we were carried along the moving sidewalk inside the Las Vegas airport.

"I would have reserved a car, but I think in this town you're a lot better off just taking taxis."

"You never told me, what hotel are we staying at?"

"I got us a room at the Quality Inn on Paradise."

"You got us a room where?"

I started laughing. "Don't worry. Only the best for you this weekend."

"I should hope so," she replied.

"Coming through, step aside, we're in a hurry."

Two men were rushing down the left side of the sidewalk, pushing and shoving people out of their way.

I pulled Karen closer to me on the right side of the walkway so that they could pass us without a problem.

The first one went past quickly, but the second one slowed down and patted Karen on her rear end.

She turned and started to say something when he lifted his right hand and placed it on her shoulder and pushed.

I reached over to his left arm and turned him facing me.

"You shouldn't have done that," I said as I dropped my left shoulder and planted my right fist into his stomach.

The other man had reached the end of the moving sidewalk and had turned around to see his friend lying on the floor coming toward him.

"What happened to Paul?" he yelled out loud.

"He had an accident." We reached the end of the walkway and we both stepped over the inert Paul.

The people behind us stepped over him as well, except they were smiling. We continued on to the taxi stand as if nothing had happened, although I saw Karen look back a few times to see if we were being followed.

Chapter 37

"This is a nice room with a great view," Karen said as she looked out the window. "You must be one of the last of the red-hot rollers. Come take a look. You can see the construction going on next door."

I looked out the window and said, "You don't understand, with my connections I made sure that they stop work when the sun goes down." I walked over to the phone and dialed information. "I would like the phone number of Lundin Partners . . . Sorry, I don't have an address . . . Do you have a number for Lundin? . . . Dennis Lundin is fine. His number is? Thanks." I handed Karen the phone. "Here, you call him. Just remember the story."

Karen dialed the number. "I'm getting voice mail."

"Tell him where he can reach us."

"Hi, this is Karen Williams. I have an investment firm in Carlsbad. I just moved in and out of SCOA and saw that you were a buyer yesterday. I'm in Vegas for the weekend and I wondered if we could get together for a drink. I would love to get some information about that company. I'm staying at Bally's with my fiancé under the name of Carlyle. Please give me a call."

"Fiancé? I don't remember practicing that line?" I held out my arms and she walked into them.

"I just wondered how it would sound," she said as she kissed the tip of my chin.

"How did it sound?" I asked as I brushed my lips across her forehead.

"Not bad. I'll have to use it a little more often to get the feel of it."

Before I could reply, the phone rang. I picked it up.

"Hello? . . . No, this is Aaron Carlyle . . . Please hold on. Karen, it's for you."

"This is Karen. . . . Hi Mr. Lundin. Thanks for calling back so promptly . . . Yes, I invested about a quarter of a million in SCOA last Monday, but because of the sudden rise, I bailed out Wednesday . . . Yes, I was lucky. I would love to get back in, but I don't know enough about the company. I saw you as a buyer so when my fiancé suggested we come down for the weekend, I decided to give you a call." She turned and mouthed the words, *Sounds better all the time.* She spoke back into the phone, "Hold on, I'll ask him. He would like to meet us for dinner. Do you feel up to it?" She let him hear her ask the question. "He says he would love to, where and when? . . . That's forty-five minutes from now. We'll be there." She hung up the phone. "Let's get started, we don't have much time."

I smiled. I was lying on the bed. "I'm ready. Come over here."

She looked at me. "I think you're becoming some mad crazed sex fiend. I meant we have to get ready for dinner."

"All you ever think about is food." I got up and started towards the closet. She stopped me halfway across the room. "You're wrong. All I think about is you. All I do is eat." She framed my face with her hands and kissed my eyes. "Now get ready."

Twenty minutes later, we were sitting at a twenty-five dollar blackjack table. It had the best view of the entrance to the Italian restaurant.

"Hit me," Karen said to the dealer.

"You have fifteen," he replied.

"I know, but you have a six showing and I want your card." The dealer shrugged and turned over a five. I stuck with a nineteen and the dealer turned over his cards. He had a ten in the hole to go along with the six on top. He turned over the next card and pulled a seven.

"I knew it," Karen crowed.

"Vegas is built by people like you that hit on fifteen." The dealer laughingly said to both of us.

"This is nice being the only two people at the table. What time do the crowds show up?" I asked.

The dealer looked around. "The town isn't full this weekend. I heard that a lot of the big rollers are over at Bellagio."

I glanced at Karen as she gripped my arm. She motioned her head in the direction of the lounge. I looked over and saw the two men from the airport.

"Something wrong?" the dealer asked.

"I don't think so. One of those guys got fresh with my fiancé at the airport and I left him sitting on the floor. Hopefully he was deciding not to do that again."

The dealer pressed a button on his table and the pit boss came walking over as Karen mouthed, "Fiancé?"

"How's everything going?" he asked.

I noticed two other men from the pit area sauntering in our direction.

"Not bad. I was just mentioning to . . . " I looked at his badge, ". . . Phil that I had a little scuffle at the airport with one of those men sitting in the lounge."

"Over anything important?"

"He got fresh with his girlfriend," the dealer answered for me.

"Mr. Carlyle, you are a guest of the hotel. If you think that you might be having a problem, I would be glad to help."

"Thanks anyway. I don't think they're looking for us. They wouldn't know we were staying here."

"Enjoy yourself. If you need anything, just ask." He walked back into the pit area, stopping to talk to someone on the phone. I knew enough about security to know that they were now taking pictures of Karen, the two men from the airport, and myself. I motioned for Phil to continue dealing.

"Blackjack," said Karen. "I'm beginning to like this game."

I stuck on twenty and Phil pulled two cards to a nineteen.

"Cash us in Phil, our dinner guests have arrived."

Karen looked up at the approaching couple and said, "His girlfriend is certainly . . . statuesque."

The pit boss returned. "Mr. Carlyle. Those two men you had the disagreement with are, how shall I put this, at best, unsavory characters. We suggest you avoid any contact with them if possible."

I removed my wallet from an inside pocket and showed him my private investigators license. "What do you mean by unsavory?"

He looked at the certificate, handed it back and said, "Those two were in Vegas last week with five others. They browbeat waiters, dealers, girls and anyone else they came in contact with. We thought they left town yesterday afternoon and I can tell you that I'm not happy to see them in our hotel."

"Thanks for the information. I'll make sure to avoid them."

We stood up and started towards the restaurant. Lundin was about ten feet from the door and about thirty feet ahead of us when Paul and his friend approached him.

I could only hear parts of the conversation.

"What do you two want?" Lundin demanded. He continued, "We will not go with you. I spoke to the general and he assured me everything was all right."

I steered Karen away from them. I didn't want Paul to see us.

"If you don't take your hands off of me, I'm going to scream." The words coming from the girlfriend were loud enough to be heard by both Karen and myself twenty feet away.

"Doesn't anyone hear her?" Karen whispered.

"Open your mouth again, bitch, and I'll slice your throat before the words reach your lips."

"Paul is definitely not a nice person. Where's the security?" Karen asked as she looked around.

"Here they come," I answered. "They must have been watching these two and realized something's wrong."

There were four security men that surrounded Paul and maybe another three or four that hung back a couple of feet.

"Is there a problem?" the lead security man asked Lundin and his girlfriend.

"Who the hell do you guys think you are?" Paul asked.

Two women who I assumed were security people moved in, took Lundin's girlfriend by the arm, and moved her out of harm's way.

"Mr. Lundin, you are a frequent guest of the hotel. If you are having a problem, we would be only too happy to help you take care of it."

Lundin looked at the two men and said, "I'm sure there's been a misunderstanding somewhere. If you could please just hold these men for fifteen minutes, I'm sure I can get it straightened out."

"Our pleasure, sir." He waved to his men and they started walking Paul and his friend towards an escalator that went down to the security office.

"Let's go," I said to Karen. "We'll talk to them outside where they parked their car." We turned to walk to the front when Paul's friend pushed the black security guard that had him by the arm.

"Take your black frigging hand off my clothes," he yelled. What had started off as a non-violent confrontation erupted. Three security guards were down before you could blink your eyes. Two other guards followed them very quickly.

"Men down, need help by the escalator!" One of the woman security guards said into a microphone attached to her collar. Paul kicked the woman as both of them headed out the side door. The whole thing couldn't have taken thirty seconds. These two men were pros.

"You were lucky this afternoon," said Karen.

"Or very good," I replied.

Lundin hadn't moved. I walked over to him, "Mr. Lundin. My name is Aaron Carlyle." I motioned to Karen, "This is Karen Williams. We had an appointment for dinner. I suggest we go ahead as if nothing happened. You definitely don't want to leave right now."

"What is it you want?" he asked.

"Just some conversation. I think we can help you out of your present predicament." I saw the security people starting to approach out of the corner of my eye.

"Mr. Lundin, we'd like to ask you some questions. My name is Johnson. I head up the security here. Do you know who those two were?" The questions came rapid fire.

I stepped in and said, "My name is Carlyle. I'm staying at the hotel. Mr. Lundin was joining us for dinner when those two men became obnoxious. I had a problem with them at the airport and I guess they were looking to get even."

"What kind of problem?" he asked.

"I thought a small one. As they passed us on one of the moving escalators, one of them got fresh with Miss Williams. I hit him and left him lying on the floor. When I saw him at the hotel, I mentioned it to the dealer. I didn't believe that it was that big a deal."

"We would like to type up a statement for you to sign. If you could come down to the security office we could probably get it done in fifteen minutes."

"How about letting us start dinner? You can have someone bring it to us in the restaurant. We can sign it there."

I could see he wasn't happy, but he was in a little bit of a box. We were guests, Lundin was a regular, and we would be in his restaurant.

"That will be fine and dinner is on us. It's the least we could do to make up for any inconvenience you've been caused." He turned to one of his people and said, "Tell Marcell that Mr. Carlyle and Mr. Lundin are our guests tonight."

Chapter 38

San Francisco

"What happened?" . . . "The general's not going to like this." . . . "Hold on Paul, I'll go get him." The man talking to Paul hated to be the bearer of bad news. He knocked on the bedroom door.

"I'm on the phone. Go away." The general's voiced sounded stressed.

"It's Paul calling from Vegas. He's got a problem."

"Tell him to call back in ten minutes. I'm busy."

He held out his hand to shake mine. "Have a nice dinner."

"I'm sure we will, Mr. Johnson. Just send up the letter whenever it's ready and thanks again for your understanding."

The four of us walked into the restaurant like we didn't have a care in the world.

"Who are you people?" asked Lundin.

"I'm the C.E.O. of a company called Be Safe Security, headquartered in Newbury Park, California. We have been hired to protect the executives of four brokerage firms located inside of California. We have reason to believe they could be in danger from a group of men who have been trying to fix the price of some stocks. Miss Williams is one of our clients. It was at her suggestion that we come down and talk to you."

"Why me?"

"I would suggest we sit down. We can talk over dinner and the food is free."

"I have a booth waiting for you over here," said Marcell, who was being very solicitous.

"I would prefer a table," I replied. "It's a lot easier to see each other as we talk. How about the one in the center of the floor."

Marcell was not happy.

"Of course. I just thought the booth would be more comfortable."

We were seated and our drink orders were taken. Karen and I ordered wine, and Lundin and his girlfriend, Teri, ordered scotches on the rocks.

Lundin started the conversation with, "I now have two questions. The first one is, what was wrong with the booth?"

"Being in the security business makes me a little paranoid. It isn't very hard to listen in on a conversation that takes place in a corner booth. It is difficult to listen in on a table in the middle of a crowded room. What's your second question?"

He looked at Karen, "Why me?"

"I told you over the phone that I manage money for many people. Last week I read a story about SCOA and decided to invest. It wasn't a lot of money, about a quarter of a million, but because of the sudden rise, I decided to get out and take the profits."

"A quarter of a million isn't a lot of money?" he asked.

"I control a little over two hundred million dollars," Karen answered him.

"At one percent you make a bundle," Lundin reflected out loud.

"I do better than that, but let me continue," Karen interrupted his chain of thought and I could see him trying to calculate her worth and pay attention at the same time.

"I noticed at the start of business yesterday that you purchased some stock. When I went back over the records, I found that you had bought and sold stock on Tuesday. Being in the business, I thought those transactions looked odd."

"Do you ever grab an eighth or a sixteenth on the trades you do for clients?" Lundin asked.

It was obvious to me his mind was still trying to figure out how much money Karen could clear.

"No. It wouldn't be ethical," Karen responded.

I could see she was getting frustrated with Lundin and his questions. I jumped into the conversation with a question of my own.

"What happened to your hand?"

"A box fell on it and broke a couple of bones," he replied as he held it up for us to look at.

"The last time I saw a hand wrapped like that someone had smashed a bottle on it."

His eyes opened wide. Teri's hand went to her mouth.

I continued, "Mr. Lundin, I would suggest you pay attention to what Miss Williams has to say. I was against her coming to Vegas, but she felt it was a matter of professional courtesy to someone in the same business. Miss Williams, if you'll please finish. I'm really not happy with what is going on."

Karen picked up the conversation. "Tuesday we got our first call from the SEC. Yesterday we got a visit from some men who claimed to be from the SEC. When they couldn't produce proper credentials, I ordered them out of my office. One of them slapped one of my associates and luckily that's when two of Mr. Carlyle's men entered the office and defused an ugly situation."

"How does that concern me?" asked Lundin.

"The only thing I can think of is that someone is checking up on all the trades that were made on SCOA. That would concern you."

"You told me on the phone you were thinking of getting back into the stock. Are you?"

"The price is back in the range that I think my clients could make some money, but I am trying to find out about the company. Why did you get involved?"

"The same reason as you. I read an article that talked about them and I thought there was some quick money to be made."

"Tell them the truth," Teri blurted out. Her voice held a hint of panic.

"Keep your mouth shut," he snarled back at her.

"I will not. These animals broke your hand, humiliated me in public and ran their hands all over my body. These two tonight were not here to just say hello."

"Mr. Lundin, I would suggest you tell us what you know. We're only here to help." I spoke the words softly, hoping not to provoke him. I thought he was on the edge.

He pushed his glasses up on his nose. He started to look deflated.

"It's very complicated. I don't even know where to begin. They hired me to oversee the buying and selling of stock for them. They were supposed to have six people in different parts of the country buying stock. Something happened and they ended up with only five. Two weeks ago, they had me manage the buying of a stock, WWSI. I cleared over three million dollars in profit for them. They paid me five percent of the profit. This week, the stock was SCOA. I thought they would clear another three, but someone started to buy before them." He picked up his glass and drank half of what was left. "They ended up losing almost two million. They blamed me for their loss. It wasn't my fault. There was nothing I could say or do. I heard from the general today. He told me they understood and would let me in on their next deal. It was probably a lie. I guess they wanted me to stay put for those two."

"Do you know where this general is?"

"He's in San Francisco. I have Caller I.D. When he called, I called the number back."

"How many men does he have working with him?"

"There were seven with him out here. I understand he has five other people around the country and I think he has someone in Washington."

"What do you mean Washington? The state or the city?"

"I think it's D.C. I'm not sure, but I think he once mentioned his friend in Washington. I took it to mean D.C."

"What are we going to do about those two monsters who were here earlier?" Teri asked.

"That's a good question. Why don't we finish up here and get you people back home. I can have some of my people here tomorrow to look after you until this mess is straightened out."

"How much do you charge?" Lundin asked.

"Two men will cost you four thousand dollars a day plus expenses."

"You're out of your mind. How much are you charging her? Or do you two have a special arrangement?" Lundin leered as he pointed at Karen.

"I normally don't give out this information, but Miss Williams has signed on for a four-week guarantee of twenty thousand per week. As far as a special arrangement, Miss Williams is a lady and I'm not that lucky. As far as your price, it no longer matters. I don't want or need you as a client. Miss Williams, I think it's time for us to leave."

"You can't leave us," cried Teri. "How much would it be for me to hire you until I can pack my clothes and get on a plane?"

"As a humanitarian act, I'll do it for nothing if you are ready to leave now."

"I'm ready." She turned to Lundin. "Dennis you have to get out of town. These men will kill you if you don't."

"They won't kill me. They need me. Tomorrow I'm going to write down everything that happened and I'll have it released if anything happens to me. That'll keep them off my back."

I rose from the table and said, "Ladies, it's time to go."

"Dennis?" Teri looked at him hopefully.

"I'm staying. You can do whatever you want."

I led the ladies to the taxi stand and jumped into the first one in line.

"Where to, folks?" The driver asked.

"I live out in Henderson, across the street from the Wild Horse Golf Course. Head out Paradise and I'll give you directions as we get close."

I watched out the back window as we got started. No one was following us, which probably meant they were following Lundin and at this point, I couldn't care less. The ride was almost twenty minutes and when we arrived I asked, "Do you have a car?"

"I have a Lincoln Continental in the garage. Why do you want to know?"

"We can let the taxi go and use your car to get to the airport." I gave the driver a twenty-dollar bill and followed the two women up the stairs. Upon entering I said, "Have you given any thought to where you're headed? If not, I have a suggestion."

"What's that?"

"You can fly to Los Angeles and I'll have some men meet you at the airport. Miss Williams and I can drive your car there and you can either sell it or drive it somewhere else. The whole idea is for you to get lost for a couple of weeks."

"Who are these people that will meet me at the airport?"

"They will be friends of mine. One of them will be a police captain and the other, one of my partners. You will be safe with them." She walked around the room picking clothes out of the closet and drawers and placing them in a suitcase.

"I might as well. I have nowhere else to go." She sounded lost. "Why don't I drive to Los Angeles with you?"

"You could do that. I was concerned with your safety. The quicker I can get you out of Vegas, the better I'll feel."

"Me too. I'll fly. Have your friends meet me."

I picked up the phone and dialed. "Barry, this is Aaron. I need you and either Scott or Tom to meet a Southwest plane coming in from Vegas. The woman getting off the plane is about five-six, blonde, wearing a green dress. Her name is Teri . . ." I looked at Teri.

"Randolph," she said.

"Randolph. That's right, Teri Randolph. Keep her under wraps until I arrive sometime tomorrow morning. I think she's on a list our friends are putting together. She will be asking for proof of who you are, so bring identification. See you tomorrow." I hung up the phone and asked for the keys to the car.

"I'm going to put the luggage in the trunk. Be ready to leave in five minutes. Karen, while I'm downstairs call Southwest and reserve a seat on the next flight." I picked up the suitcase and walked down the back stairs to the garage. I couldn't have been gone two minutes, but as I started up the stairs I heard voices.

"Where's your boyfriend, Sweet Cheeks?"

I heard Karen answer casually, "He needed gas. He said he would be back in ten minutes."

"When did he leave?"

I looked through the crack in the door. I could see her hand trembling as she checked her watch, "Five minutes ago."

"What did you do to him?" It was Teri looking at Lundin's inert body lying on the floor.

"Nothing much. Banged his hand around some, knocked out a few teeth, may have broken a few ribs. He's all right for the time being." He laughed as he stomped on Lundin's hand.

Paul came into view. He was carrying a gun in his right hand with a silencer attached. In his left hand was a knife. As he passed Lundin, he turned and fired two quick shots into the back of Lundin's head.

"One down, three to go." He turned towards Karen who promptly kicked him. She had aimed for his groin but missed and hit his leg. His friend turned and went after her as I came through the door.

I hit both of them at the same time, and the three of us ended up on the floor. I went after Paul first since he had the weapons and landed three pretty good punches before I heard Paul's friend yelling.

"Don't move or I'll slice up the broads." He had a knife in his hand and was moving towards Teri.

"Don't be a fool," I said. "The game's over. We have the general and most of your friends. Don't do something you're going to be sorry for later." I hoped he believed my bluff.

"You'll never get the general," he yelled as he took another step towards Teri. Out of the corner of my eye, I saw Karen sitting up on the floor where she had been pushed. She had the pistol that Paul had dropped.

"Don't move," she said in a staccato voice. Paul's friend turned and looked at Karen holding the pistol.

"You don't want to hurt me," he whispered as he reversed the knife and threw it.

"Karen!" I screamed. She turned in my direction as the knife hit her left arm. She turned back and fired the pistol. The sound was like that of the wind blowing between two reeds. I jumped up and ran to her. The knife had cut her slightly and fallen to the ground. I took the gun from her hand and turned back to the thrower. He was dead.

"He has a gun!" I fired a round into his head. I couldn't let Karen believe that she had killed him.

"Are you all right?"

"I'm fine. What about Lundin?"

I leaned over his body. "He's dead. Let me check on the other guy. He's gone also." I walked over to Paul who was still lying on the floor. I pulled him up and went through his pockets. "Do you have any rope in the house?"

Teri didn't answer. She was staring at the two bodies.

"Did I kill him?" asked Karen, her voice a little reedy.

"No. You only nicked him. I killed him when he started to move."

"I don't see another gun," Karen said.

"Neither do I, now. I thought I saw one earlier, but I guess I was mistaken."

"Shouldn't we call the police?" asked Teri.

Thinking quickly I said, "I have an idea. Listen carefully. If I switch the two guns it will look like Paul's friend killed Lundin and Lundin killed him. It won't hold up under too much investigation, but we might be able to pull it off until we're out of town."

"Isn't that breaking the law?" Teri asked.

"What do you think we've already done?" replied Karen.

"We haven't broken any laws yet," I interrupted. "Our next move breaks the law."

"What's that?" asked Teri.

"If we leave Paul here for the police, he'll have the rest of his friends after us so fast we won't be able to breathe. We'll have to throw him in the trunk of the car and drive him to Los Angeles where we have friends. When the police get an anonymous phone call telling of hearing gunshots, they will have to assume these two killed each other. What happened at the hotel tonight would only reinforce that premise. We will go back and check out and you will have taken the flight to Los Angeles."

"Do you think it will work?"

"If Aaron thinks it will work, it will," said Karen, her voice stronger now as she came to my defense.

I pushed Paul down the stairs and threw him into the open trunk of the car. I took the gun Paul had used and put it into his friend's hand. I took the gun that Karen and I used, wiped our prints off of it and placed it in the good hand of Lundin. I aimed at the ceiling and fired one more shot so that the residue would show up on his hand, if they checked.

"Come on ladies. We have to make the next plane." The drive to the terminal only took ten minutes. Karen walked Teri in and made sure she was on the plane for Los Angeles.

We started back to the hotel in silence. About halfway there, Karen said, "I've never been so scared in my entire life. What would we have done if I had killed him?" She thought for a second and began again. "Probably exactly what we are doing now. We have become, over the past two weeks, a team. We still have a way to go, but meeting you was one of the best things that has ever happened to me."

I held out my hand. She took it and started crying. I didn't know what to say or do, so I just let her cry.

After I checked us out, I headed to the nearest gas station and used the phone to call the police.

"I just heard what sounded like two or three gunshots from a house around the corner from where I live."

"Your name, sir?" the voice on the other end asked.

"Do I have to get involved?" I whined into the phone.

"What's the address where you heard the sounds?"

"Across from the Wild Horse Golf Course. The lights are on. My wife told me not to get involved so I'm not telling you my name."

I hung up the phone and wiped the receiver clean. I jumped into the car and drove across the street to another gas station and started filling the car up with gas. Less than three minutes after I hung up the phone, a police car pulled up and two cops got out of the car and walked slowly to the phone booth I had used. I had to admit, they were good.

Chapter 39

San Francisco

"Why hasn't Paul called back?" The general yelled into the room. No one answered. The men sitting in the room had experienced his tirades before and weren't about to call attention to themselves.

"What time was it he called?" he asked.

One of the men said, "About 6:30 P.M."

"It's 10:30 P.M. Where the hell is he? You told him to call back, right?"

"Right. Like I said, he called and said he had a problem. The hotel security got in between him and the broker Lundin and they had a scuffle. They had gotten out and were watching for Lundin to pick up his car."

"Who started the scuffle?"

"He didn't say."

"You didn't ask him?"

"He said he wanted to talk to you."

Before he could say anything else, his cell phone rang.

"Yeah!" It was all he said before his face turned red.

"Find out who's responsible," he muttered the words into the phone before he closed the lid.

"Who was that?" asked one of the men.

"None of your business," the general replied brusquely. "All you need to know is that Chuck is dead!" He continued, "They haven't found Paul, but they found Chuck and the accountant in the girlfriend's house. First indications are that they killed each other. Paul probably has the girl and is on the move. If he calls again, make sure I talk to him."

"Who gave you the information?"

"I told you, it's none of your business."

"I just thought that he might have heard something about Hal."

"If he would have heard, he would have told me." The men could tell the general was getting upset.

"Someone call the phone number of that woman in San Diego and find out if she answers the phone." He looked around the room. There were only three men plus himself left. He'd feel better tomorrow when the other five men arrived. He liked having a lot of men around. One of the men was dialing the number.

"No answer," he yelled over his shoulder.

Los Angeles

"Karen, It's time to get up." I rubbed her shoulder as I spoke.

"Where are we?" she asked.

"About ten minutes outside of Long Beach."

"You let me sleep all this time? I was supposed to drive part of the way."

"You looked so comfortable that I didn't want to disturb you."

"You must be exhausted."

"I'm a little tired. I'll catch up after we drop off our passenger."

"I forgot all about him. How is he doing?"

"Didn't even bother to look. Here we are." I flashed my lights and the gate opened. Min, Barry and Scott greeted us.

"Where's your guest?" Barry asked.

He's in the trunk. I'll pop it from here. Be careful, he put two bullets in the back of Lundin's head like it was fun."

Barry took out his pistol and said to me, "Ready."

The trunk opened and Barry pulled the scrunched-up Paul out and threw him on the floor.

"That maniac kidnapped me," Paul shouted. "Call the police."

"From what I understand, you're lucky you're still alive. If you speak only when spoken to, you have a chance of living until tomorrow. By the way, I am the police."

Paul's face paled. This was not what he expected. He was pushed into the building and shoved into a room with no windows. There was a cot up against one of the walls and what looked like a hundred watt bulb about fifteen feet off the floor.

Paul turned and shouted, "You can't do this to me. At least get me something to eat or drink." The door slammed shut.

I was watching Karen walk out the door with Soo Kim when Barry turned to me and said, "In about thirty minutes, we'll start the debriefing. We know that they're in San Francisco today, we just don't know where."

Tom continued, "We are also trying to find out who their contact is in Washington. It looks like only the general knows that answer, but you can never tell."

I looked at Barry. "We'll have to tell the Vegas police something. Someone did get killed."

"It's funny you should mention that. I was on the phone after you called and one of my friends told me a story about finding the bodies. They have your name from the hotel and they believe you left Vegas two hours before the killings. They asked me to contact you for verification of what happened."

"I guess they bought the story of them shooting each other."

"They're still looking for the other guy. I think his picture will be in the paper tomorrow," Barry said.

"I heard Karen say she shot one of the guys," Tom said.

"She did. Saved our lives," I replied.

"Did she kill him?" Min asked.

I took a deep breath, "No, I did." When I didn't say anything else, Barry, Tom and Min just looked at each other. They all understood what happened even if the words were never spoken.

"I'll take care of the Vegas police," Barry said to his friends. "We'll let the story stand as is and only change it if we have to."

"Fine by me," I said. "I have to get some sleep. Wake me if anything happens or if you get any good information."

"Aaron, you can sleep on the plane," said Min.

"What plane?"

"The one that is leaving for San Jose in forty minutes," he answered.

"What's in San Jose?" asked Tom.

"Nothing. But it is close enough to San Francisco, yet far enough away that I don't think it will be watched."

"Watched by whom?" This time Barry was asking the question.

"The Vietnamese government or their friends."

"Let me bring you up to date," I jumped into the conversation. "Min believes the Vietnamese government or some splinter group of the government is supporting the general."

"Why does he believe that?" asked Barry.

"Min, why don't you explain."

Min looked around the room. He motioned for the three of his relatives to leave. Tom and Barry both sat down at the table and looked at Min.

"Ever since Aaron mentioned to me, in error, about someone working for the Cuban Government, I have been doing some checking." He held up his thumb. "The man who we found to be disloyal had gotten instructions from someone inside of the Vietnamese Embassy." He held up a second finger. "The call to one of the brokerage firms that was used by me to buy stock was made from somewhere inside of the Vietnamese building." He held up a third finger. It looked odd. He was using his thumb, his pointer finger and his pinkie. "This general of yours, when we first met him, was doing things that someone high in the Vietnamese or the American governments had to be sanctioning. I made some discreet inquiries and found that inside the embassy there is a man, who when I knew him, was a major under my old friend General Giac. He was assigned to work with, I think you called them at the time, the Company. For him to be now in the United States and being a general in the Vietnamese Army can only lead to conclusion that they worked together."

Tom interrupted, "Assuming that all you say is true, why are you and Aaron going to San Francisco?"

"I have sent word that I would like to talk to him. He has agreed, but has given conditions."

"They are?" asked Barry.

"That I come alone."

"What did you tell him?" asked Tom.

"I told him that I must bring my friend Aaron since he must be part of conversation. I also told him the meeting must be in public place."

"And he said?" Barry asked.

"He has picked Ghirardelli Square at noon tomorrow."

"How will either of you know if the other has kept their word?" asked Tom.

"He is to be allowed two men besides himself. I think he will probably have at least six others in or around the place of meeting. I have sent today ten of my nephews and four of my nieces. Tomorrow they will either be tourists or have work in some of the restaurants. They will be watching over me."

"I don't like it," Barry said aloud.

"We do not have much of an option. He will not meet unless we agree."

"What are you going to talk about if you meet?" asked Tom.

"I will try to come to some sort of arrangement with him. I think he is the person that is in contact with the higher up in the American government. I might be able to trade for something he would like."

"What do you think he would like?" Tom again asked the question.

"His life and the lives of his family."

It was said so simply that both Barry and Tom knew he was serious.

"Even with all of your people, I still think the risk is too large." Barry's police background was taking over.

"His people will be on the lookout for any Vietnamese in the area."

"I have another suggestion," said Tom. "How about having Michael Harran go up there as a tourist? He's from that area, spent his youth with the S.F.P.D., and being black would probably attract less attention than any of your people."

"This is the man that is Tuloc's partner?" asked Min.

"Yes, that's him," I answered. I didn't want anyone to forget I was there.

Min replied, "I have heard good things about him. That is a good idea."

Tom stood and walked to the door. "I'll get him ready to leave."

I called to Tom, "Have him go straight to San Francisco. It's better if he isn't seen with us on the plane. Make sure he understands it could be dangerous."

Min rose from the chair he was in and said, "It is time for us to depart."

"I have to say goodbye to Karen," I replied.

Tuloc had entered as Tom walked out. "Miss Williams is asleep," he said.

"Do me a favor, Tuloc. When she wakes, tell her I will be back tomorrow night."

"Mr. Carlyle, I would think you should call tonight around 6 P.M.," he replied.

I smiled. "You're probably right. Just tell her I had to go somewhere and I will call her tonight."

As I followed Min to the car, I asked, "Where are we staying tonight?"

"At the hotel with the glass elevators," he answered.

I thought back over the years. Min never remembered names, but he was very descriptive.

Chapter 40

The trip to San Jose was uneventful, as was the trip into the city by the Bay. I was amazed at the way Min's people had arranged our transportation. Two men took our carryon luggage and led us through a set of security doors directly to a waiting stretch limo. I had dozed on the plane and I slept in the limo. I awoke as the car came to a halt at the hotel service entrance.

"I needed that," I said as I looked at my watch. I yawned and stretched my legs. "I probably need a little more."

"We will be in our rooms in ten minutes. You can sleep then," said Min stoically.

The service elevator door opened as we approached it.

Two more of Min's nephews were inside the elevator, dressed as hotel workers. Our driver handed them our luggage and he and his co-pilot turned and left.

The elevator went up two floors to the lobby. We exited and were met by a niece and a nephew who led us across the lobby to another waiting elevator. I entered first, followed by Min and then his relatives. We filled the elevator so that no one else could enter and were whisked away to our suite on the twenty-third floor.

"If you are interested, they have a very good commercial Chinese restaurant downstairs. It is a place we could go for dinner and not be disturbed." Min turned to me as I headed to one of the three bedrooms inside of the suite and added, "They also have what they call fine dining at the top of the hotel. It overlooks the city."

"I am going to sleep. If I wake before tomorrow, I'll call down for room service. You go ahead and enjoy yourself." I was already headed to the bedroom.

Min nodded. "Have a good sleep my friend. They have a saying in my country, that sleep is one of the two things that you can never make up for missing."

I smiled, "And the other is?"

He smiled for the first time today.

Min's face held a tint of blush. He couldn't even in a room with all men say the word "sex."

"That's why I don't ask you about the sayings from your old country." I closed the door, took off my jacket, kicked off my shoes and fell on the bed. "I'm certainly going to try," I said aloud as I closed my eyes.

"The chicken should have been a little spicier," Min said to his two nephews as they left the Chinese restaurant on the basement level of the hotel.

"The shrimp in lobster sauce was excellent," replied one of the nephews.

They entered the elevator and went up to the lobby. No words were spoken as they entered the other set of elevators that would take them to their floor. As the doors started to close, a hand was thrust between them keeping them open. Three men entered.

"Push the button for the top floor," one of the men said to Min, who was standing next to the row of buttons.

"Which floor would that be?" inquired Min.

"Are you dumb or something? The one on top," replied the man that had made the first request.

Both of Min's nephews repositioned their bodies as Min replied, "Ahh yes, I see. Sorry for my not knowing." Min pushed the button with a thirty-two on it.

"Not that one. Here let me do it."

"Sorry," Min again replied as he pushed button number thirty-three.

"Idiot," said the man as he shoved Min aside and pushed button thirty-five.

Min stood back as the elevator rose. His eyes were riveted on the hands of one of the men. The man stood against the glass wall clenching and unclenching his hands.

The elevator stopped on the twenty-second floor. Min and his nephews exited. Min had pushed number twenty-two instead of twenty-three as a precaution when the other men entered the elevator.

"Americans are sometimes very rude," said one of the nephews.

"They will have time to reflect as they stop on the wrong two floors," replied the other nephew.

"These Americans may be the ones we are to be on the lookout for tomorrow," replied Min. "The making of a fist again and again is the trait of their leader."

Min pushed the up button. When the elevator arrived they entered and pushed twenty-three.

"Maybe we should ask one of them some questions. Call Mai Ling and tell her that we need her here as soon as possible."

Both nephews nodded the understanding of the instructions they were given.

"Has Aaron gotten up yet?" Min asked one of the two men watching television.

"No. We have not heard a sound since he went to sleep."

"I'm up," I said as I walked into the room. "I think I'm more hungry than sleepy. I'm going to go down to the restaurant on the main floor and get myself a steak. Anyone want anything?"

"I think you should order room service," Min replied quietly.

"What's wrong?" I asked.

"In the elevator we met some unpleasant men. The one who seemed to be in charge kept clenching and unclenching his hands. His face was not familiar, but his eyes were. They were on their way up to the place to eat on the top floor of the hotel. If fate has dealt us a winning card, it would be a shame to waste it by letting them see you."

"What are you planning on doing?"

"I have requested the presence of one of my nieces. She should be able to separate at least one of them from the pack thus enabling us to talk to him."

"When will she be here?" I asked Min.

Min looked at one of the men in the room.

"She will be here by 8:30 P.M. I have also requested two more men to come with her, just in case."

Min nodded. "You have done well." He looked at me and said, "Aaron, order some food. It may be a long night."

I looked at my watch. "Shit, I forgot to call Karen."

I looked over at the two men that had not eaten. "Are you two going to order from room service?"

They looked at each other and then at Min. He nodded and one of them said, "We will call room service while you make your call. What should we order for you?"

"I'll have a steak, medium. Baked potato with sour cream, no chives. A piece of apple pie with vanilla ice cream and a large Coke. Tell them to make it a large steak. I'm starving." I walked back into the bedroom, picked up the phone and called Karen. Soo Kim answered the phone.

"Hi Sookie. This is Aaron. Is Karen there? Sure I'll hold . . . Hi . . . I thought they told you, I'm in San Francisco . . . You were sleeping and the plane was leaving . . . Don't worry, this is just a negotiation to make sure there will be no loose ends when we're finished . . . Bad dreams go away once they're replaced by better thoughts or actions . . . No, you didn't kill him. I did. It's easier if you think that by his actions he just committed suicide . . . Tell your mother what? . . . Fiancé? . . . When did we agree to that? . . . I know I said it had a nice sound to it . . . Can we talk about it when I get back tomorrow night? . . . Yes I miss you and yes I will be careful . . . See you tomorrow." I hung up the phone and sat on the edge of the bed. I thought about Marcia. Three weeks ago I never would have believed that someone would be able to replace her. Now I wasn't sure. Thirty minutes later, after a shower and a shave, I felt I could take on the world. In the middle of dinner, Mai Ling arrived.

"Aaron, may I introduce my niece, Mai Ling." Min spoke to me with a twinkle in his eye.

I stood and shook her hand. I looked at Min and said, "They have a saying in my country. It is impossible to have so many beautiful nieces in one family."

Min smiled. "You are probably right. Now let's get on with business at hand." There were now six nephews plus his niece in the room with Min and myself.

"David, you will go to the top of the hotel with Du and point out the men from the elevator. You will then leave making sure that they do not see you. When you come back down, you two," he turned and gestured at the two newest additions to our group, "will go upstairs and take direction from Du. Ten minutes later, Mai Ling will enter the lounge. She will be told which men we are looking for. It will be her job to separate at least one of these men and bring him to a room on the fifteenth floor where David, you will be waiting. Remember, Mai Ling is to be protected at all costs against any bad things happening, which is why there will be three of you upstairs. You all have cell phones. Make sure that you have each other's numbers. Let us get started."

David came back fifteen minutes later. "There are now five of them. The one you thought was the leader is no longer with them. They are easy to notice. They are loud and vulgar."

The two men nodded and left the room. Ten minutes later, Mai Ling got up to leave.

"Mai Ling, be careful," said Min.

After she left I said, "Old friend, there was a note of concern that is normally not in your voice."

Min stared at the door as he replied, "She is Soo Kim's older sister. Their mother, who was my oldest child, is still in Vietnam. She was a most beautiful woman. I call Mai Ling my niece to protect her from any enemies that I might have. Nephews and nieces have different status than children and grandchildren."

His use of the word "was" told me his daughter was dead. There was nothing I could say. This was the first time he had opened up about his private life.

Chapter 41

More than a dozen people turned and followed Mai Ling with their eyes as she entered the lounge on the top floor of the hotel.

One of the men from the elevator nudged the man sitting next to him. "Look at her."

Mai Ling, with heels, stood at five-foot-six. Her jet-black hair hung down around her shoulders. She had high cheekbones and softly chiseled features that were not quite perfect, but because of the imperfections, she became more beautiful. Her skirt was about three inches above her knees, which made her legs look that much longer. She looked around the room and walked over to the bar.

"I'll have a glass of white wine, please."

The bartender tripped over himself trying to be of service. "Shall I run a tab?"

"No, thank you." She said loud enough for the men sitting a few stools away to hear. "I'm only having one or two before going to bed. It's been a tough day."

"Hey lovely lady, how about letting me buy you a drink?" said one of the five men.

She smiled and shook her head no.

"Do you think you're too good for me?" he countered.

"No, it's not that," she answered. "I find that when I let someone buy me drinks, they think it entitles them to something more than conversation. I don't mind talking, but I don't like people getting the wrong impression."

"What do you do for a living?" he asked

"I'm a legal secretary. I work for a firm in Los Angeles, but I'm up here to take a deposition. I started at 8 A.M. and just finished a half-hour ago. What do you do for a living?"

The man looked a little uncomfortable. "We work for the government. We're here investigating a stock fraud. I'm originally from Texas. Bill here," as he pointed to the man sitting next to him, "is from Arkansas."

"My roommate is from Shreveport, Louisiana. She says it is only a short distance to Arkansas. Too bad she's not here. She'd love to talk to you. It's like someone from back home."

"Where's your roommate, back in Los Angeles?"

"No, I meant my roommate up here. I live alone in Los Angeles. She's changing her clothes. She wanted to get something to eat."

"Give her a call. I'd love to join her for some food. How about the two of you getting something to eat and all four of us can talk."

Mai Ling smiled. "I could do with some food. Let's go get Amy."

The three of them started to the door.

Du, who was standing by the elevators, motioned to his two friends. He entered the elevator as his friends got behind Mai Ling and the two Americans. He called the suite and brought them up to date as he got off on the fifteenth floor.

"She has attracted two of them. I am heading to the room on floor fifteen."

Mai Ling and the Americans entered the elevator. As the doors were closing, one of Mai Ling's followers jumped into the glass-enclosed elevator.

"Please to push button number six."

Mai Ling pushed the number six as the elevator descended. On the fifteenth floor the doors opened. They walked down the hall to room 15-131.

"Let me knock first," Mai Ling said as she took out her key. "Amy might not be dressed."

The two men looked at each other and smiled.

After knocking twice, Mai Ling opened the door. "The shower is on. That is why she didn't hear me."

Mai Ling started towards the bathroom when one of the men grabbed her by the shoulder and threw her down on the bed. "I'll get Amy. You just lie there and don't say a word. We can all party in about two minutes."

He opened the bathroom door and found himself staring at a man holding a pistol aimed straight at his head. He turned just as his friend came face to face with another man that came out of the closet.

Mai Ling got off the bed and opened the door for the two other men that were part of their team.

They searched the general's two men and then tied their hands behind their backs.

"Time to go," said Du as he put small towels from the bathroom in the two prisoners' mouths. They walked them to the service elevator. The doors were open and waiting. The ride to the twenty-third floor was quick. Upon entering the suite, the gags were taken out of their mouths and they were seated back to back on two straight chairs.

Bill spoke first. "What do you people want from us? I can't believe you're upset about our trying to put the make on one of your women."

I started circling the men. Tied as they were, only one of them at a time could see me. I passed in front of Bill who had a pink shirt with a frayed collar and asked, "What's your friends name?"

"Sam. Sam Duncan," replied Bill as I passed from his line of sight.

"Mr. Duncan, what do you do for a living?" I continued walking ,looking at a scar that was on his neck.

"None of your goddamn business," he shouted as I passed from his view.

I approached Bill and backhanded him across the face.

"Bill, let me ask you. What does Sam do for a living?"

"He works for the government. Why did you hit me when he didn't answer?"

I approached Sam. "If one of you lies or refuses to answer, the other one will be punished." I backhanded Sam.

"Sam, you know he lied. What do you do for a living?"

"I told you, it's none of your business."

"I'm afraid it is." I again backhanded Bill. Blood started to run from his nose and his lip.

"Don't hit me. I'll tell you the truth," cried Bill.

"The truth from one of you isn't enough. You both have to decide to tell me the truth."

"The general is going to fry your ass in oil," said Sam as I approached his side.

"You think this general knows who I am?"

"He knows who you are and where you live. I was with him when he was watching you."

"What's his name?" I asked.

"Screw you," replied Sam.

This time I backhanded Sam. "A little change in plans."

"Bill, where is the general?"

"I don't know. He had to go meet someone tonight."

I stopped in front of Bill. "Who did he go to meet?"

"He didn't tell us."

I backhanded Bill again.

"I told you the truth, I don't know"

I continued walking. "Sam, you haven't been very cooperative up until now. Let me tell you what I want and you can decide how much you would like to help me. I know in the beginning you started with about eleven people plus the general. By the way, we know his name is Waldman. I know that you must be looking for four of them that seem to have dropped off the face of the earth." I continued to circle and now stopped in front of Bill.

"Bill, I hope you've been listening. Only one of you is probably going to leave here alive, the one that helps me the most. Personally, I hope that it's you. I don't like Sam." I again started walking. Min nodded his agreement on what I was doing. "There are three things that I need. The first is, are there any plans for tomorrow? The second is, who does the general get his information from? And finally, who does the general report to?" I stopped in front of Sam.

"Would you like to go first?"

Sam was now starting to look worried.

"He doesn't work for anyone and I don't know where he gets his information. I do know he only talks to someone over the cell phone after he calls an 800 number."

"And about tomorrow?"

He wet his lips and glanced around the room. "I'm not sure. I've been on the road. We're supposed to discuss it tonight."

"I don't think you've been honest with me." I turned towards Du and one of the other men and simply said, "Take him into the bathroom and drown him."

A cloth was shoved into his mouth as he started to scream. He was lifted out of the chair and a stain appeared down the leg of his pants. He was carried in front of Bill to the bathroom.

"Bill, it's now your turn."

"I'll tell you anything you want to know. Please don't hurt me." His eyes never left the closed bathroom door. He could here the water running in the bathtub. "Anything, I'll tell you anything."

"You might as well start at the beginning."

Chapter 42

Bill asked for a glass of water and I held it in front of his face. He nodded his thanks and proceeded.

"The general is a hero from the Vietnam War. He was part of a special group put together by the President to insure ongoing relations with people inside of Vietnam after the war was over. He has friends in very high places in both Washington and Vietnam. They put together this plan to raise over one billion dollars by buying stocks low and selling them high inside of a four- or five-day window. They were going to use a different brokerage firm as the lead every two or three weeks. Can I have another sip of water?"

I held the glass in front of him again. As he finished, the door to the bathroom opened and Du and the other man walked out and smiled. Bill paled and started stuttering.

"Slow down and continue your story," I said.

"I, along with five others, were sent to different parts of the country to buy the stocks. They didn't want all the money coming from one place. We started out with two hundred and fifty thousand each, but something happened to the one woman we had as part of the group. She got herself involved in an accident and there was a lot of concern about somebody maybe finding the list that we were going to work off of. We still made a couple of million on the first transaction. The second deal didn't work so well. It seems that someone got in ahead of us and cost us about two million, no one is quite sure exactly how much. The general told all of us to come to San Francisco to regroup. There are two guys missing from a San Diego trip and another two from a trip to Vegas. We know that one of the guys in Vegas is dead. The broker we used killed him and we think he may have killed the broker. The general got a call on his cell phone during dinner and left for a meeting. He said he would be back later to go over our plans going forward."

His eyes darted to the closed bathroom door. "I swear to God, that's all I know."

I looked at a list I had written, containing all the questions we needed answers to. “One more thing, what room is the general staying in tonight?”

“He usually stays in the suite on the twenty-sixth floor with four or five of the guys. The suite has three bedrooms. I don’t know which of the rooms he has taken.”

I nodded and Du opened the bathroom door. Before he could move, Bill screamed, “You promised if I told you what you wanted you wouldn’t kill me!”

Du entered the bathroom and dragged out a trussed up Sam.

“He’s alive!” said Bill. “You told me you killed him.”

“Not yet, but I will if either of you gives us any trouble.”

Min picked up the phone and dialed.

“Our people will arrive shortly.”

For about three minutes, no one said a word. The two of them kept looking at each other like they were trying to communicate without saying words. There was a knock on the door. I opened it. Two men entered and they both nodded at Min. They put duct tape over the mouths of Sam and Bill before they put hoods over their heads. No one said a word; they just went ahead and led both of them out like it was an everyday occurrence. After they were gone, I asked Min, “Where are they being taken?”

“I have a van downstairs. They will be driven tonight to Los Angeles where they will be handed over to Barry for further questioning.”

Sixteenth Floor

“It’s been over three hours since Bill and Sam took off with that broad. Does anyone remember her name or her room?"

“I never heard her name, but her roommate’s name was Amy.”

“Just great. When the general gets back, he’s going to have a fit.”

The six men were sitting in the living room of the suite watching a double x-rated movie as the phone rang.

“Hello . . . This is Vic, General . . . No, Sam and Bill picked up some broad and they’re not back yet. The rest of us are here . . . I’ll tell them and we’ll see you tomorrow.” He hung up the phone and said, “Lower the sound on the television. The general won’t be coming back tonight. I think he’s staying at the Embassy Suites or something like that. Anyway, he wants us to pair up tomorrow and have lunch in four different restaurants in Ghirardelli Square. We are to keep our eyes open for people that might be interested in a meeting that will be taking place between two Vietnamese and an American. He wants them identified, not touched."

"I've been on the road. How about bringing me up to date with what's been going on?" interrupted Tony from Chicago.

"You know what I know," Vic answered him.

"Maybe that's not enough," chimed in John.

"When we started, there were thirteen of us. I heard we lost one to an auto accident. We lost two more guys in Vegas and two in San Diego. That leaves only eight of us and maybe only six if we don't hear from Bill or Sam."

"The general has always taken care of us," answered one of the men who had been traveling with the general. He continued, "What makes you think we won't hear from Bill and Sam? They only picked up some broad in the bar."

"I know, but for over two years we have had ourselves a ball. We travel all over the world. We make some money and we party. We did some things even a hardened city priest would blush at, but we are all part of the team. All of a sudden, we're involved in a deal that we're left out of. We aren't told who's funding the operation or whom we're working for. Then we run into this guy that the general has a hard-on for from his Vietnam days and everything starts turning to shit. He's made this personal instead of business."

"What are you suggesting?"

"I'm not suggesting anything. I just don't like being led around by my nose. Waldman has got to let us know what's going on."

The men looked at each other and nodded. One of them said, "Let's get some shuteye. Tomorrow looks like a busy day."

Chapter 43

My first reaction was to reach over to the left-hand side of the bed to stop the ringing. When I realized the phone wasn't on the left side, I started wondering why it was so loud. I turned the other way and picked up the receiver.

"Hello."

"Aaron?"

"Hi Barry." I squinted at my watch as I asked, "What time is it?"

"It's 6:30 A.M. Did I wake you?"

"I had to get up today sometime and it might as well be now. Everything all right down there?"

"Everything's fine. Hold on, someone wants to say something."

"Morning Aaron. Not jogging today?"

I smiled at the sound of Karen's voice. "Not today. Today was my day to stay in bed."

"You didn't meet any lady cops on the way up there, did you?"

"You have an evil mind," I replied.

"How did you sleep?" she asked.

"Not bad until the phone rang. What's Barry want?"

"I'll put him back on. You be careful," she whispered.

"Aaron, this is Barry. Where the hell did you find these guys? I could become an instant hero probably all the way across the United States. The one you brought back from Vegas is wanted in three states for murder. The one we got from San Diego is a parole violator. He was on parole after serving sixteen months for rape and is wanted in connection with the rape of a nine-year-old girl in Petaluma and the slicing up of a fifteen-year-old high school student in Santa Barbara. The two guys that were delivered this morning both broke out of jail while being transferred from the lockup to the courthouse. Two policemen were killed in that escape. I can't wait to see what today will bring."

"Don't turn them in yet," I said. "We can't let the general know we have them. That Webster guy may be a conduit of information and he may have access to your computers."

"I feel the same way you do, but you know the rules."

"I know, but rules were made to be broken, or at least bent a little."

"You're starting to sound like Min."

I thought to myself, *At least he's smiling.* "We have the meeting this afternoon. After talking to those two last night, we believe Waldman is going to have his people in and around the square. Has anyone spoken to Michael?"

"Aaron," Scott interrupted, "I'm on the extension. That must have been some meeting you had. One of those guys was screaming for another pair of pants when he got here this morning."

Looking back at it, it was funny. "What about Michael?"

"He will be in place. He called about an hour ago. He's joined a band that plays at the square every day. He will blend in. Those are his words, not mine."

"Great. I'll talk to you guys after the meeting." I hung up the phone. I sat on the edge of the bed and realized I missed Karen. As soon as this was over, I was going to get away for a few days and really relax.

After a shave and shower, I went in and briefed Min as to my conversation with Barry.

"My people have a saying. The only ones that can decide what is good and what is evil are the people that are left alive."

"What does that mean?" I asked.

"Make sure that you are left alive," Min replied. "If not, you become the evil one."

I nodded and said, "Let's get some breakfast." The words weren't out of my mouth when there was a knock on the door. Min motioned to his nephew who opened the door and escorted in a tray loaded with food. He never ceased to amaze me.

We took a taxi from the hotel to the Maritime Museum across the street from the Square. This meant we would have to walk up two sets of stairs. We hoped if we were being watched they might split their people and start looking at the North Point Street entrance, which was higher. We wanted them to think we would be trying to sneak some people into the square. Hopefully our people were already in place.

Min touched my shoulder and pointed to a man sitting at a table outside one of the restaurants. At the tables on each side of him, other men sat drinking coffee. He stood as we approached.

"General Min, it is a pleasure to meet you again." He bowed slightly from the waist and turned towards me. "You must be Aaron Carlyle. I have heard much about you."

"I hope it was good things." He did not offer his hand so I kept mine at my side.

"It would depend upon who was doing the listening." He smiled as he replied, but his eyes were showing an animosity far beyond anything that was taking place at this meeting.

"Have we met before?" I asked

"Not face to face." He was still smiling as he snarled his answer. "You placed an explosive device in the back door, after the war was over, of what was the U.S. Consulate in Vietnam. My younger brother lost his life opening that door."

"That was ten years ago. It was a different time and a different place. We were at war and people get hurt in war."

"To my brother, it was not war," he shouted. "To him it was a game."

"This is not why I asked for the meeting," interrupted Min.

"Why you asked for the meeting is not important. Only yesterday I was told the name of the person who was responsible for the death of my brother. Did you think you would bring this person to this meeting and I would let him walk away without letting him know he was going to die? Maybe today, maybe tomorrow, but he can now start wondering when it will happen."

I looked at him. There was no doubt in my mind he was a raving lunatic. I forced myself to stare straight into his eyes. "Everyone dies, but let me tell you of a saying that I learned from Min. If you are hell-bent on vengeance, you better dig two graves." I turned away and spoke to Min. "I am leaving this meeting. I will meet you in front of the museum when you are finished."

I walked slowly down the steps toward the street. I could see Michael Harran playing a clarinet with the band on the first landing. I was about ten feet away when I felt myself being grabbed. I turned both ways and saw that two Asians were holding me. They kept walking, forcing me to walk down the stairs with them.

One of them leaned over and whispered in my ear, "Do not make a disturbance or we will kill you on this spot."

The band had walked right into our path and they parted as we came rushing past. I hoped Michael could see what was going on.

The move was so fast that I didn't even see it coming. One of the members of the band tripped into the Asian on my right as Michael brought the clarinet down on the head of the one on my left. The band I noticed was made up of eight black musicians who handled themselves like a precision drill team. As the two Asians hit the floor, Michael said, "Follow me, Mr. Carlyle. My friends will make sure we get out okay."

I looked back and saw six or seven other Asians come to the aid of their two friends.

"The men in the band are going to need help." I had stopped to look back.

"I don't think so," he laughed, "They're part of the S.F.P.D. special tactics squad. They play in the band on their days off. In fact, you wouldn't believe it, but another twenty or so happen to be on duty today. They're around the corner practicing crowd control. They should be here in a minute."

I looked at him. "I believe it. It's certainly nice to have friends in the right places. I told Min I would wait by the museum."

"No can do, boss. I can hear the sirens now. You take a taxi back to your hotel and I'll get word to Mr. Min."

I walked back into the hotel room as the action news station was showing everyone the scene at Fisherman's Wharf. Peter Carlson, their staff reporter who was on the scene, was telling the story.

"Two staff members from the Vietnamese embassy were apparently intoxicated and started an altercation with an off-duty unit of the San Francisco Police Department. Other members of the embassy in an effort to help their friends found themselves knee deep in police. There were a few bruises, but no one was badly hurt. In a separate but related event, a Vietnamese national who we originally believed to be a senior member of the embassy was killed in an attempted holdup about two hundred yards from the scuffle. His name is being withheld pending notification of family. It is our understanding the two events are being investigated as separate occurrences. We will continue to monitor this tense situation."

The scene shifted: "This is Carol Wilson of the *Channel Two News* action team. I am in front of the Vietnamese embassy. As of this minute they have no comment about either the fight or about the person that was killed in the . . . hold it, someone has just come out."

"Ladies and gentlemen. I have a brief statement."

Carol Wilson whispered, "This gentleman in the three-piece suit is obviously a spokesman for the Vietnamese government. We will try and get his name for you."

"The Vietnamese government protests the handling of our embassy people." He stood nervously reading from a piece of paper.

"They have diplomatic status and as such the police have no right to question or detain any of them. We will be filing an official protest unless they are released immediately. On the second issue, we have just learned the name of the Vietnamese citizen that was killed by someone that has no regard for human life. This person was not a part of our staff, but a businessman visiting the United States in an attempt to better relations between our two countries. When his family has been notified, we will release his name. We have nothing further to say at this time." He turned and retreated into the embassy, leaving reporters scrambling for something to say.

"This is Carol Wilson. As you have just heard live, on *Channel Two News,* someone from the Vietnamese embassy has demanded the immediate release of all of its nationals from police custody. They have also said they will advise us on the name of the dead man as soon as his family has been notified. We will now take you back to our studio to continue with the program in progress. We will of course keep you apprised of any details as they become available."

I turned off the television as the door to the suite opened. Min came in, followed by two of his nephews.

"I was watching the news. For a second, I thought you might have been the one that was killed."

"He was not smart. He decided to argue with a thief and fell on a knife. There are other people in the Vietnamese government that I know from the past. I had conversations with them and they have decided it would be better to disavow any knowledge of him. He has no relatives, and as such that avenue of concern is now closed."

I nodded my understanding and asked, "How did the rest of our plan work out?"

My people have taken pictures of what we believe are at least four more of your general's men. He is now almost alone. His only ally is this Daniel Webster, and when Barry finds him, he will be alone. My people did not see the general, but I believe he was close by. I would suggest we return to Los Angeles quickly. Everything we know about him points to his trying to get revenge at any cost. Being unbalanced, he might attempt to strike out and hurt someone we know."

"I'm ready, just let me call Scott and Tom and bring them up to date."

Min started giving instructions as I called the office.

"Carol, can I speak to Scott or Tom please?"

"Aaron, I want to apologize for the other day. Barry wasn't in a good mood and I guess it rubbed off."

"You don't have to, but your apology is accepted. Can I talk to one of the guys?"

"They're with Barry in the conference room, I'm putting you through."

"Scott here."

"Scott, this is Aaron. Put me on the speaker."

"Aaron, this is Barry. What the hell is going on up there? All the news stations are carrying the story of the fight and of some guy getting killed. Is that us?"

"Slow down. The fight was them. The guy Min had the meeting with tried to pull a fast one. He had about six or eight people and they tried to grab me. Michael and six of his friends stepped in. Before you knew it, another twenty or so police showed up. Michael got me out without a scratch. As far as the guy that died, he was Waldman's contact. Scott, Tom, remember the hand grenades we left behind when we left Vietnam? It turns out that his brother was killed when the door was opened. He has held a grudge since then. His only problem was that he didn't know who did it until this week."

"How did he die?" Scott asked.

I took a deep breath. "It looks like the Vietnamese government decided he was expendable. With him gone, they have made peace with Min that they both can live with."

No one asked any more questions, which was fine by me.

"Let me get back to the main reason I called. Waldman has six men left. Min believes that he is a certifiable lunatic and will probably try and get even in a hurry. We are coming back the quickest way, but he may be a couple of hours ahead of us."

"Aaron, this is Barry. Reports are continuing to roll in. If the six people he has left are the same types as the ones we have down here, we may be able to close over fifty major crimes. I've even gotten a few inquiries from Interpol. They were busy people."

"I'll see you in a couple of hours. Keep our people safe." I hung up the phone and headed home.

Chapter 44

We walked off the United shuttle as the sun was going down. Burbank was warmer than San Francisco, but the weather report called for cooler temperatures, probably before morning.

"Are you sure I cannot drop you off?" Min asked as I stood waiting for Karen to come get me.

"No thanks. Karen will be here any minute. It's been an interesting two days. Get some rest when you get home. We'll talk tomorrow."

He closed the door and both cars that came to meet Min started moving at the same time. I looked up and saw Karen waving to me from the second floor of the parking structure. I waved back and crossed the street. I walked up the stairs into Karen's arms.

"Miss me?" she asked.

"I was only gone overnight."

"I know how long you were gone. That's not what I asked."

"Okay, I missed you."

"Did you miss me a lot?"

Karen's back was against the rail and I was facing the terminal entrance. As she asked the second question, I looked over her shoulder in mock frustration.

"Of course I missed you . . . Son of a bitch."

"What's the matter?"

"Don't move. It's the general. He just came out of the terminal." I should have known better. Her head was already turning as she asked, "Which one is he?"

I stepped back behind the wall. "He's the one with the blue windbreaker jacket. Where's the car?"

"It's down about six or seven on the right."

I pulled her down the aisle.

"Let's go. I want to see if I can find out what he's driving." I was hoping the general was taking the freeway. At the Burbank Airport, you had to drive completely around the parking structure to exit on a street that would take you to a freeway. As I paid the parking charge, a blue van passed in front of the exit. I could see the general sitting in the front right seat. I counted four other men with him.

"Karen, write down the license number." I opened my cell phone and called the office.

"Be Safe. How may I direct your call?"

I didn't recognize the voice. "This is Aaron Carlyle, please connect me with Scott or Tom."

"I'm sorry Mr. Carlyle, they have a meeting going on and are not taking messages."

"Do you know who I am?"

"I think you said Mr. Carlyle."

"Where's Carol?"

"She's on her break."

"What is your name?" I was starting to lose my patience.

"Please hold."

"Aaron, this is Carol. Sorry about that. Here's Scott."

"Aaron, where are you?"

I'm with Karen. The general landed on another plane right after us and I'm following him. His license number is Peter, Peter, Young, Three, Three, Four, King."

"Got it. I'll put someone on it at once. Where are you now?"

"We're on Hollywood Way. He's turning right. I think he's going west on the 134 . . . That's what he's doing. He's headed out towards us."

"I've put some cars in motion. The closest one to you is at Haskell. As long as he doesn't take the 405, we've got him cornered."

"Scott, I only counted four people with him. That leaves at least two others unaccounted for."

"Aaron, hold on a second, I'm going to patch Barry in on the call."

"Aaron, listen carefully. I received a call from Webster. He was fully briefed on what went on up in San Francisco. He believes that the general is headed down to Los Angeles and wants to be notified immediately if he is spotted. He is claiming National Security is at stake."

"Bullshit!" I yelled into the phone, "We tell him and it's like telling the general."

"Aaron, listen to me. Five minutes after I spoke to Webster, I received a call from the governor's office. I can't disregard a call from the governor."

"I understand. All right, if you see the general you call Webster. I'm coming up on Haskell. Where's my backup?"

"He should be two or three cars ahead of you. He just went up the ramp."

"I see him. Tell him to stay there."

"Aaron this is Barry. Can I be of any help?"

"Have one of your cars standing by. If we cross into Ventura County, it becomes your baby."

"Aaron, you should see a second car about now."

"I see him. This should be enough. Every time one goes off, have another one get on. See if you can get some unmarked ones up ahead."

"They'll be there."

Karen tapped my arm. "They're signaling. They're getting off."

"Guys, they're getting off at Topanga. Do we have anyone near there?"

"We have one ready if he goes south."

"Have one of the cars on the freeway move in front of him and head north. Remember we just want to know where he's going. I'm dropping out and heading home. I'll check in later." With Karen in the car, I wasn't about to take any unnecessary chances.

"You're headed home because of me," Karen said.

"You are absolutely correct. If I don't get you alone somewhere soon I'll go bonkers."

She leaned over and kissed my cheek. "You are an absolutely wonderful liar, but just in case you're telling the truth, don't stop for any red lights."

I started laughing and moved the speed up a notch.

As we pulled up to the house, the car phone rang.

"Don't answer it," Karen whispered.

"I'll only be a second. It might be important." I kissed her lightly on the lips as I activated the hands-free button.

"Aaron here."

"This is Tom. I have some bad news."

"How bad?"

"Min has been shot."

"How bad is he hurt?" For the first time I felt really afraid.

"We don't know. Tuloc got a call about ten minutes ago and shot out of here like a bullet. Let me put Barry on. He's been making phone calls."

"Aaron, as close as I can determine from here, as he got out of his car another car approached at a high speed and opened fire. Min and two of his people were shot. The shooter's car didn't get two hundred yards before it was shot so full of holes it exploded. The police are saying it was a gang fight because of the Asians. The two bodies in the car have not yet been identified and my source says from the way they look, they may never find out who they are."

My mouth started working, but no sound came out. Karen looked at me and then asked, "Is Min alive?"

"I don't know," Barry replied. "I do know at least one of the Asians is dead and the other two are under guard at the hospital where at least one is being operated on."

I looked at Karen. She had tears running down her face. I put my arm around her and gave a squeeze.

"Is Michael back from Northern California?"

"He checked in about a half hour ago. He was headed home."

"Get in touch with him and tell him he's in charge of the detail that will guard Min. I'm on my way to Min's house to see if I can find out what's going on. I'll be at the hospital after that. You know how to reach me."

"Aaron, make sure you have some firepower with you. You could be next on their list."

"I have something in the trunk that will suffice, but do me a favor. Have a couple of our people meet me en route so that I can offload Karen. I don't want to leave her alone at my place."

"The hell with that!" Karen exploded at the top of her lungs. "Don't bother sending someone to get me because I'm staying with Aaron and it's not open for negotiation."

"Aaron?" Tom's voice was asking me the question.

"Don't send anyone. I'll handle it . . . along with my future fiancé. I'll check in with you later."

I started backing my car out of the driveway when Karen said, "Hold it. What do you mean future fiancé?"

"I was thinking about it and decided it was something I would like to do in the future."

"You weren't even going to discuss it with me before you announced it to the world?"

"Well, when we were in Vegas you were using the word indiscriminately."

"We were play-acting in Vegas."

"I can tell the guys we changed our mind. It's no big deal."

"That would make me look foolish in front of your friends. I'm going to have to go along with this, just to save face." With that she leaned across and placed her lips on mine. She didn't kiss me and she didn't touch me with her hands. She just sat there.

"Thank you," she said as our lips continued to touch. "Let's get to Min."

The drive to his house took about forty minutes. Police cars were still on the street, directing traffic.

"You can't park there," said a policeman waving a flashlight.

"I'm visiting this house."

"I don't give a damn who you're visiting, there's no parking on this street."

I turned to see Tuloc come running down the steps with another man. "Mr. Carlyle, let us park it for . . ."

I cut him off. "Min?"

Tuloc almost smiled, "He is alive and giving orders. Du was killed and Tran Wan was wounded seriously." He was telling us what happened as we moved up the steps. Soo Kim opened the door as we reached the top step.

She held out her arms and said, "Karen, I am glad you are here." She turned to me and bowed. "You do us a great honor with your presence. Please, both of you come in."

We entered the living room where we had met just a short time ago.

"Any news on your grandfather's condition?"

"Mr. Carlyle, my grandfather has checked himself out of the hospital. He has told anyone that would listen that his wounds were not of a serious nature. He will be here within the next thirty minutes. He has made a statement to the police that he hasn't the slightest idea of why he was shot. The police are still trying to find the men that killed the two people that shot my grandfather."

"Where are they looking?"

"In all the wrong places, probably."

"How are you going to insure your grandfather's safety?" Karen asked.

"Tuloc has suggested that I hire Be Safe. It is his belief that you have trained professionals with licenses that could insure my grandfather's well-being."

"Tuloc suggested this?" I asked in amazement.

"It is not good idea?" she replied.

"It's a great idea, I just didn't believe you would listen to anything Tuloc suggested."

She looked at her feet. "It is strange, he is always the one that is present when I need help."

"Who needs help?"

We all turned as Min came walking through the door. He was walking with a noticeable limp that he was obviously trying to hide. His face had about four or five bandages and his clothes looked like they had been dragged through the streets.

Before I knew what she was doing, Karen was across the room with her arms around him.

Min caught my eye and winked before saying, "I repeat, who needs help?"

"Now that you are home, no one needs help," Karen whispered.

I stepped into the conversation. "Old friend, it is good to see you still alive. A suggestion has been made that I think you should follow."

"What is that suggestion and who made it?

"A thought has been put on the table that you hire my firm to protect your home and people. The police are looking for the men that shot up the car, and the use of licensed people is our best way of insuring your safety."

Min looked around the room and sat down resignedly.

"You are probably right. I am tired and must take a nap. When I awake, we must talk. There are things that must be done."

"Grandfather, a cup of tea to help you relax?"

He nodded as he left the room.

Chapter 45

I fell asleep on the sofa watching television. I was dreaming that I was walking on the beach with Marcia when she somehow changed into Karen. I was trying to figure out why Karen was calling my name when I opened my eyes.

"Aaron! Aaron, wake up. Min is awake and wants to talk to you."

"How long was I sleeping?"

"About three hours."

I looked around the room. We were by ourselves.

"What's going on? Where is everyone? Is Min okay?"

"Slow down. Everyone I think is with Min. I haven't been able to figure out how many people there are in this house, but those that I know are in his room. He is cranky and ornery, so I guess that means he's okay."

"Lead me to him. Have you heard from Tom or Scott?"

"That's the bad news. They called about an hour ago. It seems the van the general was in stopped for a red light and the general and three of his men got out and walked away. There was no way to follow them."

"That being the bad news, I suppose there's some good news?"

"Your man continued to follow the van and when it parked in a garage, the driver was grabbed and taken to the warehouse. Barry interrogated him and decided he didn't know where the general was and wants you to call him when you get a chance."

We entered Min's bedroom. He was sitting up in bed with three or four pillows propped behind him. He smiled when we walked in.

"Will you look at the way they are treating me. They think I am an invalid. Aaron, tell them how we walked out of Vietnam. These children don't know what real hardship is."

"Min," I smiled, "If I tell them the truth, they'll know I had to carry you out on my back. After twenty minutes of walking, you had blisters, and after another twenty, you were out of breath."

Tuloc, Sookie and the other two people smiled.

"Some friend you are," he blustered. "All of you get out. I must speak to this forgetful one alone. Karen, I'm afraid that includes you. What I am going to tell Aaron must be between him and me."

"I understand. I will be in the kitchen with your family."

I closed the door behind them and walked over to the bed. "How are you really feeling?"

"I am feeling terrible. This general has again been responsible for a person's death. This time the person is someone very close to me. We must stop him."

He closed his eyes and rested for a few seconds. He started talking with his eyes closed. "I spoke to Barry a short while ago. The man who was picked up driving the van has confessed that the general and the other three men were on their way to even the score with you. Barry has gone with Tom and Scott to your home. They have let themselves in with a key from your office. With the lights off, they will be waiting inside. They said to tell you to arrive home at approximately 2:30 A.M. If the general has not shown his ugly face by that time, you will then discuss the next plan of action. Barry has a concern that this high official will help free the ones we have in the warehouse. Their outcome must also be discussed. I am unable to join you for this meeting. I want you to remember our conversation. These animals cannot be set free."

I looked at my watch. It was almost 1:30 A.M.

"I must go. I don't want to be late for this meeting. I will not forget our conversation. Get a good night's sleep and we will talk further in the morning."

He reached out and took my hands. "Be careful, old friend. You must come back to tell the young ones the truth about how we walked out of the jungle."

"I will." I turned and left the room. In the hallway leading to the kitchen, I stopped and thought about what I would tell Karen. She walked up behind me.

"Are we ready to leave?"

"Karen, you'll have to stay with Min. I'll be back in a few hours. Get some sleep and dream about our vacation to Hawaii."

"We've had this conversation before. Where you go, I go."

"I'm sorry, but not this time. If something happened to you, I wouldn't forgive myself."

"Aaron, listen to me. We've only known each other for a short time. I've been competing with a ghost and I think holding my own. If you shut me out now, we'll never have a chance."

She stood there looking at me. Her eyes told me she was not running a bluff. I stared back. She had to know how I felt. "Karen, I'm sorry. I can't take you with me."

I turned and walked out the front door. Tuloc and Sookie were standing by my car.

Sookie looked behind me, "Where is Karen?"

"I can't take her with me," I replied.

Tuloc coughed. When I looked at him, he said, "We were going to ask you both to be part of the bridal party at our wedding. I guess this means the answer will be no."

"You're getting married? When did you decide this?"

"Tonight. We decided with what has happened, we don't want to take a chance of not being together."

I shook his hand and leaned over to Soo Kim. "Is it proper to kiss the intended bride?"

"It is proper and eagerly anticipated," she grinned.

I put my arms around her and kissed her on the cheek. "You're getting one hell of a snake in the grass." I stepped back and looked up at the house. I glanced at Tuloc and Sookie and said, "What the hell." I took the steps two at a time. As I reached the top step the door opened. Karen walked out.

"It sure took you a long time to decide."

"I figured if I didn't come back, I'd never get my hair dried. Come on, we'll talk in the car."

"No hug or kisses?" she asked.

I took her in my arms and held her tight. "Kisses come later." On the way home, I contacted Barry and he brought me up to date with what was going on. I pulled up in front of my house at 2:20 A.M. It was almost a full moon and the shadows through the branches of the trees cast eerie shapes on the ground and the side of the garage.

"Remember, if there's any trouble you run like hell."

She nodded her acceptance as I pushed the garage door opener. I drove the car into the garage and pushed the button to close the automatic doors. As I exited the car, I was thrown down on the ground and kicked in the side.

"Don't move, you son of a bitch."

I felt a gun against my neck.

"Lady! Get out slowly. Don't make any noise or make any quick moves."

I was dragged to my feet and asked, "What's the code for your alarm system? If we see one of your cars come anywhere close to this house, we'll kill both of you on the spot."

"Be Safe. Just put in B, S, A, F."

They took my keys and opened the door that entered the house through the garage. One of the men, I could now see three of them, punched in the code.

Two of the men went into the house with their guns drawn. The third stood with his gun pointed at Karen and myself.

"It's clear in here. Come on in," one of the men shouted.

I had Karen go first so that I would be between her and the man with the gun. The only light on was in the hall, keeping the rest of the house dark. As she entered, she was grabbed and pushed into the living room where she was thrown on the floor.

"Don't move. Just sit there and be good."

I walked in and said, "I don't have much money. Take what you want and leave us alone."

"You just stand there and keep your mouth shut."

After saying his big line, he walked to the front door and opened it. In walked ex-General Waldman.

"Remember me?"

"Who could ever forget you?" I remarked.

He was opening and closing his hands. He had a sadistic smile on his face that could only mean he was enjoying himself.

"The last time we met you put a bullet in my shoulder that still bothers me when the weather changes. I think it's time to get even."

"I guess you don't want to know how to get your money back?" I taunted.

"I'll get around to that after I enjoy myself." He looked over at Karen. "You always seem to find good-looking women. That bitch in Nam, the lady cop and now this one." He walked over to where she was sitting. "Stand up." Karen didn't move. "I said stand up, or don't you understand English?"

"I didn't hear the word *please.*" Karen spit the words out.

He looked at her. "I like a woman with spunk. Stand up, please."

Karen stood and he hit her with his fist. I leapt towards him and got hit by the one standing behind me.

"Now stand up," he said again to Karen, "without the smart mouth."

She stood and I could see it coming. She lashed out with her foot and caught him squarely between his legs. He doubled over and fell on the floor.

The one watching me turned his attention towards Karen and I hit him at the knees. Two shots rang out. Everyone turned towards the sound. Scott and Tom had fired at almost the same time. I looked around and the other two men were on the tile floor with blood running like a river between the tiles.

"I was starting to wonder where you guys were."

"You saved his life by knocking him down," said Barry as he holstered his pistol.

I walked over to Karen. "You've got a real set. That had to be one of the bravest and dumbest things I have ever seen."

The general sat up. "What now, hotshot? Another couple of years before I get a chance to get even?"

"Aaron, I'm putting a call in to my office. These two on the floor broke in and were killed by Be Safe security people. I would suggest that you and Karen take the general and his friend to the warehouse and decide later what we're going to do with them. I can handle it here with Scott and Tom."

"Scott, Tom, are you guys okay with this?" I asked my two closest friends. They both nodded yes.

Karen and I delivered the general and his cohort to the warehouse. Min and Tuloc were waiting for us to arrive.

Tuloc walked up to me and said, "I am tendering my resignation from Be Safe. I wish to thank you for all that you have taught me. I am joining a company that is owned by Soo Kim's grandfather. Since I am going to be part of the family, we thought this best."

"We'll miss you, but I have a feeling we will still get to see each other."

"Of that I am sure."

I walked over to Min. "You should be in bed."

"I had to see with my own eyes that this monster has been captured."

"I just heard you have taken on a new employee. Treat him well."

"If I don't bring him into family, I will end up eating on Saturdays by myself." He looked back at Tuloc and smiled. "I never told you, but he is my friend Giac's son. I never told this to Soo Kim. I didn't want her to think I was arranging a marriage for her. This had to be her idea."

"Don't tell me, but I bet they have a saying for this in your country."

"Where do you think Shakespeare got his idea for Romeo and Juliet if not from my country?" He was now laughing and coughing.

"Old friend, I need one more favor," I said loud enough for everyone to hear.

"What is that?" he asked.

"I have promised Karen a vacation. I am arranging for tickets for tomorrow leaving for Hawaii. Could you have your people keep watch on these . . . animals until I return and we can then decide what to do with them?"

"This I can do. Have a good time and do not worry about anything. She is someone you should get to know very well."

Karen leaned over and kissed him on the cheek.

I took her hand and we walked out together.

"You have very nice friends."

"I think so."

Next Day

"This first class lounge is nice. I wonder who does the decorating." Karen downed a planter's punch.

"I don't know, but it certainly is bright. We'll probably start boarding in about ten minutes. Do you want to start walking down to the gate?"

I looked in the mirror on the wall and saw in the reflection a man watching me. He had short-cropped hair and a thin white scar that ran down the side of his face. He was talking on a cell phone as he noticed me looking his way. He closed the phone, nodded in my direction and smiled.

"Aaron, look at the television. Isn't that Min's warehouse?"

"It looks like it, but in that neighborhood they all look alike."

"What are they saying?"

"Can you turn that up please?"

"This is Peggy Durant reporting live from the Carson area of Los Angeles. As you can see behind me, a fire started in a maintenance warehouse of a cleaning service company. The fire quickly spread to the adjacent building. It was contained where it originally started, but the building next door, which was supposedly empty, has burned to the ground. The fire department has found six bodies inside of that building. The building is known to be a place where homeless people congregate. A police official doesn't know if the bodies will ever be identified. We will keep you advised of this late breaking story."

Karen looked at me with a face that had a million questions.

I looked back at where the man had been standing. He was gone. He looked vaguely familiar.

Karen took my arm. "Our plane is boarding. It's time to go."

"Do you have a legitimate handicap?" she asked.

"Are you getting personal or are you talking about golf?"

We both laughed as we entered the first class cabin of the plane. It was then I remembered.

Singapore

After repeatedly telling us we couldn't land, air traffic control finally directed us towards the end of the runway and had us stop the plane over two miles away from the rest of the planes. Armed police and people from the U.S. Consulate greeted us. Our story was poles apart from our prisoner's and it turned out the pilot did belong to the CIA. We were placed under house arrest while our stories were checked out. For two days, we were questioned and threatened. The only time I saw Marcia was out of the window that didn't open in my room. I was told she changed her story and she told me later that she was told I changed mine. I didn't have the slightest idea of what happened to Min and my requests to see someone from the military were denied. I was told this was a civilian matter that involved attempted murder, highjacking and the possible theft of government property. During the third day of questioning, the door was thrown open and in walked a Marine colonel along with a sergeant and two other Marines. The man that was questioning me, whose name I was never told, asked, "What the hell do you people want?"

"First I want your name and Captain Kellog brought here now."

"Do you have any idea who you are talking to, Colonel?" asked the civilian. He was starting to look uncomfortable, which brought a smile to my lips.

"How are you doing, Lieutenant Carlyle?" The colonel asked the question, pointedly ignoring the CIA man.

"I'm fine, sir, just a little concerned about Captain Kellog."

"My name is Colonel Ewing and I have been given instructions to make sure you and the captain are treated with the utmost respect and returned to the States forthwith." I liked that he stood ramrod straight. His hair was cut short and I noticed he had a thin white scar that ran from the tip of his left ear down the jaw line, halfway to his chin.

The CIA man closed his folder and said, "We'll see about this." He rose and started out of the room.

"Sergeant, if he puts his hand on the doorknob, shoot him."

The words were said in a quiet voice that left no doubt as to their sincerity. The sergeant took out his gun and held it at a ready position. The CIA man stopped in his tracks. "The only thing I want to hear out of your mouth is your name, your organization and the instructions to someone to bring Captain Kellog here pronto."

The CIA man moved closer to the colonel. In a whisper that was heard by everyone in the room, "This is a career threatening move you are making. If you will just back off for ten minutes, I will have someone call you and . . ."

That was as far as he got. The colonel backhanded him across the mouth, sending him to the floor.

He turned to the sergeant and, pointing to the other man in the room, said, "I want his name and Captain Kellog here in five minutes. I don't care how you get it done, but get it done."

The sergeant nodded; turning to the other CIA agent, he smiled and asked, "Your name and organization is?"

The CIA agent looked at his partner lying on the floor and said, "I don't think I am allowed to tell you."

The sergeant motioned to the other marines and two of them lifted the first agent from the floor. They held him loosely by his arms as the sergeant quickly kicked him in the groin. He turned back to the second agent and again smiled. "Your name and organization is?"

The agent paled as he stammered out, "Conner, Rangoon Group, Central Intelligence."

"That was easy," said the sergeant to no one in particular, "and now tell me how fast you can get Captain Kellog here. I still have three and a half minutes left."

Conner grabbed the phone and after a three or four second wait, yelled into it, "Bring the bitch over and do it quickly."

Two of the Marines stepped outside of the door and about two minutes later, they entered with Marcia.

She started towards me when she saw the colonel. She stopped, saluted and then asked, “Colonel, why are we being held?”

The colonel answered, “You’re not being held anymore, young lady; we’re going home. Some of our men ran into a patrol walking out of Vietnam. A Colonel Miller and Major Greenberg headed it up and they told some wild-ass story about some clandestine operation in the middle of the jungle. They also told us about some love-sick lieutenant who was going to somehow fly out of there to freedom with his lady love.”

Marcia’s face reddened as her eyes moved from the colonel to me. I felt my face flush as I stared at my shoes and listened to the rest of the story. “We had some serious doubts, until yesterday when we got word about a Viet officer that was causing a ruckus in Singapore. He was easy to find, but no one seemed to know where you two were.”

We had started walking while the colonel was bringing us up to date and as we reached the street I asked, “Where are we headed now, Colonel?”

“Miller and Greenberg have been flown Stateside, which is where you two are headed for further debriefing. The Viet officer is at this moment in the air, headed in the same direction. It is my understanding that he and the one who was with our troops are going to be given permission to live in the States and become citizens, to make good on some promise that was made to them.”

True to his word, Marcia and I were flown back to the States. The plane developed some unexplained engine problems during the refueling in Hawaii and we were forced to spend two nights at a hotel on the beach, compliments of the United States government. We were given a suite that had a fully stocked bar, a huge living room and two bedrooms. We were told to use room service and not to leave the premises. When the plane was ready, they wanted to be able to find us. If I thought I was in love with Marcia before we arrived in Hawaii, after two days I was positive.

They came for us early during the morning of the third day. The plane took off into the sunrise, which meant we would arrive in the States mid-afternoon, West Coast time. We were in a Boeing 747 that looked like something you would expect Air Force One to look. About an hour after we took off, we were asked to join a two-star general and a man with credentials from the CIA. They proceeded to explain the facts of life. We would both be given honorable discharges and our records would be sealed. We had stumbled upon a rogue operation that had been dealt with by the military. To go public would only hurt the country in what was going to be a tough time for healing. As part of the deal, Min and Giac were being allowed into the country and we could keep the money. They told us that Scott and Tom were given the same option and that we would meet with them before we had to make a decision. There was also another option open to us. They could court-martial the four of us under any one of six different articles and were prepared to guarantee we would be found guilty.

On a Plane to Hawaii

"These were people from our government?" Karen asked with disbelief in her voice.

"They didn't answer. They just smiled. They were sure we would make the right decision. They thanked us and suggested we return to our seats, contemplate what was said, have breakfast and enjoy the flight."

Standing against one of the pillars watching the plane pull away from the gate was the man with a closed cell phone in his hand. His hair was cut short and a thin white scar ran down the left side of his face. He said aloud to himself, "Thank you, Aaron Carlyle. I owe you one. I've been trying for years to figure out how to get rid of that piece of garbage and his friends. You probably don't remember me. We only met that one time in Singapore. I'll be around and who knows, maybe I'll be able to repay you some day."